THIS HAS TO BE A DREAM

The man in the embroidered rob̶e̶ ̶.̶.̶.̶ you're one of his followers?"

Michael wasn't sure how to a̶n̶s̶w̶e̶r̶.̶ ̶.̶.̶ ̶No."

"Good." The man nodded approvingly, then added, "But your daughter has committed a crime."

"No, she hasn't!" Michael said desperately. "My daughter and I were only trying to help this man. We didn't know he was a murderer."

Michael looked over at Elizabeth. She was starting to weep again, and he felt powerless. She looked much smaller surrounded by as many as ten soldiers. *I love you,* Michael mouthed, causing fresh tears to roll down her face.

A soldier stepped forward. "Your Excellence, what would you like us to do with these prisoners?"

The man commanded his soldiers: "Bring me Barabbas!"

"Michael J. Sullivan draws us quickly in . . . [and] provides the detail and heart that make us want to believe. There is real emotion here. . . ."
—Eric Wilson, *New York Times* bestselling author of *Fireproof* and *Haunt of Jackals*

"Michael J. Sullivan is a born novelist. . . . This entrancing tale of mysteries both temporal and spiritual is sure to take up residence under your skin."
—Sam Hamm, screenwriter (the *Batman* movies)

This title is also available as an ebook

NECESSARY HEARTBREAK

A NOVEL OF FAITH AND FORGIVENESS

MICHAEL J. SULLIVAN

GALLERY BOOKS

New York   London   Toronto   Sydney

G

Gallery Books
A Division of Simon & Schuster, Inc.
1230 Avenue of the Americas
New York, NY 10020

Copyright © 2010 by Michael J. Sullivan

First Gallery Books trade paperback edition March 2010

For information about special discounts for bulk purchases,
please contact Simon & Schuster Special Sales at 1-866-506-1949
or business@simonandschuster.com.

The Simon & Schuster Speakers Bureau can bring authors to your live event.
For more information or to book an event, contact the Simon & Schuster Speakers
Bureau at 1-866-248-3049 or visit our website at www.simonspeakers.com.

Designed by Stephanie D. Walker

Manufactured in the United States of America

1 3 5 7 9 10 8 6 4 2

Library of Congress Cataloging-in-Publication Data

Sullivan, M. J.
Necessary heartbreak / Michael J. Sullivan.—1st Gallery Books trade pbk. ed.
p. cm.
1. Single fathers—Fiction. 2. Teenage girls—Fiction.
3. Fathers and daughters—Fiction. 4. Time travel—Fiction. 5. First century,
A.D.—Fiction. 6. Jerusalem—Fiction. 7. Faith—Fiction. I. Title.
PS3619.U44N43   2010
813'.6—dc22   2009044471

ISBN 978-1-4391-8423-3
ISBN 978-1-4391-8425-7 (ebook)

TO MY WIFE DEBBIE, MOM AND DAD, AUNT RUTH AND UNCLE ED,
AND BROTHER LEO RICHARD,
FOR GIVING ME LIFE IN FOUR DIFFERENT WAYS

1

INTO THE TUNNEL

"Let's save each other some time today, Elizabeth. What are you wearing?"

"In a sec, Dad."

Michael sighed and looked in the mirror. His head was pounding from a few glasses of pity wine the previous night, and he noticed a web of inflamed capillaries spreading across the corner of his left eye. *I look awful,* he thought.

Disgusted, he retreated to his bedroom and pulled open the top drawer of his worn dresser. A thin layer of dust was across the top, and absentmindedly he brushed it away. He stared down sullenly into the contents of the drawer and pushed aside a few pairs of socks. There it was at the bottom—a simple gold band. He turned it sideways to read the inscription: I'M GLAD I FOUND YOU. LOVE, VICKI.

Michael sighed and rubbed it gently against his T-shirt. He rarely wore it, except when he wanted to prevent any awkward encounters with unattached women. One look at the ring and they would be sure to leave him alone.

He slipped the ring on his finger and rubbed his stomach, uncomfortably aware of how his belly was gaining a foothold over the worn elastic waistband of his pajamas. He was beginning to understand why women complained about feeling bloated all the time. Adding to his misery was the humidity of the April day, so he chose a simple white T-shirt, light gray sweats, and a pair of his favorite old sandals. He pulled the sweats above his belly and sighed. *Now I look like Fred Mertz.*

He dressed conservatively these days even though he was just forty. With his daughter now a teenager, he believed he needed to set a good example. Michael had seen what the kids wore at the local middle school, where Elizabeth was in the eighth grade. She was becoming a young adult, and sometimes he felt alone against the world in protecting her. No matter how hard he tried to be open, there was no way he could agree with belly rings and low-cut shirts.

I hope she doesn't come down in another skimpy tank top. He was well trained by this point. She would wait upstairs until they were miserably late, with no time to spare. Then it would be a last-second struggle: he would barely see her run past him on the way to the car, leaving him time to register only the most horrific thing she was wearing.

Today, though, he felt ready for the dress-code war.

His determination was swayed by the startling ring of the phone. "Elizabeth, are you going to get that?" Michael shouted upstairs. He chided himself for waiting for an answer; her friends called almost exclusively on her cell, meaning that she wouldn't waste time picking up the house phone.

He ran into the living room and saw the phone out of its holder, along with the empty wine bottle sitting on the side table near his recliner. He bent down and dug furiously along the cushion of the chair. "Got it," he muttered. He noticed the caller ID said UNKNOWN. His stomach lurched and he threw the phone back onto the recliner. *Probably the bank again. Why can't they leave me alone?*

Elizabeth, sandals on her feet, T-shirt tied up to her navel, and oversize shorts hanging low on her waist, sprinted down with the upstairs phone in her hand. "Sure, he's here, hold on." She glanced up and saw her father scowl. "Oops," she whispered as she handed it to him.

"Hello?" He paused, looking annoyed. "Yes, I understand my financial obligations. I'm working as hard as I can and as fast as I can to keep up. I need a couple more weeks. My boss cut my salary in half, sir. So I'm trying to find other ways to make it up. Can you give me more time?"

Elizabeth stood motionless on the stairs, watching her father's brow furrow. For the first time, she noticed some strands of gray hair peeking through the sides of his head, near his ears.

"Good-bye." Michael sighed. He clicked the phone off and looked down. *I really need to clean this carpet,* he thought randomly.

"Everything okay?" Elizabeth asked, noticing the shiny gold ring on his finger.

Michael gazed at his growing daughter, undeterred.

"No. Change the shirt."

"Why, Dad?"

"Change the shirt. Change it or we won't go."

In this rare case, Michael knew he held the upper hand. She needed him to take her to this event to receive the proper credit for school. Every student in the honor society needed a certain number of community-service points, and she was still short.

"Oh, fine. Whatever." Elizabeth rolled her eyes dramatically but then scampered up the stairs back to her bedroom.

Michael was aware that Elizabeth was gradually becoming less attached to him, which meant that the most positive aspect of his life was slowly eroding. He tried hard not to think about it. But on this Saturday morning, he didn't mind the power-broker role for, if nothing else, it kept her with him.

Elizabeth walked down the stairs in an oversize, faded-white Springsteen concert T-shirt. Michael was slumped in the recliner, still clenching the phone and staring off into space. She smiled, trying to cheer him up. "Hey, Dad, does this shirt go down far enough?" The shirt fell past her shorts, well below her knees.

He looked up. "I see you were in my closet. Did you ask?"

"No. I wanted to pick out something you would approve of."

"So you took one of my favorite T-shirts?"

"Bruce wouldn't mind, right?" asked Elizabeth as she flashed an angelic smile.

Michael smiled weakly. "Bruce isn't your father, I am. But this time I approve. C'mon, let's scoot." He slapped his knees before standing up.

Opening the front door for her, he was happy to see that the rain had finally stopped. "Who's my baby?"

Elizabeth didn't answer, knowing from experience that it would only encourage him to ask it again.

Michael smiled as they climbed into the car, deciding it was probably best not to tease her more. He had finally upgraded to a Camry a few years back because it gave Elizabeth more room in the backseat to keep her video games, DVDs and CDs. However, Elizabeth had now taken a liking to sitting in the front. He still couldn't get used to it. He watched as she put in the white earbuds and began playing with the iPhone. Michael once again felt a mingled sense of pride and worry as her fingers rapidly began moving.

"Who are you texting?"

"My friends."

"Boy? Girl?"

She looked at him. "Both."

"What's the boy's name?"

"Matt."

"How old is he?"

"I'm not sure."

"You're not sure?!"

"Okay, okay, he's a couple of years older than me. So?"

Michael grimaced and took a deep breath. "Is that perfume?"

"Yes."

"Where did you get it?"

"Mommy's drawer. You said I could have anything in there."

He glanced over at his daughter and noticed how much she had grown up over the past year. Her hair was neatly brushed, the once girlish curls now straight and pulled into a tightly wound ponytail wrapped in a simple green elastic band. The smell of sparkly nail polish filled the car.

"You're not meeting him here, are you?" asked Michael.

"He might be here later. Do you want to meet him?"

"Um . . . no . . . ah, yeah, yes . . . I don't know."

Elizabeth laughed. "Well, which is it?"

"Let's just get through this day first, okay? I can only manage one crisis at a time."

Boys, he thought as he turned onto Ocean Avenue, watching a few teenagers pushing and shoving each other playfully on the adjacent street corner. Michael remembered he used to be one of them, though he had been quiet and shy when he was fourteen, not outgoing like Elizabeth. Plus, when he was young, there was none of this texting immediacy in getting a girl to like you: you spent days, months even, trying to figure out how to bump into her in the hall, or to find the right friend of hers who would deliver a note for you. At that age, it was all about trying to be alone long enough to just kiss a girl. Well, one special girl.

He shook his head, thinking of her again. *I wonder if Valentina is married,* he thought, remembering his first true love back in elementary school. He drifted off briefly, only to be distracted by Elizabeth's feverish texting. Her phone chirped and she giggled as she read the new message.

Michael nudged her shoulder with his hand. "Who's that?"

There was no response. Unfazed, Elizabeth kept swaying to the beat of My Chemical Romance. It was so loud Michael could hear every lyric that leaked out through the tiny earphones. The scary thing was that he couldn't be sure exactly what they all meant.

He could see in the far distance the boats docked side by side in the harbor. The wind had stopped its howling and a shaft of sunlight struck the cross atop the old church, casting a long shadow across Main Street. Children were pulling their parents into the local toy store, where another birthday party was about to begin. Old men and women were rummaging through the contents on an outdoor table, searching for the best bargains at Perry's Five and Dime. Just another ordinary Saturday morning in Northport.

"Elizabeth? Elizabeth Ellen!" Michael gently lifted his daughter's chin upward while she kept up with her digital connections.

"What, Dad?" Elizabeth asked, pulling out one of the earbuds.

"We're here." He scowled to himself in the rearview mirror, for this was the last place he wanted to be.

Michael parked the car near the corner of Main and Church Street. From there he could see scores of young kids and adults pulling food off trucks parked awkwardly on the sidewalk in front of Our Lady by the Bay Church. They were all there to help organize the food-drive donations.

The next thing he knew, the passenger-side door swung open and Elizabeth threw her phone back onto her seat before jumping to the curb. "Elizabeth!" Michael said as he climbed out quickly. "Wait . . ."

Elizabeth was already across the street heading toward her best friend, Laura. He sighed as he locked the car. "Always following, always following . . ."

"Hi, Laura!" Elizabeth squealed.

"Hey, Liz! Ah, hi, Mr. Stewart."

"Hi, Laura. Hey, *Liz,* remember you're here to help out and get your community-service credit for school."

"Only my friends can call me that." Elizabeth rolled her eyes.

Wow, Michael thought, *that's two eyerolls for today; the day's getting off to a great start!*

He watched her turn to Laura and whisper, "Fun killer." Elizabeth had been using the phrase more often lately. Despite some residual hurt feelings, Michael had become resigned to it.

"Hey, Mike!" shouted a woman in a pretty blue dress from across the street, startling him. "I tried calling you last night. Were you out?"

He smiled as he walked over to give the woman a quick kiss on the cheek. "Susan, you know me better than that."

Michael couldn't help but notice how her light reddish brown hair touched her bare shoulders. "You look great today, Sue."

She looked quizzically at him, casting a quick glance at the ring on his finger. "My, Mike, did you have a hard time getting out of the chair again?"

He nodded. "I've had a rough week, Sue. There are so many things changing in my life. I'm not adjusting at all."

"Well, call me then. Or come by and we'll talk." She rubbed his right arm gently. "I know what you've been through."

"Believe me, I know you know. I appreciate your kindness." Michael meant it, too. Of all his neighbors, Susan Horn was the only one he considered a true friend. Ever since her husband walked out on her almost ten years ago, Michael and Susan had spent many hours talking about everything from child raising to life without a spouse.

Susan smiled. "I guess we've got some work to do today, right?"

He shrugged his shoulders. "Isn't that why we had kids?"

She laughed and tapped his forearm a couple of times. "Good one."

Susan walked back to the front of the church. Kids and parents were already going back and forth up the steps that led to the three big open doors of the church. To the far right stood Father Dennis, watching his flock work like little bees, and chatting with volunteers.

Oh, no, Michael thought, *I'm going to be spotted.*

As if on command, Father Dennis immediately saw Michael in the crowd and waved to him. Michael cringed. He hadn't been to mass in over a decade. It seemed as if every time Father Dennis saw Michael, he would ask, "Where have you been?"

As Father Dennis approached, Michael quickly grabbed a carton of food and ran up the stairs two at a time. "Hi, Father!" he said as he passed the priest.

Father Dennis smiled. "Good to see you working so hard for the church, Michael."

"Glad to help out."

Michael moved past the holy water sitting on the table near the entrance of the church, quickly dipping his fingers inside the bowl. He touched his forehead with it. Inside the building, it was cool and dark, with only four lights illuminating the lip of the altar. Michael could see the gleaming figures of Jesus in the center of the altar, Mary on the left, and Joseph on the right.

Michael knew his way around a church. As an altar boy, he'd helped serve mass four or five times a week. Sometimes Michael would do a mass, funeral, and wedding all in the same day. He liked weddings the best. Everyone was happy, and he would get a big tip from the best man. Michael knew the words from the mass by heart. When he graduated from Holy Child and his life as an altar boy ended, part of him was extinguished, too.

Today the church created in him mostly feelings of fear and pain. He and Vicki always used to go to church together. She felt that she had to pray for those who needed help because someday they might need some.

Ha, Michael thought, *what help did I get?*

To him, church was filled with a bunch of phonies who sat inside an air-conditioned building on a wooden pew without ever really hearing a word of the mass itself. Then the same parishioners went out on the street gossiping about each other and their neighbors. He didn't need or want any part of it.

And yet, he couldn't escape it: Father Dennis was walking right behind him.

"Michael, isn't this a beautiful church?"

Michael looked around the church. He saw the five arched windows along each of the two long sides of the building, under one of which were engraved the words MY FRIEND, YOUR SINS ARE FORGIVEN. The stations of the cross depicted in wooden carvings were affixed to the right of each window, while big white candles with green ribbing sat below. He took in the organ situated high above the pews, the altar made of white marble, and the podium from where the lector read.

It's beautiful, sure, Michael thought, *but where's he going with this?*

"Michael, your church awaits you," Father Dennis said with a pat on the back.

"Thanks, Father."

"Michael, we could really use your help."

"In what way, Father?"

"What about joining the choir?"

"Are you kidding? With my voice?"

"Michael, God doesn't care what you sound like. He only cares what's in your heart."

"No offense, Father. But I think I would turn even God off with my voice."

Father Dennis laughed and patted him on the shoulder. "What about being a lector?"

"I'm not sure . . ."

Father Dennis smiled. "Well, if you think you'd like to help out, let me know."

Michael looked up one more time at those carvings of Jesus' last moments on earth. "Well, I should go help the kids some more," he said, walking away.

He didn't want anyone calling him *lazy*. That word tore at his spine. Michael winced, remembering the dark days of living in Queens, defending his sanity against the daily verbal battering.

"You're not even trying to find a full-time job, you lazy jerk!"

Michael sat there quietly in the living room recliner. Silence was his most effective weapon in the Richmond Hill house. His older sister would not get the satisfaction of knowing she got to him. Of course, she couldn't see his knees rising slightly as his toes curled into the carpet.

"Look at me! When are you going to get a job?" she demanded.

I am *working,* Michael thought. He had a part-time job writing for a weekly football publication in Port Washington. Since he had no car and it was such a long trip by bus and train, on the weekends he slept overnight on the floor beneath his office desk. *That's* not working?

He knew he could have tried to do something noble and become a policeman or fireman or gone back to school to become a teacher. But he really loved sports and was willing to work his way up by doing all sorts of part-time work. For some reason, to his sister Connie this just wasn't enough.

"Say something!" she screeched.

"Okay," Michael shouted, boiling over, "how about 'shut up'?"

"Don't talk to her that way!" his father bellowed, rushing in from the kitchen.

Michael instinctively stood up and pushed past him as he made for the stairs. *Great, now he gets involved.*

"Get down here!" his father screamed. "Get down here, you moron!"

Michael didn't obey him; instead, he slammed his bedroom door. He listened to his father run up the two flights of stairs, wondering whether the old man was going to come through his door and finally confront him. He knew it wouldn't be much of a match: Jim was fifty-three years old while Michael was only twenty-two and in the best shape of his life. He lifted weights constantly and had little fat on his body. Meanwhile, his father smoked two packs of cigarettes a day and spent his nights drinking scotch.

But he's still my father, Michael thought, listening to him climb the stairs. Michael's stomach tightened as he leaned his 180-pound frame against the door.

"Let me in. Let me in!" Jim was trying to barrel through the door.

Michael didn't answer; instead, he planted his weight more firmly against the wood.

Thump! Thump! Thump! His father was angrily throwing himself against the door. Michael grew afraid that he might physically hurt the guy if he got in. He knew his father had such an overstated view of his own importance that he wouldn't be expecting Michael to fight back. *I'd like to punch him . . . although he's my father.*

Still uncertain, Michael continued to lean against the bedroom door, his hands clenched tightly around the doorknob. He listened for any movement, then cautiously opened the door. His father stood there glaring at him. Michael hesitated, then stepped aside and let his father into the room.

"What are you doing talking that way to your sister?"

"Why are you always defending her?"

"You have to stop mouthing off to your sister. Are you going to stop it?"

Michael didn't respond. Instead, he turned and flung himself face-down on the bed.

Jim took another step into the room. "Answer me," he demanded.

In an effort to avoid his father's menacing stare, Michael focused on the torn curtain covering the only window in the small room.

"Do you hate me?" Jim nearly whispered.

Stunned, Michael grimaced. *Are you serious?*

"Look at me," his father said forcefully as he moved closer. "Do you hate me? Are you angry about your mother? Do you hate me for what happened to her? Don't you think I did my best?"

Michael was silent for a few seconds before turning to him. "I know you did your best," he finally replied weakly.

Jim walked to the bookshelf, his thumb scrolling across the book spines, with his back to Michael. "Then why do you hate me?"

"I don't."

"Then why won't you be like the rest of us? Why won't you be part of this family? Why won't you talk to me about how you're feeling?"

Michael looked up slowly. "You're always yelling. You never listen."

Jim spun back to him quickly, his hands clenched in front of him. "Stop acting like a child. Then I'll listen."

Michael shook his head slowly.

"Do you miss your mom?"

"Of course."

"You're so silent and quiet. You're never around us. You never go out with us for dinner. It's like you're not even here."

Michael rolled onto his stomach, his head resting on his pillow. Glancing down, he noticed some crumbs that had fallen from his dinner last night. He pushed himself up, swinging his legs over the side of the bed to kick the crumbs under it.

He sighed. "I miss Mom. But I love her in my own way. I'm not angry at you. Just because I haven't cried in front of you doesn't mean I don't care. I'm angry at the way she died. Okay?"

"I tried, Michael. I really did."

"I know, Dad. . . . I guess she's in a better place now."

In one explosive motion, Jim whipped a book off the top of Michael's dresser, hurling it against his closet door. "A better place? What do you mean by that, you dumb—"

"Nothing!" Michael shouted.

His father scowled at him. "Yeah, in a better place. Better than here. Yeah, I know you don't like it here. You've made it very clear."

Michael shook his head and gave up. "Go away. You'll never understand. Please just go away."

"Sure, whatever. You'll just use this as another excuse. I wonder if you really cared about her at all." With that, Jim left the room.

Michael leaped up and slammed the door. He crumpled onto the floor, glancing at the contents of his tiny room: the steep piles of sports books around his bed, several empty soda cans littering the desk and bookshelf, even Bruce Springsteen's *The River* album, nestled under his dresser. A Springsteen poster draped the back wall while a photo of tennis star Chris Evert hung crookedly over his bed.

He thought about what he'd said. He'd meant heaven, but his dad had totally misunderstood. *I didn't mean it that way,* he thought. He wondered why he could never properly communicate with his father. It had always been difficult, but it was bleak now without his mother.

It seemed like only a few minutes later when he heard a soft knock.

"Michael, Father Pete here. Can I come in?"

"Sure."

Father Pete was a friend of the family's, particularly his father's. They had grown up together, and Father Pete handled all the family religious functions such as weddings, funerals, and baptisms. He was often over at the house during the holidays.

Michael stood up and opened the door. He cleared some papers from his desk chair and invited the priest to sit.

Father Pete wasted no time. "Michael, your father thinks you need psychological help."

"My father is the one who needs the psychological help."

"Why don't you talk to him?"

"I can't talk to him because he never listens. He's always yelling."

Michael reached down and grabbed *The River* album and turned it over to show Father Pete the lyrics to the song "Independence Day." It was a sorrowful description of Springsteen's relationship with his father and the inevitable parting between them. Michael played it over and over in his tiny room, the lyrics echoing in the attic, as if the pleas from Springsteen's voice would resonate with his father. He so wanted his dad to be a positive part of his life.

"It's well written," the priest said, looking up at Michael. "I like the part about the son leaving St. Mary's Gate. It's very symbolic. Why can't you two talk to each other like we're doing now?"

"He won't listen. I can't talk to someone who's always yelling."

"Well, Michael, he says his conditions are you either get psychological help or move out of the house."

"That's interesting, Father. So he's saying he feels I need help mentally but he'd throw me out of the house if he doesn't get his way. I'm not sure I could ever treat my son like that."

Father Pete didn't answer.

"Look, Father, I'll go for psychological help if he comes with me. I want him there with me so we can both discuss things, like about Mom and everything."

Father Pete looked encouraged. He stood up and headed toward the door. "Great! I think that will be fine."

It wasn't long before he returned with Jim's answer. "Michael . . .

he won't go with you. I think you're either going to have to go alone or else leave. He's ranting about something he said you almost did. He said something about you and your mother. He wouldn't explain it to me. Did you do something to your mom or say something before she died?"

"Father, he has it *all* wrong. I'll just say this: I wasn't going to do it."

Father Pete stared at him, perplexed. "Michael, that's between you and your father." He paused. "Do you have a place to stay?"

"I guess so," Michael said, wondering if he could move into his friend Steve's apartment in Flushing.

"God will take care and serve you, Michael."

Michael laughed bitterly. "Ha! I have to do this on my own."

As Father Pete stood there watching him, Michael started to pack his belongings: a few T-shirts, some torn shorts, a faded pair of jeans, and several socks, none of which matched. He grabbed some loose change and put it into the front pocket of his sweatpants. A dollar was lying near the side of the bed. He reached over to put it inside a shoebox.

He gathered up several of his own poems, including one about his father, and stuffed them inside the shoebox. Thoughts of the past year since his mom died almost overwhelmed him.

He turned around and looked at the priest. "Is this how God serves me?"

Father Pete glanced down at his folded hands, a sad look on his face.

"I'm sorry. I know, Father Pete. But can I just catch a stinking break?"

Father Pete shook his hand, passed him a hundred bucks from his dad, and told Michael it was time to leave.

Michael grabbed more boxes of food, following Laura's and Elizabeth's giggles and smiles up to the front of the church. An hour had passed, and now the area was cluttered with cartons leaning against the white marble fence surrounding the altar.

"The pile is getting too big," Father Dennis told the volunteers. "I need two helpers to bring some of this down to the basement for now."

He looked around. By now, most of the students were bored and tired. The parents looked pretty exhausted from climbing all the stairs. He spotted Michael and Elizabeth.

"What about you two?"

Michael looked suspiciously at Father Dennis. *Why does he think we're not tired from all the lifting and carrying?* "Yeah, sure, Father."

He felt a pat on his back. "You're a good man, Mike," said Susan, flashing a big smile at him. Michael returned the gesture with a wink.

Catching the exchange, Elizabeth's eyes widened. "We'd be happy to do it. Right, Dad?"

"Ah, sure," Michael said, his voice echoing throughout the big church.

He felt the bulky cell phone and keys inside his pockets. "Father, can I leave these here?"

"Of course."

"No one will steal them?" Michael said, trying to lighten the mood.

"I will bless them to make sure," the priest responded with a smile.

Michael had already left his wallet behind in his car. He hated to be weighed down by items of any sort when working. In fact, he'd stopped wearing a watch in high school, feeling it restricted him too much.

Elizabeth and Michael began moving some of the cartons. The doorway to the basement stairs was just to the left of the altar. It was about fifteen steps down before they reached the floor of the darkened room.

He looked around. The room was fairly large, maybe forty by sixty feet. Collection baskets and random piles of outdated hymnals littered the floor. There wasn't much room for more boxes.

"Great," Michael said, annoyed. "We'll have to move some of this mess before we bring down the rest of the cartons."

"Chill, Dad. This is supposed to help the needy."

"Chill? Okay, I'll chill. But, you know, I'm pretty needy. When is someone going to help me?"

"Oh, Dad. You have to lighten up a bit. Life's too short."

He turned from her and muttered under his breath, "Yes, I *know* life's too short."

Elizabeth began bouncing around the room. She picked up all the baskets and stacked them in one corner. Then she sprinted around the other side of the room, grabbing outdated missalettes and organizing them into piles on a nearby folding table.

"Look, Dad, the Empire State Building," she said with a smile, placing an old mustard-colored book on top.

Michael looked at the tall pile of books. "Great, but what about the cartons of food on the floor? How about making the Eiffel Tower with that so we can get out of here."

"Chill, Dad."

"Stop with the *chill* stuff . . . or *I'll* start using that word."

"Yuck, don't use that word," she said, laughing while picking up a discarded penlight in the corner and shining it on him. "You're old people. You can't talk like that."

"Old people? Ouch!" Michael peered at her with puppy-dog eyes and his bottom lip stuck out. He sucked in his stomach and pulled up his sweats higher than his belly button. "Now I am as old as Fred Mertz!"

"Um, Dad, Fred Mertz is dead."

"Yeah, so what's your point?"

As if on cue, they both fell into a fit of laughter. "Okay, you're totally freaking me out now," Elizabeth said with a grimace.

"What is this?" Michael asked with interest, picking the mustard-colored book off the pile. He thumbed through it while Elizabeth continued to work. It appeared to be a worn diary. The word on the cover—*Miraculum*—was faded and barely legible. Michael thought the word might be Latin. Many of the pages were falling out and the handwriting was mostly faint and spidery. The first entry was not legible. But the next one said 1797. Michael let out a low whistle. "Wow. I should show this to Father Dennis."

"Ah, Dad, don't you want to get out of here?"

"Yeah, sure, but . . ."

"We're almost done, Dad."

Michael put the small book in his pocket. When everything had been cleared away and nearly all the boxes were neatly stacked, he noticed for the first time a steel door marked with a gold cross in the center of the floor.

"That's strange."

Elizabeth walked over to check it out. "What is it?"

"I don't know and I don't want to know." Michael could hear Father Dennis up above thanking the volunteers for their help. "Let's get out of here, Elizabeth, and get the rest of those cartons."

"Go ahead, Dad. I'd like to see what's in there."

"Do me a favor: don't open it. Just leave the door alone."

Michael ran upstairs to grab the last of the cartons but bumped into Father Dennis, who was helping parishioners locate empty areas to place their food cartons. "I need to show you something, Father, when I'm done."

"Okay. I'm a little busy right now. And thanks, Michael, for staying around to bring the last of these downstairs."

"No problem, Father, glad to help!" Michael called over his shoulder. When he reached the basement, he dropped the cartons on the floor and looked around.

"Elizabeth?"

Oh, no. Michael saw that the steel door in the floor had been pulled back. *Are you kidding me?* He walked over to it and peered down. It was pitch-black, but he could make out a dark stairway.

"Elizabeth! Are you down there?"

The only response Michael heard were his words echoing below.

I can't believe she's going to make me come after her. He took a few steps down the old, wooden stairs. They creaked a bit under his weight, making him nervous.

"Elizabeth Ellen! Answer me!"

He started counting the steps, and by the time he came to the ninth one, he stopped. "Elizabeth Ellen Stewart. Come up here right now or I'll really be a fun killer!"

Michael had thought that should sufficiently scare her to return, but there was still no answer. With the complete absence of light, the darkness below felt sinister.

He took a few more steps. *Nah, she's always been afraid of the dark. Why would she go down here?* Michael climbed back up the stairway, convinced that she must be somewhere upstairs.

Michael ran back into the main part of the church. He spotted Father Dennis chatting with some parishioners. "Hey, Father, did Elizabeth come up here? Have you seen her?"

Father Dennis turned around and shook his head. "I haven't seen her up here." He noticed the book sticking out of Michael's pocket. "What's that?"

"What, Father?"

The priest pointed. "That book in your back pocket. Let me see it."

Michael pulled it out and handed it to him. Father Dennis started paging through it.

Michael grew impatient. "I've got to go find Elizabeth."

The priest looked concerned as he scanned through an entry before placing the book in his back pocket. "Michael, I'm going to hold on to this. I've never seen it before and yet there are reflections from many of the previous pastors of this old church."

"That's nice, Father . . . but about my daughter: do you know where she is?"

"Maybe she went outside with her friends?"

"I don't think so." Quickly he ran to the open front door and looked up and down the street. There was no sign of her.

Michael ran back to the basement stairs. He reached the trapdoor and called again. "Elizabeth? Are you down there?"

He started descending the stairs now at a rapid clip. He could feel panic beginning to set in. *What if she's fallen and hurt herself?* He was so far down into the subbasement that he wasn't sure anyone would be able to hear him from above if he needed to call for help.

Suddenly, his feet hit solid ground. He stretched out his right arm and felt a concrete wall. Leaning slightly to the left, he reached out and touched another wall. They were about six feet apart, creating a tunnel, although he could only see complete blackness ahead.

"Elizabeth!"

Still no answer.

Michael shuffled slowly forward. As he took each step, he kept the fingertips of his right hand against one wall while his left balanced him upright on the other. Every five steps or so, he took a deep breath. The air felt cold and damp in his lungs.

"Elizabeth, I'm really getting worried now," Michael said, trying to sound calm and rational. "Come back and we'll talk. I'm sorry if I upset you upstairs."

Michael tentatively took more steps, trying not to think about the assortment of rodents that must live down here. After traveling about thirty more feet, he stopped when he felt the floor underneath him shake slightly. "What was that? Did you feel that?" he called out, trying to remain calm and hoping that Elizabeth would respond.

The ground underneath his feet felt different. *Has the floor changed to sand under me, or is that my imagination?*

"Elizabeth, you are going to be grounded! Yeah, I know you're fourteen, but I can still ground you! You can even kiss your iPhone good-bye for at least a month!"

He paused. "She won't care. She's a teenager. Yeah, I'll chill out. Hear that, *Liz*? I said I'm going to *chill out*!"

While he was wondering why he kept expecting Elizabeth to respond to the word *chill*, he felt the floor shake again; this time it had a more defined feel, more intense.

"Great! Thank you, Elizabeth. Thank you for making this lovely experience at the church even *longer*, and *much* more fun."

He stopped walking when a gust of warm air hit him. "Oh, God, please let her be okay."

The shaking under his feet became more frequent. His eyes had adjusted to the darkness, and in the distance he could now see what looked like the beam from a miniature flashlight. The light remained steady, like a beacon drawing him near.

"Elizabeth!" Michael shouted, stumbling toward the light. "Is that you up there?"

Suddenly his head struck the ceiling. He winced and ducked, realizing the tunnel was narrowing. He heard a muffled sound in the distance, then felt the floor shake more violently.

"What is that?"

"Dad!" cried a voice faintly.

Michael's heart raced. "Elizabeth?"

There was no answer.

Michael moved more quickly now, hands skimming over the walls, stumbling a few times as he tried to reach the light. *"Elizabeth, can you hear me?"*

The ground shook again and the muffled sounds became more discernible.

"Dad?"

Even though he could hear her, Michael still couldn't see her. "Where *are* you?"

"Over here, Dad!"

The ground shook again and Michael could make out a small figure in front of him. She was partially blocking the light coming from above, and seeing her silhouette was a relief.

"Elizabeth!"

"Dad!"

"What were you thinking?"

"Shh!" she whispered. "Shh!" She reached out and grabbed his back. "Dad! Oh, Dad!"

"Why did you come down here? I said not to. You could've been hurt, you could've—"

"Look!" Elizabeth pointed, cutting him off. "Look! Look at this!"

Michael shielded his eyes and gazed through what appeared to be a sewer grate at the end of the tunnel. Beyond it, he could see dirt bouncing up from the churning wheels of carts and the sandaled feet of men running past them.

"Where are we?"

2

MEETING A MURDERER

Michael and Elizabeth stared up through the grate, startled by what they saw. Just above them soldiers wearing metal helmets and chest plates were mounted on horses. They jogged by in two-by-two formation, carrying long, narrow spears in their hands.

They could see other soldiers lining the street, pushing back a large crowd that had gathered. The men and women were strangely dressed in floor-length tunics and veils, some wearing tattered sandals. Michael couldn't help but notice that their hair looked unwashed.

"Elizabeth, did you hear anything in school about an Easter play going on in town?" Michael whispered.

"No, Dad. I wonder if we're in East Northport or maybe even Kings Park?"

Michael thought he had walked for a considerable distance inside the dark tunnel before finding Elizabeth. Maybe they *were* in one of the neighboring towns. But then again, maybe it had just felt that long. He tried to calculate the distance and the direction in his head.

Could we have gone farther than I thought?

"I'm not sure where we are, but we could be in Huntington," Michael whispered back, trying to think of anything that could help him rationalize what he was seeing. "But I don't know what's going on there. That town always has something going on."

The uncertainty of everything made him grow angry again at Elizabeth. Turning to her, he whispered, "Why didn't you listen to me? Why did you go in this forsaken tunnel and scare me? Do you know what my life would be like without you? Do you?"

"I'm sorry!" she exclaimed. "I wanted to see what was down here. There were all sorts of great drawings all along the tunnel." To make her point, she shone the light on the side of the wall, illuminating pictures of men being pulled in chariots.

"Interesting."

"Interesting? I thought you loved history. Look at this one." Elizabeth turned toward the other side and sprayed the wall with her penlight.

Michael bent down to get a closer look. "It looks like a soldier putting a spear through a man's heart," he said, revolted.

"That's what I thought."

Michael rubbed his hand along the wall. "That's odd. This feels like it was drawn recently." He looked up again to the street. "It looks so real." Then he turned and looked back at the darkness of the tunnel behind them. "We should go back."

But his attention was drawn to the crowd above them. They could hear gasping and shouts as a man was dragged by a soldier through the streets. The man's robe was bloodied and torn, and he had shackles around his ankles. He was badly bruised, with a large, bleeding gash in his right shoulder.

Michael was a big fan of history. It was probably the only subject in school that he had really enjoyed. He was always fascinated by famous people and events from the past. It showed in his schoolwork— it was the one subject he didn't have to worry about repeating in summer school. He stared in awe.

"Wow, Elizabeth. Look at the metal spears. They look so real. These guys totally look like they're Roman soldiers from those documentaries I watch."

Elizabeth was unimpressed. She was more interested in the clothes.

"How could kids back then enjoy these clothes?" she asked, shaking her head. "I bet these guys will probably be happy to get home and change. And look at the girls. Their faces are all covered up."

"They're just veils." Michael laughed nervously. This was almost too real. He glanced over at Elizabeth and saw her mouth drop. She covered her eyes and looked away.

"What's wrong?"

She pointed through the grate. Three soldiers had gotten off their horses and were poking the man in chains with their spears. The roar of the crowd grew louder.

Michael again felt a surge of panic but tried to keep his tone light. "It's just playacting." He craned his neck to get a better look and saw one soldier stab the man in the leg, causing him to scream in pain as blood gushed from the wound. The other two soldiers started beating him on the back with the shafts of their spears.

"No!" Elizabeth yelled before Michael could put his hand over her mouth.

"Shh!"

She pulled away from him. "Dad, we've got to do something!"

The soldiers hit the man in his back and legs repeatedly. He lay on the ground trying to cover his head with his hands.

This can't be real. "Maybe that's fake blood?" Michael suggested. "You know, like the blood you see in the movies and on television?"

"It looks real to me."

Michael felt helpless. "What kind of play is this anyway? I can't believe the town approved this kind of street play. I'm sure the cops are going to stop it. Those people out there should be doing something. But they're all standing around like nothing is going on."

"We're doing nothing, too, Dad!"

Michael could see the fear in his daughter's eyes as they watched the soldiers now kicking the man, who was obviously in terrible pain. The look on her face gripped Michael's heart. But love for his daughter—and fear that Elizabeth would get hurt if he tried to intervene—paralyzed him.

He couldn't let anything happen to her. She was his reason to live.

Michael reached into his pocket. Empty. Then he remembered. "Oh, no, I left my cell phone back at the church."

"I don't have mine with me either, but we have to do something. We can't just watch this and do nothing."

The soldiers started spitting on the man. Elizabeth screeched in horror. "No, no!" she shouted through the tiny opening. "Stop it!"

"Quiet, Elizabeth!" Michael hissed as he put his hand up to her mouth.

But Elizabeth slapped his hand away and pushed forward against the metal grate. Its frame cracked slightly.

To Michael, the crowd outside seemed to be getting louder and the soldiers' laughter more defined. "No, Elizabeth, stop. Please stop pushing!"

"I have to help, Dad. I have to help him!"

With one last thrust, the grate broke free of its frame, falling out onto the road above. Elizabeth pushed against Michael, hoisting herself through the opening, and dropping her miniature flashlight pen. Getting to her feet quickly, she ran over to the bloodied man.

Michael grunted as he pulled himself up onto the road. "Elizabeth, stop!"

He ran over to Elizabeth and grabbed her arm, pulling her away from the bleeding man. "Sir, are you okay? We need to get you some medical attention."

He turned toward the crowd. "Someone should really call 911!" he shouted, exasperated.

Several soldiers surrounded them, one of whom pulled Elizabeth away from the man.

"Get your hands off my daughter!" Michael screamed.

"Κατασιγάζω!" a soldier shouted.*

---

* Koine Greek, a language spoken by the Romans and others in first-century Jerusalem. Translation = Silence!

Another soldier waved at the crowd to quiet them, then turned to Michael. "Πώς σας λένε?" *

Michael and Elizabeth looked at each other, unable to understand what the soldiers were saying. One began to scream at him. "Αποκρίνομαι!" †

"What?" Michael muttered. "Who are you? What is going on here? This guy is seriously hurt!"

The soldier pushed his spear into Elizabeth's chest. "Αποκρίνομαι!"

"Stop! Please don't hurt her!" Michael screamed.

"Αποκρίνομαι! Πώς σας λένε?"

"What . . . what did you say?" implored Michael as he was pushed to the ground.

"Dad!" said Elizabeth weakly as the soldier continued to press his spear near her neck.

Michael reached up with his left hand, grasping at the spear, his ring sparkling in the sunlight. The soldier relaxed his stance slightly and leaned over, grabbing his hand. He pulled at Michael's ring.

"No!" he shouted at the soldier.

The soldier pressed his spear with one hand against Elizabeth's shoulder and reached for the ring with the other. Still unable to comprehend the soldier's demands, Michael hesitated. The soldier took his spear away from Elizabeth and jabbed at Michael's hand, gesturing at the gold ring.

"No," Michael said, shaking his head. "Not my ring. Please."

The soldier swung his spear wildly around, whipping it past Elizabeth's face.

"Okay, okay, whatever you want." Michael looked at the ring quickly, kissed it, and slowly slid it off his finger. "I'm sorry . . . I'm so sorry," he whispered.

He weakly reached up to give the ring to the soldier, who seized it violently. Suddenly a big gust of wind bent the fig trees in the dis-

*Translation = Who are you?
†Translation = Answer!

tance, tossing the fruit in the air and whipping up the dust from the ground. The onlookers in the crowd covered their faces while the soldiers cowered sideways, putting their shields up to protect against the thrashing particles of dirt. Some fell to the ground, coughing, gagging from the soil that was filling their throats and ears. Michael lowered his head to avoid the swirling dust, expecting any moment that he, too, would begin to choke.

A moment later, he glanced over at Elizabeth in surprise. He actually felt fine. A feeling of warmth embraced him, and he found himself breathing normally. Elizabeth nodded at him. She seemed to be having the same experience, while all around them soldiers dropped to the ground, wheezing, and some vomiting. Michael felt as if he were floating, yet his feet remained firmly planted on the ground. The pinging of the sand against their faces didn't sting at all; instead, he found it soothing.

The wind died down as suddenly as it had started, and the swirling dust in the air settled. The soldiers, grimacing and gasping, staggered to their feet and looked around in wonder. Still clutching the ring in his hand, the one soldier wiped furiously at his eyes and assumed his menacing stance.

"How would you like your daughter to watch you die?" he asked clearly.

Michael was stunned. He looked at Elizabeth and saw that suddenly she, too, could understand the soldier's words.

The soldier thrust the metal edge of the spear toward Michael, jabbing him slightly. "What the . . . ? Stop! I gave you what you wanted," Michael said angrily. "You got my ring!"

He turned toward the man who was still bleeding. "You really hurt him. You need to call an ambulance, right now."

A soldier rode up to the crowd and quickly dismounted. Michael could hear his flat-soled sandals slapping against the stone road.

"Oh, it's you," he said coolly. "Tell me what your interests are here."

Michael turned to the swarming crowd. "Someone call 911, please!

Call a cop! This man is really hurt. Jesus, the poor man is bleeding. Help him!"

The soldier drew near. "So, you are a follower of Jesus. Just like your friend. Do you want to join him?"

Michael looked confused. "What?"

Elizabeth tried to help the bloodied man to his feet. Another soldier cut between them, pushing her to the ground.

"Ow." She flinched. "My arm!"

"Leave her alone!" Michael yelled.

As she tried to stand, her foot caught in the hem of the T-shirt, tearing it. Michael leaped at the soldier who had hit Elizabeth and struck him on the side of the head. Another soldier hammered Michael with his shield, driving him to the ground.

"Dad, are you okay?" Elizabeth cried, pushing her way past the soldiers.

"I'm okay." He winced and looked up at her. "I'm fine."

The crowd was cheering with excitement. The soldier who had crushed Michael down with his shield bent over and picked up the piece of Elizabeth's torn shirt. Laughing, he put it underneath the back of his helmet and turned to Elizabeth with a leer.

"Is she the one, Marcus?" one of the soldiers asked, his eyebrows raised mockingly.

"Yes!" he hissed, with a menacing smile. "She will be mine. Soon."

Michael was furious. "You put your hands on my daughter and I'll kill you."

Marcus lunged at him, causing Michael to roll backward. The soldier towered over him. Jamming his spear against Michael's chest, he warned, "The next time you challenge me will be the last time you breathe."

Another soldier grabbed Michael and roughly pulled him to his feet. The other soldiers began dragging him and Elizabeth through the streets.

"Keep away from her," Michael shouted angrily.

The hot, dry air around them was stifling as they moved through a maze of dusty streets. Michael noticed that all the buildings they passed had flat fronts and were simply made; it was hard to tell one from another. They were constructed of stone, and many were no more than two stories high. There was a carnival-like atmosphere, people milling around near makeshift tables. The aroma of frying fish and fresh fruit lingered in the air.

"Where are we? What town are we in?" Michael shouted to one of the soldiers.

"Just keep moving!"

The soldiers swung the sides of their spears into his back, and Michael's legs buckled. "Keep quiet!"

He looked around, searching for a friendly face, even someone he would recognize from the parish—perhaps his friends Tom, Karen, Anne, Dennis, or Donna from the soccer league? As he scoured the multitude of people they passed, panic set in.

He couldn't find anyone he knew, and everyone seemed to be mocking them. Tears dripped down Elizabeth's cheeks, which rattled him emotionally. Michael couldn't help but cry, too.

As he tried in vain to wipe his face clean with his dusty hands, a woman in a black veil traveling in the crowd around them gave him a cloth. She looked at him quizzically, while signaling him to clean his face. "I'm so glad to see you. But why did you come back?" she whispered to him. Then she softly kissed him on the cheek.

Michael shook his head in confusion. "Who are you? What do you mean?" But there was no time to hear her answer as the soldiers dragged them on.

The crowd started to thin as the soldiers brought the bloodied man, Michael, and Elizabeth through a gate into what appeared to be a giant courtyard. There was no grass, just stones that paved the massive area. On the far end, a formidable series of steps led to a huge marble building supported by eight stanchions.

This isn't like any building on Long Island, Michael thought. *Is this a dream?*

Elizabeth looked over at her dad. He could tell that she was frightened. Earlier, her desire to help the man had overshadowed any anxiety she might have felt. But now, he could see the fear in her eyes.

Prodded by the guards, the three of them climbed the marble steps. The sun was strong and Michael could feel the sweat splattered on his forehead. His sandals were filthy and the knot in his stomach was growing. He was about ten feet away from Elizabeth. He tried to reassure her.

"Relax, Elizabeth, someone will call the cops."

She nodded and managed a slight smile.

A man clothed in a heavily embroidered robe strolled out gallantly from the building. His shoulders were lean and muscular. Another man, apparently some sort of servant, approached him with a bowl of water. He dipped his hands in it, then splashed his face.

"Your Excellence," shouted a soldier standing next to Michael. "We have three rebels. They have committed crimes against Caesar."

Michael was stunned. "What?" he yelled. "Caesar?"

"Silence!" bellowed the court guard.

"I won't be silent," Michael shouted back. "This man was being viciously beaten. All we tried to do was help him. I've had enough of this. Where are we?"

The man with the embroidered robe looked at Michael. "Why do you care if this man is beaten?"

"I don't like seeing anyone being whipped or kicked or anything. It's not right."

"Not right?" the man responded incredulously. "Was it right that this man murdered a Roman soldier?"

Michael's jaw dropped. "Roman soldier? What Roman soldier?" *This has to be a dream.* "I don't think a murder in an Easter play is a crime," he added sarcastically.

"Easter?"

Elizabeth broke the silence. "Easter. When Jesus rose from the dead."

"Jesus of Nazareth?" the man asked. "Are you talking about the so-called prophet?" Turning toward his servant, he asked, "Has anyone else heard this? He's dead?"

The servant threw his hands up in the air and shook his head.

"Of course he's dead," Michael said impatiently.

The man stared at him. "How dare you mock me?" He paused a moment, then continued, "So you're one of his followers?"

Michael wasn't sure how to answer. Then he weakly replied, "No."

"Good." The man nodded approvingly. "But your daughter *has* committed a crime."

"No, she hasn't!" Michael said defiantly. He turned to the crowd. "Hey, can somebody help us here? Where are the cops? We need to get this man to a hospital."

The man in the embroidered robe looked back sternly at Michael. "Don't you understand that the man you tried to help killed a Roman soldier?"

Again with the Roman-soldier bit, Michael thought incredulously. He looked up at the sky and realized that he hadn't seen any airplanes, nor had he noticed or heard any cars or motorcycles, for that matter. This certainly wasn't Main Street in Huntington. There were no shops, nor teenagers on skateboards or adults riding bikes.

Where are we?

"I don't know anything about any killing," Michael said desperately. "My daughter and I were only trying to help this man. We didn't know he was a murderer."

A soldier stepped forward. "Your Excellence, what would you like us to do with these prisoners?"

"Let us go," Michael demanded. "We haven't done anything."

"Yes, you have," the man in the elegant robes responded. "You were trying to help a murderer. You interfered with the actions of the Roman empire." Turning his back on them, the man put his hands into the large basin of water and again splashed his face.

Michael could feel his own perspiration dripping onto his dirty sandals. He looked over at Elizabeth. She was starting to weep again and he felt powerless. She looked much smaller surrounded by as many as ten soldiers with spears.

He stared at Elizabeth until she met his eyes. *I love you,* Michael mouthed, causing fresh tears to roll down her face.

"Bring me Barabbas!"

Hearing the command, the soldiers dragged the bloodied man up the steps to stand in front of the man in the embroidered robes.

"Barabbas, until your fate is determined, you will remain in prison for the killing of a Roman soldier."

"Barabbas?" Michael whispered in disbelief. "This guy's name is Barabbas?"

Elizabeth had recognized the name, too. She stared back at her father, puzzled and horrified.

Suddenly the man in the fancy robes turned back to them. "Come here!" he ordered.

The soldiers pushed Elizabeth and Michael up the last few steps until they stood on the lip of the grand platform. The man had re-treated to an area off-center from the crowd. He pulled at his heavy robes, arranging them with great care as he sat back on an ornate stone chair, raised a foot off the floor like a throne. A tufted pillow was pro-vided for his back by a young male servant, his robe shorter than that of all others around him. The soldiers pushed Michael and Elizabeth again from behind, maneuvering them closer.

The stone walls arched over them, providing a hint of shade. A loose white cloth hung between the wall and a pillar ten feet above the man, who seemed to languish in his distance from the crowd. His gaze on them was unsettling.

"Who are you?" Michael asked, his voice barely a whisper.

The man glanced up at the cloth above him, watching it billow in the wind before glancing back at them. "The only thing you need to know is that as the high priest, Herod has given me the authority to punish you."

"What? Herod? Punish us for what?"

"You will be punished for helping a murderer, the murderer Barabbas." His voice was cold, yet even and measured.

Michael stepped toward him, hands clenched at his side. "I said we didn't know that he was a murderer."

"Please, sir, we were just trying to help," Elizabeth pleaded, grabbing Michael by the arm.

The man turned and studied Elizabeth for a moment. His hands swept over the fine threading of his robe, smoothing it out in his lap. He cocked his head quizzically. "While your father claims he isn't a follower of this Jesus of Nazareth, you do. Why is that?"

"I just am."

"Silly girl, you could get yourself into a lot of trouble thinking that way." The corners of the man's mouth turned upward, pressing deeply into his wrinkled cheeks. "At least your father is wiser. You should listen to him. He knows it is our imperial government that provides for you and rules over you. *Not* that criminal."

"Please, sir . . . Your Excellence," Michael interjected as he shifted his weight to the right, blocking Elizabeth behind him. "Please, she's just a kid and doesn't know much. Please let her go."

The guard spoke urgently, "Your Excellency, please remember that they were trying to help a murderer, a criminal who viciously killed a Roman soldier."

"I know what the crime is," the high priest snapped back, clearly annoyed. Michael again scanned the crowd for help and met the eyes of the woman in the black veil. She seemed to be studying him; he caught her squinting at him, lost in concentration. She looked away immediately, as if he would recognize her.

"Who are you and your daughter staying with for the festivities?" the high priest asked, his eyebrows rising mockingly.

Michael's eye searched the area, trying to make sense of the scene. "What festivities? Are you talking about Easter? I'm not sure . . . I don't know where I am. What town is this?" He glanced over his shoulder at the group of people gathered by the foot of the steps. "Maybe I could call someone? I can call my sister. She can give me a ride home."

The high priest chuckled, misunderstanding the request. He lifted his arm, indicating the crowd still watching from a distance. "Go ahead, call someone."

Michael was even more confused. They were in a town on Long Island with no cops, no air-conditioning, no streetlights, no recognizable shops, and, apparently, no phones.

"Your Excellency!" The woman in the black veil stepped out from the massive crowd. "Forgive my insolence, but I have no other to speak for me. Your pity, please."

The high priest looked down at her with interest. He smiled again before gesturing for her to join them.

Michael watched as she drew a breath to steady herself. Then, head down as if in penance, she moved toward the steps. When she reached the top, she paused.

"May I?" the woman asked, indicating her veil.

"You may."

The woman pulled the veil back from her forehead, her hands trembling ever so slightly before she clasped them. She appeared prayerful, though her countenance belied any sort of peace. Her green eyes were striking, the pupils fixed in concentration. A lock of light brown hair fell forward at her temple, softening the edges of her thin, angular face. Michael realized she was much younger than her slow gait had indicated.

"Come no closer," the high priest called out to her, his chin high and proud. He settled back into the chair. "What is it that you want?"

"My name is Leah. You asked if they had any family or friends," the woman replied. "This is my brother and his daughter. Please let them come with me."

The man nodded at the soldiers flanking Michael and Elizabeth before gazing back at her. "Did they know Barabbas was a murderer?"

"They are not from here," she said. "They wouldn't know."

"Everyone knows Barabbas is a murderer," the soldier on Michael's right said with a snicker.

"Obviously, not everyone knew," the high priest said, mocking him. Many in the crowd laughed, irritating the soldier even more. He glared at Michael, lifting his spear in a menacing way.

The high priest turned back to Michael. "You have a daughter to take care of. I have one myself. We should both shoulder our responsibilities and keep them from harm."

Michael nodded.

"Sir, we'll upset many in the army if we allow them both to go," the court guard pleaded.

The high priest rose and strolled thoughtfully back and forth in front of the prisoners. He then stopped at the side of the soldier and spoke in a monotone, "How much anger do you see?"

"Sir, enough to cause a problem during the festivities."

The high priest turned to Elizabeth. "Where is your husband?"

Elizabeth shook her head, puzzled by the question. "Husband? What?! I'm not married!"

"Perhaps it's best you find one."

"She will be with me," the woman with the black veil said. "Let me bring her back to my home."

The high priest slowly looked around. Sensing the animosity building up among the impatient soldiers, he quickly made his decision.

"You've disrespected me and my soldiers," he said firmly to Michael and Elizabeth. Then he walked down a few steps and surveyed the crowd, enjoying the attention. Suddenly he spun back up the steps and faced Elizabeth and Michael again.

The high priest pointed at Leah. "Woman, take your brother's daughter and show her the way home." Then he turned toward Elizabeth, hissing, "Do not disrespect me again, woman. Cover your face or you'll find a place with your father."

Gesturing at Michael, the high priest shouted loud enough so that even those in the rear of the crowd could hear him, "Take him to the prison to await sentencing. Let it be known that if you help a murderer, we will treat you like one."

The soldiers chuckled in agreement and the high priest seemed to revel in the moment.

"No," screamed Elizabeth as she struggled away from the soldiers to reach her father.

Leah swiftly moved toward her and grabbed her arm. "Stop. Or you'll get hurt."

"I don't care, they're taking my father!"

Leah's grip tightened around Elizabeth's arm as two Roman soldiers led Michael away. He turned slightly to get a last glance of her. "Go, Elizabeth, go with the woman, get back to Northport," he pleaded.

"Listen to him, woman!" the high priest said, gliding toward Elizabeth. "You are to go with your father's sister and stay with her while you are here for the festivities. Do not travel at night. Not everyone will show mercy like I have today. The soldiers will remember you for what you tried to do. Next time I will not help you." His hand slapped at the air, his palm upturned. "Go now!"

"Thank you for your mercy," Leah said, her face turned downward. She leaned into Elizabeth, pulling her back slightly. "Come, come with me quickly," she whispered, nodding once to Michael. "I'll take care of her."

Elizabeth watched as her father was led off into the courtyard below. She struggled to follow him as closely as she could, but the crowd only parted for the soldiers, trapping her behind the mob.

"Take this," said Leah, ripping a piece of garment under her robes and then handing it to Elizabeth.

"I'm not wearing this," said Elizabeth, giving it back.

Leah grabbed her arm and tightened her grip. Staring at Elizabeth she implored, "Do you want to die? Listen to me!"

Elizabeth remained silent, glaring, then adjusted the veil over her face.

3

A MARCH
TO DEATH

The crowd started to disperse as the soldiers dragged Michael farther from the courtyard. People still lined the sides of the dusty stone road, eyeing the three of them as they walked past. Some boldly hissed and taunted the soldiers from afar, while others mocked Michael.

The noise and catcalls unnerved him briefly, but then a strange calm took over. He began to register every unusual sight and image, mentally making note of each unique landmark. He took a deep breath in an effort to shake off the fear that threatened to suffocate him.

The walk was slow and measured. The soldiers scanned the restless crowd, monitoring everyone as if a skirmish could erupt at any moment. Their path took them around the back of the courtyard, and Michael was astounded by how large the high priest's enclave must be, given how far they had already traveled.

He hesitated slightly, wheeling back to determine if Elizabeth and the woman were following him. The road behind him appeared nearly empty. A sharp blow to his back sent a surge of pain shooting to the top of his head.

"Keep moving," yelled the soldier on his right.

"I am!" Michael replied angrily.

The soldier on the left whipped the end of his spear into Michael's right leg, causing him to stumble in pain. The other soldier laughed menacingly.

The men on the side streets continued to yell but this time directed their jeers at the soldiers. Michael noticed that the women, all veiled, looked down as the soldiers paraded by. One of the soldiers followed his gaze. "Keep moving," he ordered.

All the blows he had taken reminded Michael of his early childhood days when he misspoke or did something wrong. A whack on the head was sometimes the punishment, but more often than not, it was a painful hour on his knees in a corner of his bedroom with his hands folded on top of his head. In retrospect, that penance was nothing compared to this.

As they walked, Michael realized in panic that they were traveling in the opposite direction of the tunnel's entrance. But then this thought brought him a sense of solace: he was drawing the soldiers away from the tunnel, which meant that Elizabeth would be free to go back home, where he would soon join her. *If I don't wake up first.*

He tried to compose himself but an overpowering fear for Elizabeth's safety nearly sidelined him as the soldiers turned the corner onto a new street. Before him loomed a majestic building, cut into the hillside sweeping upward behind it. Four gigantic towers, one higher than the other three, shot up into the skyline above him. He was mesmerized by how much it resembled a medieval castle. As they drew closer, Michael wondered how this could possibly be the prison.

They approached five soldiers flanking the grand entrance, around which small clusters of people huddled. Some of the soldiers, dressed in shining gold helmets and silver breastplates, held spears in their hands while others lazily swung round cement balls dangling from chains. Michael's captors nodded their heads toward the front guards and were immediately allowed admission. Once inside, the retaining wall soared above them, and Michael was impressed by its grandeur. His gaze followed it upward for as high as he could see.

The soldier to his right cracked him on the back of the head. "Don't worry. You're not going there," he chuckled.

The other soldier shoved Michael hard to the right, propelling him sideways through a small archway. The passageway was narrow and led to a dark, steep stairway. It was so tight that one soldier had to stand in front of Michael while the other held on to him from the back. Michael tried counting the steps but lost track at forty-five; the oppressive heat distracted him.

At the foot of the stairs, Michael immediately detected a pungent odor in the humid air. *What is that smell? Dead fish?*

The soldiers pushed him farther down the dank hallway before them. The smell intensified, causing Michael to put his shoulder to his nose. The soldier on his right looked at Michael and grinned. "Is this your first time coming to Antonia?"

"What is this place?"

"It's where Jews like you come to die." Both soldiers laughed.

"I'm not a Jew!" Michael protested.

"Oh, you're not?" asked the soldier on his left. "Then what are you? You're not a Roman."

Michael didn't answer right away, measuring the consequences of what he was going to say. Obviously, this was no place for a Jewish man or woman. But there appeared to be an anger regarding Jesus as well. So he chose the safe route. "I'm just a guy who wants to get home and see my daughter. That's all."

The soldiers laughed again. "Welcome home," one of them sneered.

The hallway emptied out onto another stairway, which descended below them. A waft of stale air overpowered them. Michael tried not to gag.

"What is that smell?"

"Rotting flesh," the soldier on his left answered. "Smells good, doesn't it?"

Michael stopped, shocked at what he'd just heard. "I'm not going down there!" Instinctively he gave a swift, measured kick to the back of the soldier's leg, and he released his grip. Michael staggered back but the other soldier still hung on gamely.

Several soldiers from below heard the commotion and came rushing up, swinging their spears at Michael and knocking him to the ground. He curled up in a fetal position with his arms covering his face in a vain attempt to stop the blows.

"Enough!" shouted an authoritative voice. Michael lowered his arms and looked up. A soldier with a white piece of cloth dangling from the back of his helmet stared down at him.

"Help him to his feet and put him in the dungeon. But leave him alone, he's mine!"

"Yes, Marcus," said one of the soldiers. "Is there anything else you need to be done?"

"Keep him handcuffed to the wall. I'll take care of him later myself."

The soldier bowed to Marcus. He tried to drag Michael to his feet but he wouldn't stand.

"So, you're going to be difficult?" another soldier asked. Michael cried out as his arms were yanked up and he was forced to walk. As they half-dragged him down the staircase, he heard one mutter, "I wonder why Marcus has an interest in this prisoner."

The other soldier shrugged. "It's usually the women prisoners he cares about."

Michael felt like a mouse inside a maze as they made their way through the twisting, filthy corridors below. *The prison must be huge.* But what struck him most was the noise. Muffled screams and the sounds of whips penetrating human flesh echoed from all sides. The sound of cloth tearing and a woman's cry for help made Michael wince helplessly. It was hard to believe that only a few hours ago he'd been worrying about what Elizabeth would wear.

He turned to the right to catch a glimpse of the cells and saw a skeleton, arms and legs still shackled, hanging from the ceiling by what appeared to be a grimy rag around its neck. To his left, he saw a man and a little boy huddled together, weeping, their clothes torn and blood dripping from several gashes on their faces. They turned away and covered their faces in shame. In the cell next to them, a soldier was swinging a metal ball against a fallen man lying near the cell's entrance. As Michael drew closer, he felt a splatter of blood hit his face. He retreated in horror and furiously tried to wipe his cheek.

The soldiers moved him along more quickly. "Let's get rid of him so we can get some dinner," the soldier on the left said.

The other soldier nodded. "Move!"

After passing another bank of cells, each containing more horrifying scenes of suffering, Michael came to the last, where he heard low groans and weeping. He was startled to see Barabbas chained to the wall in the adjacent cell.

The murderer greeted him like an old friend. "Ah, so they got you, too?" he mumbled, a faint smile spreading across his bruised and swollen face.

The soldier on Michael's left opened the metal gate and shoved him into the ten-by-ten cell. The other soldier locked Michael's arm into a chain protruding out of the wall and then tightened the clamp so it pinched his skin. "Now you two killers can die side by side," he sneered. He smashed Michael against the wall with one last parting kick in the gut. Michael's knees buckled, and he fell to the ground, his right arm still tethered to the chain at a grotesque angle.

"Are you all right, my friend?" Barabbas asked.

"I've been better," Michael groaned.

He pulled himself to a sitting position and looked around. It was so dark that the only image he could decipher was the outline of the bars that covered the cell opening. Muffled sounds of men and women crying, begging for leniency, were all around them. He could hear Barabbas jiggling his chain, trying to jerk it out of the wall.

This has got to be a nightmare. I'm going to wake up from this soon and I'll be back in Northport. Michael closed his eyes briefly and opened them quickly when a drip of blood from the top of his forehead ran into his eye. He wiped it away quickly. *This isn't a dream. But where am I?*

He got to his feet slowly and jerked on the chain. No luck. The harder he jerked, the more the clamp dug into his wrist.

"Keep trying," Barabbas urged. "We've got to find a way out of here."

"Here?" asked Michael wearily. "Where is here?"

"Here is the Roman prison."

"I just don't understand how that can be—"

Barabbas interrupted him. "Yes, that happened to me the first time they got me."

Michael shook his head in confusion. "You've been here before?"

"Yes."

"So we'll get out of here soon?"

"My friend, you may never get out."

Stunned, Michael slid back down the wall and shook his head as the enormity of the situation sank in. "I don't understand," he muttered. "What did I do wrong?"

They both started pulling on the chains, attracting a soldier's attention. "Stop!" he shouted. He then slid his spear through the cell opening, poking Barabbas and then Michael. "Try it again, and I'll come in there and make sure I reach you," the soldier yelled.

Michael sat back against the wall. His only thoughts now were on Elizabeth. *If I had only stopped her from coming down into the tunnel. Why did I have to go back upstairs? I should have made sure she came with me. Maybe she can get home and find help?*

The chain in the wall made it impossible for him to lie down completely as exhaustion overtook him. The heat of the dungeon seeped into Michael's body, and his throat was parched. "Barabbas, do they give you any water?"

"When the sun comes up."

Michael tried not to think about how thirsty he was. It was probably best to keep talking. "Barabbas, would you—"

Another Roman soldier bolted toward Michael, slamming his spear against the rusty rods. "Stop!"

The clanging of the metal weapon against the front of his cell set

Michael's teeth on edge. He briefly forgot about his physical ills. He had mixed emotions about Barabbas and helping him. After seeing the cruel methods of the Romans, he understood how anger could build up in its victims. He wondered if prayer could save him this evening, but struggled to remember a time when it actually had.

Michael's stomach twisted in pain as he sat on the E train. He leaned down to gasp for some air as a woman sitting next to him got up and moved away.

It must be my breath, he thought with embarrassment.

He rubbed his chest in an effort to ease the nausea. *It has to be from that tuna fish sandwich. I shouldn't have saved it from yesterday.*

It was a cold December night. Michael sat near a heater, absorbing the warm air like a dog rolling on grass. *Ah, this feels good.*

He moved his feet closer, aiming the right one at an angle so the air would warm the part of his sneaker that was ripped. *Embarrassing. I can't afford new sneakers. Who would think I'm a college graduate?*

Michael looked around the train, avoiding direct eye contact. He could see fellow passengers dressed in winter coats, scarves, and woolen gloves. Many people had presents and brightly colored holiday bags filled with packages either next to them or on the floor. One man, dressed in a suit, was holding a woman's hand, talking gently while stroking the back of her neck.

He tried hard not to look at their faces. A quick glance got him some snickers from the couple. *I would laugh at me, too. Go ahead, mock me. What do I have to live for? I hate myself.*

Michael got up from his seat and walked to the far end of the train. He dropped down into a seat, pulling his hood over his head, partially covering the side of his face. When he looked up briefly, he saw his reflection in the window. *Wow, I am ugly.*

He hadn't shaved in almost five days, and it had been almost a week since he had brushed his teeth. Michael tried keeping his mouth fresh by eating Life Savers mints. But his teeth felt grimy. The fingers on his right hand peeked through his torn, ratty gloves. He clenched his fist so no one could see.

"Fifty-third Street, Fifth Avenue," a voice sounded over the PA system.

So I guess this is home for tonight.

Michael kept his face hidden as he walked with a big crowd up the stairs. When he reached the outdoors, the beautiful lights of New York City greeted him. Santas on the corners peppered New Yorkers with pleas to help the needy. They jingled their bells with glee, smiling and giving tourists merry greetings. He could see the pots filled with coins and dollar bills.

Should I?

The Santa on Fifth Avenue swung his bell wildly. "Can you spare some change for the poor?" the man in the red suit asked Michael.

"I *am* the poor."

"That's what they all say. Go back to your fancy house and keep saving your money."

Thanks a lot, jerk, Michael thought after giving Santa a searing glare.

He walked away, stealing some quick glances at the storefront windows. A toy store had shiny cars, elaborate dolls, and speedy trains that captivated all the little kids passing by.

Almost there. It's freezing out here. Got to find a pew near a heater.

Michael climbed the many steps to St. Patrick's Cathedral and opened the big door. He pulled his hood partially off his head, leaving it halfway up his face. His hair was flat and greasy.

God won't care. Stop worrying.

The evening mass was still going on inside the famous church. So he sat down in the last row. When it was time for Communion, he bolted quickly to be the first to extend his hands to the priest to receive it. *I'm so hungry. I need to eat.*

As the line dwindled, Michael got up a second time to get Communion. The priest looked at him curiously but gave him the host again. He knelt down and said a prayer. *Mom, I wish you were here. Things are going bad, Mom. Why did you have to leave? This never would have happened if you were alive, Mom. Why did God take you from me? Why?*

Michael shed some tears as he ended his prayer. The priest finished the mass. *Now what do I do? I've got nowhere to go.*

He reached into his right pocket and found a couple of quarters. Michael dug into his left pocket and found only some tissue paper. He wiped his misty eyes and stared straight ahead. Most of the parishioners had filed out of the church. Others were lighting candles, while some were chatting with friends in the back.

It had been a couple of days since he had had a chance to close his eyes. Michael mainly got his rest ten minutes at a time, when the E train moved into the tunnel from Queens to Manhattan, affording him a break between stops.

He sank gratefully against the back of the pew, then jumped forward, startled, when he caught himself snoring as he began to doze. But there was no one around. Slowly his body began to relax. Peace . . .

Thump! Wham! The noise startled Michael awake. He lifted his head up, banging it against the back of the pew. "What the . . . ?"

"Church is not for sleeping," an old lady sternly lectured Michael. She walked back toward the candles, lighting them, and placed some coins into a box. Michael stood up and glared at her but she didn't notice. He staggered out of the pew and made a direct line toward her. Too late. The lady walked out the front door and down the steps.

A light rain had begun, wetting Michael's head. He sat down on one of the steps and buried his face in his hands. *Mom, I need your help. Oh, why, God? Oh, why? I don't have anywhere to go. Oh, God, why . . . why . . . is there anyone out there who can help me?*

Michael let the rain hit his unwashed hair. *No better way to get it clean, right?* he thought sarcastically. Drips of water fell from his hair, gently removing the crust that had built up in his eyes. He wiped his face with the sleeve of his soiled jacket, forcing him to spit out some grains of dirt from his lips.

He put his head down again, allowing the big drops to slide down the back of his neck. He shivered. *I've got nowhere to go. Nowhere.*

The woman in the black veil easily navigated the bustling, congested streets, and Elizabeth followed closely behind. The roads were unlike any she had seen back in Northport. They were paved entirely of stone yet still dusty, and already her legs were aching from walking on the uneven surface. People were milling about, chatting and laughing with marketplace owners. Despite the strangeness of her surroundings, it felt like a carnival to Elizabeth, as if she were back in Northport at the Firemen's Fair in the Pit. There were no midway games or rides, but a variety of foods and items were being sold on both sides of the street.

The scene was so chaotic and absorbing, especially under the veil, that Elizabeth almost forgot that she was holding the hand of a complete stranger. Her thoughts flew to her father and she stopped abruptly. Leah, a few steps ahead, unintentionally yanked her hand. "Please," Leah begged, "we must get you back. There's no time. You have to show me exactly where you came from."

Elizabeth looked all around, her eyes now focusing on not just movement but the myriad of buildings surrounding them. She quickly pulled her hand away from the woman. "It's over there," she said, pointing to a fruit and vegetable stand about thirty yards away.

"By that marketplace?"

Elizabeth nodded. The woman walked a few paces ahead, but when Elizabeth stopped, the woman turned around.

"Why are you stopping? We're almost there. We can get you home now. Hurry. You're in danger."

Elizabeth shook her head. "My father is in more danger."

"But the soldier, he'll come for you if you don't leave now."

Elizabeth shook her head. "I don't know anything about any soldier. I'm not going home until my father is with me."

Leah walked back to Elizabeth and spoke urgently. "You are obviously from another place. There isn't much a woman can do to help. The Roman soldiers are brutal and vicious. They know you helped a murderer who killed one of their own. Every step you take and every day you spend here will only bring you more risk."

"I don't care about what you think or what they think of women in this town. I'm not going without my father!"

They stood in silence and looked at each other awkwardly for a few seconds. Then Elizabeth relented, her eyes glistening with a new round of fresh tears. "Can you help me? Please?"

The woman glanced back at the tunnel's entrance. She hesitated a moment, then turned back to Elizabeth and nodded. "I'll try to help you in any way I can."

Elizabeth let out a sigh of relief. "Thank you." She paused, then smiled uncomfortably. "You know, um . . ."

"I am Leah. And you are Elizabeth? Did your father not speak of me?"

Elizabeth shook her head, puzzled, yet certain that this woman must have heard her father call her by name earlier.

"Elizabeth, let me get you something to eat and drink. Then we can discuss what we should do." Leah reached out her hand in a display of friendship, and Elizabeth took it with some apprehension. They started toward the fruit stand across the street.

"What kind of a place is it where my father is being held?"

"It's a place where they hold people before they are put on trial. And there are many soldiers."

They both stopped walking. The breeze picked up slightly; even though it relieved some of the heat that had bothered Elizabeth only moments ago, it had a chilling effect. She turned around resolutely and began walking back. Leah followed behind. She noticed that Elizabeth was looking up at the sky and then putting her hands to her eyes.

"Oh dear," Leah said, walking quickly alongside the teenager. She wrapped her arm gently around her shoulders, but Elizabeth pulled away.

"I'm sorry."

"What are you sorry for?"

"It's all my fault," said Elizabeth, her eyes red.

"It's not your fault. You were only trying to help someone in need."

"But if I hadn't gone into the tunnel . . . and if I didn't run out to help that man . . ."

Leah patted Elizabeth's back reassuringly. "Come with me. Let's get something to drink and eat. You'll feel better."

"No."

Leah frowned. "I'll take you to the prison. Then perhaps we can find out more about your father. But first, why don't we get you something to drink."

She guided them to a nearby well, where she cupped the water in her hands.

Elizabeth pulled back in disgust. "Aren't there any cups or anything? My hands are really dirty."

"You can rinse them first."

Elizabeth peered at the water. It looked cloudy. "You drink this?" she asked doubtfully.

"What else is there?"

Elizabeth hurriedly poured some water on her hands, hoping that it would wash away the dusty grime. Even though it was warm, she was overcome with thirst. *Oh, well,* she thought. She gathered the water in a tight clench and downed it in three quick gulps.

Leah grinned. "My, you were thirsty. Do you want something to eat?"

Elizabeth scanned the many marketplace storefronts. She spotted a stand selling what looked like miniature watermelons. "That looks interesting," she said halfheartedly.

Leah smiled. "Let's go."

It was only a few yards across the street. A woman had just bought a piece for a little girl, who giggled while taking her first bite. Elizabeth was ecstatic to see that it was indeed her favorite summertime fruit. Leah handed the vendor a couple of coins and bowed. Elizabeth bowed, too. She munched heartily and quickly finished off the large piece as Leah watched in delight. "You were hungry, too," she said with a faint smile. "Would you like another piece?"

Elizabeth shook her head and wiped her mouth. "No, I'm fine now, thank you."

Leah adjusted her veil slightly, covering more of her face. Elizabeth did the same.

"Our path to the prison is not a safe one. You must stay close to me and keep your head down. Do you understand me?"

Elizabeth nodded as Leah began to lead the way again through the labyrinthine streets. The older woman seemed anxious. When she next spoke, it was with urgency. "Remember, when we get there, don't look up until I tell you."

"Do you have a plan?" Elizabeth whispered from beneath her veil. She noticed the slight variations in color of the stones in the road; from this angle, she could see little else.

"I think so."

Elizabeth shrugged. The evening's remaining light started to slip away beneath the horizon and the shadows on the ground lengthened and blurred into each other. She looked up briefly and saw a majestic mountain ahead, into which miles of buildings were carved. It looked like the mountains she saw in Colorado on television. She looked at it in wonder and thought for one brief moment that the peak must surely reach to heaven. Then she looked down again at her dirty feet trudging through the dust and felt nothing but despair.

How will this woman in this barbaric town ever be able to help us?

4

UNDERSTANDING THE LANGUAGE

Elizabeth could see the outline of the Antonia Fortress against the skyline. It was magnificent, looking so much like a storybook castle that she momentarily forgot about the evils and horrors that Leah had described.

"I will do the talking," said Leah in a low voice. "Keep your veil high on your face. We don't want anyone to recognize you. If a Roman soldier addresses you, look down, like a hyena would do when faced with a lion."

"I'll do whatever I have to do to free my father."

Leah gently rubbed her back. "Whatever you do, don't get angry or raise your voice to the guards there. They're going to be curious who we are. Just treat them with respect."

Near the front gate, they could see another woman talking to a Roman guard, who was listening intently. Leah and Elizabeth slowed their pace, waiting for the outcome. The woman, clothed in a beautiful blue garment, gestured forcefully. The soldier, who had now taken his helmet off and was holding it in his right hand, nodded several times. Then the woman with long black hair and a white veil handed him something. The soldier laughed, then suddenly knocked the woman down, startling her. He then reached down and pulled her up by the arm. "Come with me!" he yelled as the woman's feet slid along the ground. "I know someone who will be happy to see you."

Leah and Elizabeth both gasped in unison. Leah grabbed Elizabeth's arm and pulled her back in the direction of the city. "Come with me!"

They could hear the woman's muffled screams behind them as they fled.

"We're not going to help her?" Elizabeth asked, swinging her head around to get another glance at the commotion.

Leah dragged her forward. "How do you expect me to help her?"

Elizabeth stumbled and again felt tears coming to her eyes. "I don't know. What about my father?"

"We'll go back to my home. Maybe I can find someone to help me."

Elizabeth stopped suddenly. "I'm not going to your home. Didn't you see what just happened? What kind of a place is my father in? This place is sick. Don't you have any friends here that can help us? Where's your husband?"

Leah looked away. By now they were back within the city walls. She watched the crowds milling around the many marketplaces. "I don't have a husband," she said softly, grabbing Elizabeth's arm.

"Where are we going?"

"You're going home."

Elizabeth yanked her arm away. "I am not!"

They stood in the street about fifty yards from the grate. "This is too dangerous a place for you to be here alone." Leah looked around helplessly. "I'm not sure we can save your father. Didn't he know the soldiers would be looking for him?"

Elizabeth shrugged in confusion. "I have no idea what you're talking about."

Leah shook her head in disbelief. "He had to know. I don't understand why he came back." She turned away from Elizabeth, deep in thought as she remembered that tragic day.

Leah climbed to the second floor and looked out the window with concern. On her left she could see a few neighbors retrieving some fruit that had fallen from the fig trees. Over to the right, several Roman soldiers milled around in the distance, not too far from the aqueduct.

She went back downstairs to the kitchen, picked up some grains from a bucket, and tossed a pile on the ground for the sheep that was nursing her lamb. Everywhere she moved in her now silent home seemed to have tragic reminders of a terrible time.

Leah had taken up weaving over the past few weeks in an effort to escape the horrific memories. It was a way to stop reality and briefly regain the happiness she had felt only a short time ago. She fingered a pretty white robe, hoping she would be able to sell it in the market-place.

Leah started to stitch the bottom of the garment, then dropped it. Restlessly she walked back to the window again, looking left and then right. She repeated this several times, never adding more than a stitch or two at a time.

On the seventh try at working on the robe, she tossed it in a basket and retreated to an empty adjoining room. There, lying on a small mat, was a tiny blanket. Leah picked it up and held it to her face. She breathed deeply several times, allowing the scent to engulf her body as if the aroma would strengthen her soul.

It felt like another sunset had passed when she removed it, her tears soaking a section. Leah fell to the floor, clenching the garment. She stared at the room, absorbing all the details—a wooden cradle, a small robe she had recently made, and a plate and cup.

"Why? Why? Oh, why?" she moaned in a broken voice. "My Sarah. Oh, my Sarah. Oh, my Sarah. I miss you."

Leah tightened her grip on the blanket, rubbing it softly against her eyes. She touched the cradle, placing her hand inside it. Her body heaved back and forth. "Why? Why? I need to know why!" she cried with more anger. "Tell me, why?"

Her body gradually began to relax but she never released her hold on the blanket. Leah went downstairs to the kitchen and poured a cup of water. Sitting down at the table, she dabbed her eyes. She laid her head down on her folded arms, listening for any sounds.

The muffled noises of boys and girls playing outside shook her momentarily. Eventually, Leah drifted in and out of consciousness. As her shadow on the wall dissipated, she was vaguely aware that the sounds of the children had gone silent. She rose and headed back upstairs, placing a cup and plate on one mat next to where another neatly arranged set was waiting. The plate had several nuts, while the cup was filled with wine and water. The odor disturbed her so she replaced them with fresh wine and food.

She sat down, transfixed, on the opposite mat. Leah shook her head, deep in thought as she remembered the last time she had shared a happy meal with Yochanan. "We are blessed, my love," he had said that glorious evening. "We are going to be a family."

Leah touched her flat stomach and sighed. She got to her feet a few moments later, hearing some noises outside. *Could this be Yochanan?* she thought hopefully. *Yochanan?*

Her heart thumped as she ran to the window. "Yochanan?" she said forcefully. She could see a brown-haired stranger gesturing wildly near the well.

"John, get out of here!" the man shouted.

"I'm coming. Go. Now. Run!"

That sounds like Yochanan, she thought. *He is home. Thank you! Thank you!*

Leah scurried up the ladder to the top of the house to greet him. The commotion outside turned violent and intense, confusing her as she stepped to the side of the roof to see what was happening. Several Roman soldiers were chasing two men, throwing rocks. One struck the brown-haired man on the back of the leg, and he cried out.

"Keep running. Don't stop."

Leah's excitement turned to horror. "Yochanan! Yochanan!"

A man, tall and with arms like tree trunks, looked up toward her. "Leah!"

He collapsed suddenly, struck by a rock hurled by a Roman soldier. Yochanan hit his head hard against the side of a tree, not too far from the well. From the roof, Leah could see that he was bleeding heavily.

"John," the other man yelled. "John!"

"Get that rebel! Kill him if you can!" a soldier shouted.

The stranger ran off as Leah held her hands over her face. "No! No! No!" she wailed. "Yochanan. Oh, my Yochanan. No! No! No!"

No breeze was to be found inside the Antonia Fortress that evening. The solid walls were dense and unyielding, and Michael felt alone and cut off from the outside world. He yearned for another chance to take a stroll along Crab Meadow Beach, then smiled ruefully to himself. How often had he thought about taking a walk down there, only to be quickly distracted by life's mundane problems?

He coughed slightly, trying to gather up some saliva to relieve the itch in his throat, and forced himself not to think about water. The heat was stifling, exhausting him. The screams he had heard earlier seemed to have diminished, or perhaps he'd just grown accustomed to his surroundings. He struggled to find a comfortable position but without success.

"I need water," Michael shouted with the last bit of energy he had. In the next cell, Barabbas lay silent, a veteran at survival.

"Sleep, my friend, sleep," he whispered.

Michael ignored him. "Help! I need water!"

He heard heavy footsteps approaching, then a soldier appeared outside his cell door. He rattled the metal bars with the shaft of his spear. "Shut up!"

"Leave him alone," ordered a familiar voice. "He hasn't done anything wrong."

A tall man strolled past Michael's cell and stopped in front of Barabbas. "This sick murderer deserves to die, though."

"I'll get you before you get me," Barabbas retorted, but with far less energy than he had displayed a few hours ago.

The Roman soldier laughed mockingly. "You'll rot here or we'll get you before you do die!" He shoved his spear through the opening and taunted Barabbas with the sharp, shiny point, allowing it to ping his neck, drawing blood. A group of soldiers standing nearby cheered.

"Kill him, Marcus. Let's give his cell to someone worthy. He isn't much of a rebel, is he?"

The soldiers laughed louder. One pulled out what looked like dice and another tossed several pieces of silver on the floor. "Are you in with us, Marcus?"

"How much do you have?" Marcus asked, half grinning.

"Enough to make you happy, Marcus."

He walked past Michael, then suddenly turned to look at him. "No one will hurt you here."

The three other soldiers sitting on the floor exchanged confused glances. "But, Marcus, we have orders to kill him."

Marcus leaned over and grabbed the soldier by his neck. "The orders have been changed," he said menacingly, then pushed the man back. He sat down beside the others and pulled out a light brown pouch, dumping several coins on the floor. Then he removed his helmet and wiped the beads of perspiration from his forehead.

Marcus looked back at Michael, now paralyzed against the wall. "Get my friend a cup of water," he ordered, gesturing toward the soldiers.

"This is against the governor's policy," the soldier to his right replied. Without warning Marcus grabbed his arm, pinning it to the ground.

The soldier winced in pain. "My arm. You're breaking it, Marcus."

Marcus paused a moment longer, then let go. "I make the policy here. Get a cup of water for my friend."

The soldier bolted to his feet and ran off, leaving the suddenly quiet dice game. Marcus got to his feet, stretched, and took a deep breath. "Are you fine in there?" he asked Michael conversationally.

Michael felt a sense of foreboding. There was no reason for Marcus' sudden concern. Michael studied the soldier's face, noticing several small, thin scars that stretched a couple of inches down the sides of his cheeks. His black hair was plastered to his head from the heat, and his teeth were dirty and chipped. The warrior didn't hide his battle tattoos either. Several fresh gashes lined his muscular biceps.

Marcus ignored his silence and continued, "You have nothing to fear, my friend. I'll make sure you stay out of harm's way while you are here with us."

He opened the cell door and pulled at Michael's arm. The rusty clamp had pierced his wrist, leaving a line of dried blood along his hand.

"My friend, are you in pain?"

Frozen in fear, Michael tried to respond but couldn't. Marcus didn't wait for the answer. He unlocked the clamp and tossed it to the ground, removing the chain. The two other soldiers remained sitting, watching in utter confusion. The third soldier returned with a cup of water.

Marcus took the cup and offered it to Michael. "Take this."

Michael looked at him. But overwhelming thirst destroyed any caution. He reached up and took it, not caring how muddy the water looked. He downed it quickly, never taking his eyes off Marcus.

"Tastes good now, doesn't it?" Marcus smiled.

Michael nodded.

"How about another?"

"Yes," Michael said weakly. He was surprised at how calm he sounded.

Marcus took the cup, spun around, and tossed it in the middle of the soldiers, scattering several pieces of silver. "Get my friend another drink!"

None of the soldiers moved. They looked uncertainly at the cup. "Get it now!" Marcus roared.

Together as one, all three lunged for the cup, banging heads as they reached for it. If the situation had been different, Michael might have found it comical. He watched in fear as one man grabbed it and ran off. Marcus let his body settle against the wall, scraping the cement with his armor, much like the sound Michael's sixth-grade teacher, Miss Pavotti, made with her fingernails grazing the blackboard to awaken a sleeping classroom. Marcus was now shoulder to shoulder with Michael, whose body twitched.

The soldier laughed. "You needn't be afraid. I'm your only friend here."

Michael was silent.

"Where are you from?"

"A place far away," he mumbled.

"How far?" Marcus demanded.

"I'm not sure."

Marcus laughed again. It was unlike the previous times he had done so. This time it actually sounded friendly, and for a moment Michael felt reassured.

"I believe you," Marcus said, nodding. "Your clothes are odd. I haven't seen such."

Michael looked down at his sandals.

"Do you know how to get home?" Marcus asked.

Michael's spirits lifted slightly. Perhaps Marcus did want to help him after all. He straightened up and spoke more forcefully. "Yes, I think I do."

Marcus grinned and slapped him on the shoulder. Michael nearly fell over. "Good! I think I can help you."

"Great!"

Marcus put his hand to Michael's mouth. "Quiet," he said in a soft, reassuring tone. He pointed at the group of soldiers. They had moved their game of dice farther away and appeared to be completely engrossed.

The soldier came back with the cup of water and handed it to Michael. Marcus waved him away. He leaned closer to Michael's ear.

"Stay awake. I'll come by later and free you. But you must go directly to where you came from. You remember the place, right?"

"Yes, yes, I do!" Michael said with excitement.

"Good. I'll make sure you get back home safely." Marcus smiled.

Michael stood up with a thrust of energy. "Thank you for being so kind to me. Could you help me with something else?"

Marcus stopped and turned around, frowning slightly. "What is it?"

Michael held up his hand slightly. "My ring. The soldier with you in the street took it from me. It means a lot to me."

"I will do my best to find it. You can trust me. Now get some rest."

Leah wiped her eyes as she lingered by a nearby well, then pulled up a bucket and dipped her hands repeatedly in the water. After the fourth time, she muttered, "Come with me, Elizabeth."

They began walking toward the Antonia Fortress. "I thought you were getting some help before we went back there," Elizabeth said with concern.

"We aren't going there. We're going to the only place where I can ask for true help."

"Where is that?"

"We're going to the Temple."

"The Temple? Why? Who can help us there?"

Leah didn't answer. She picked up her pace as the outline of the Fortress loomed ahead. But instead of heading toward the entrance, Leah turned abruptly to the north side.

"Where is it?" Elizabeth asked, looking around.

"Not too far away. Keep your veil on while you clean."

"Clean? I thought we were going to the Temple?"

"We are."

Leah stopped in front of what appeared to be a series of small, square-shaped in-ground pools. They looked ancient to Elizabeth.

No lining held the water, just stone walls. Without warning, Leah pulled off her clothes, then her shoes. Elizabeth quickly looked away as Leah walked down the four steps into the water and began splashing her body and face. "Come quickly." She gestured, pointing to the stairs.

"What? Are you serious? No way!"

"Come in. Don't stand there. Don't you do this where you live?"

"Um . . . *no.*"

"Hurry! You'll stand out and draw attention to yourself. You'll upset the high priest."

Elizabeth hesitated, looking around to see if anyone was watching. It was quiet now. Dusk was settling in and the hustle and bustle of the day was gone. Still, she felt shy.

"Are you bleeding?" Leah asked.

"Bleeding? What do you mean?"

Leah gestured toward the lower portion of her body. "Down here."

"My period? No, no . . . that's not the problem."

"Good. Because if you are, then you mustn't come in."

Elizabeth reminded herself that they needed to find her father. If this was going to help, then she would do it. She looked around quickly, then hurriedly removed her shirt, keeping her bra on. Then she kicked off her sandals but left on her long shorts. Leah looked at her oddly.

On the far end, two men were bathing. Elizabeth made a face and quickly scurried down the steps into the water with her back to Leah.

"Clean quickly."

"No problem there," Elizabeth muttered as she bent down to let the water rise above her shoulders. By the time she stood up, Leah had climbed out and was putting her clothes on. Elizabeth sprinted up the steps and did the same. "Now what?"

"Over there." Leah pointed to a large building about a football field away. Even at this distance, Elizabeth could see how splendid it was. Rows of towering, white marble columns lined the front, capped with tinges of gold that glowed in the early-evening sky. Sharp gold spikes rose on the roof, reflecting a soft light across the several acres of the plaza. She felt mesmerized by a feeling of holiness about the place, her body tingling with excitement. She pointed toward the bronze doors. "Is that where we go?"

"No. We must go through on the other side."

They walked around the wide structure and entered through another gate made of steel. Elizabeth noticed that it wasn't as ornate as the main entrance.

"Stay with me," Leah ordered. She led the way down several steps and into a tunnel. Carefully placed candles on either side shed light on the ceiling, which was covered with crude drawings of people and animals.

"Stay quiet," Leah whispered.

The tunnel opened into a large area, surrounded by several rooms. "Over here," Leah said in a hushed voice. "We must always stay in this part of the Temple. Always remain with me."

Leah closed her eyes and knelt. Elizabeth briefly looked around in confusion. It was a simple room, large enough where several people could kneel and pray. It wasn't as elaborate as the outside of the building. She could hear Leah whispering something but was unable to decipher any words. As Elizabeth looked around, she realized a few other women were praying, too. But no men.

Leah's whispers became louder. Elizabeth began to understand some words, including a plea for help. Elizabeth felt a stab of disappointment. No one here could help them.

But as she looked around, the meaning of Leah's words dawned on her. Slowly Elizabeth sank to her knees and bowed her head. *Lord, can you please help my father? Please. It was my fault, Lord. Punish me. Please. Don't let anyone hurt him. Please. Punish me.*

The quiet inside the Temple moved her. A tear slipped out of her eye and coursed down her cheek as she continued to silently say, *Punish me. Punish me. Not my dad. Please.* She let the tear stay there in hopes God would see it. *Lord, please. Please. Please. Help him. Please help me to find my dad.*

She clasped her hands together and bowed her head, and the veil slipped over her face.

Wow. Look at all these people. Well-dressed adults and children filled the pews on both sides as Elizabeth tugged at her veil, making sure it didn't obscure her eyes. *Daddy told me to keep it out of my eyes. I want him to be proud of me.*

Organ music suddenly boomed out around them, jolting everyone in line to straighten up and pay attention. A woman, dressed in a soft brown suit with a beautiful blue corsage on her wrist, gestured to the boys and girls to follow her. After one last pull on her veil, this time making sure it wouldn't fall off, Elizabeth clasped her hands together. She glanced at the boy to her left, looking for guidance on when to begin walking.

When he started, she did, too. Smiling, and imagining that this was how Mommy felt when she married Daddy, Elizabeth floated the first few steps. She glanced first to her left, then to her right, spotting Mrs. Horn. Elizabeth beamed and her neighbor waved. Elizabeth gave a quick half-hello in her direction.

She fell a few steps behind her partner as the line continued to stroll two by two up the aisle toward the altar. *I wonder if this is how the animals felt going onto the ark.* Elizabeth giggled to herself.

She skipped a few steps, prompting a few smiles from the adults nearby, then Elizabeth brushed back her hair, fixing her veil once more. *I hope Daddy thinks I look pretty.* The children started filling the front pews where the families were waiting. As Elizabeth approached her family's pew, she caught a quick smile from her father. She glowed with pride, keeping her hands folded tightly, head up and eyes wide-open as she joined him.

Just like Daddy told me to do it.

"You look beautiful, Elizabeth," Michael whispered into her ear.

Aunt Connie leaned across Michael and gave Elizabeth a big

thumbs-up while Aunt Sammie gently reached over to touch her shoulder. "You look like a bride!" she whispered, her face fixed in a huge grin.

"Thank you," Elizabeth said shyly.

Ruth and Ed, her great-aunt and great-uncle, beamed at her, and Elizabeth remembered how grown-up they had said she looked when they had met earlier in the church's parking lot. Farther down the pew she could see her cousins and Uncle Bill, Aunt Connie's husband. Elizabeth leaned over the front of the pew to see them.

Michael gently pushed her back as the priest greeted the parishioners with his opening prayer. After she made the sign of the cross and strained to pay attention to the opening prayer, the first reading began and Elizabeth could finally sit. She instinctively grabbed her father's hand as she leaned back onto the hard wooden pew. Michael smiled briefly at her, then looked up and wiped his eyes with the sleeve of his new jacket.

Is he crying?

She tried to turn her attention back to the front of the church, but her veil was caught on the back of the pew. She leaned forward to free it, delighted that everyone around her seemed to like what she was wearing. She reached down to touch the box that contained the blue rosary beads that her aunt Sammie had left for her. They had been Elizabeth's grandmother's and she felt so special, even though she had never known her.

It surprised her when the priest came to the edge of the altar— usually it seemed as if church took forever—and she knew that she was about to receive Communion for the first time.

As the children in the front pews went up to the altar with their parents, her thoughts wandered to Aunt Connie and her father. When Aunt Connie came to the house that morning, they had argued loudly.

"I don't need you to tell me what to do," Michael had said angrily.

"But Elizabeth should have someone with her when she goes up. All the other kids will have two parents up there. Be fair to her."

"In case you forgot, Connie, Elizabeth doesn't have two parents. If Vicki was around, she would. But it's just me here, okay? Or have you forgotten already?"

"How dare you talk to me like that! I know what you went through!"

"What do you know about what I went through?"

"Please, Michael, please. Let me stand up there with her."

Then Aunt Connie's eyes had narrowed in a funny way and her voice stayed firm but softened, although Elizabeth could still hear her. "Or should we just get your neighbor Susan to stand there? Are you sleeping with her? I wonder what Vicki would think of that."

"You're way out of line. Like today isn't hard enough—leave it to you."

"All I'm saying is that everyone else will have two people up there. Vicki would have wanted it this way."

"How do you know what Vicki would want? Nobody can replace Vicki. Drop it!"

The woman with the pretty blue corsage snapped her fingers from the side of the altar, jolting Elizabeth out of her trance. The woman looked over at both her and Michael. Aunt Connie stared straight ahead, giving no indication of her mood. Michael put his hand on Elizabeth's arm, urging her to walk to the aisle.

After checking her veil one last time, she clenched her hands firmly together and stood up. As she started up the aisle, her father's hand on her shoulder, she began to silently whisper a prayer.

Dear God, I don't care about getting any money today. I really don't. Well, maybe a little, God. But, I want Daddy to be happy. He's been so sad lately. I thought this would make him happy. I tried to look pretty for him, God. But he still seems angry. He's angry at Aunt Connie, too. I don't like it when they fight. I get nervous. Can you make it better? Can you tell them to stop fighting? Please, God. Please. I really don't want any gifts. I just want him to be happy.

As she reached the priest, one last thought went through her mind.

God, you're not mad that it's just Daddy and me up here, right?

The dice game had broken up a while ago and Michael was alone again in his cell. He dozed briefly but the noise nearby kept him from any extended rest. He could hear Barabbas sleeping in the adjacent cell, his snores echoing through the corridor. *How can he sleep in such a place?* Michael thought, shaking his head.

An eerie quiet filled the prison. Occasionally someone would cry out for water, only to be met with more silence. Michael wondered if all the soldiers had left.

Chains clinked back and forth, reminding Michael of beads falling off a strand. He couldn't tell what time it was as the last few flickers of candlelight cast their snakelike shadows on the concrete walls.

He agonized over a plan to return to Northport, mapping out the details in his mind: first, find the woman who took Elizabeth. Second, take Elizabeth back to the tunnel. Then find Father Dennis and have him call the police. Finally, call his brother-in-law Brian at the FBI.

He mulled over that last point and then thought better of it. He had had enough problems there. It was probably best not to get him involved.

Michael tried to settle his nerves by closing his eyes. But sleep was impossible. He continued to mentally go over his escape plans. How could he find that woman? he wondered. Perhaps she was looking for him. If all else failed, he knew that Elizabeth would try to find him. Then again, perhaps Marcus could help.

His body straightened and he could feel his blood rushing to his head. Yes, he felt sure that Marcus could help.

Footsteps echoing in the distance woke him just as he was starting to doze. He stood up. "Marcus? Is that you?"

A Roman soldier, helmet on and spear in hand, appeared and pulled open the door. Michael looked at him in confusion. "Where's Marcus?"

The soldier gazed at him for a few seconds. "He went home. He wishes you the best on your journey. He said to make sure you take the same path home that you came from. It's the safest way back. Do you understand?"

Michael nodded. He wondered if this soldier was trustworthy. Perhaps he would be able to help him find Elizabeth.

The opening of the cell door awoke Barabbas. "Where are you going, my friend?" he slurred, still heavy with sleep.

"I'm going home."

"What? Be care—"

"Shut up," shouted the soldier as he whipped his spear against the rods of Barabbas' cell. "Move," he demanded, pushing Michael from behind.

"Be cautious, my friend," said Barabbas, his voice growing faint in the distance. "Watch your back. They just don't let anyone . . ." Barabbas' words were no longer audible.

5

WATER TO WINE

The remaining inches of wick were still burning in the dark hallway, and Michael peered into the cells they passed. He could only see shadows huddled against the walls, some sleeping, a few weeping softly. They turned the corner and approached a long stairway. Brightly lit torches were strategically placed along the route, giving them plenty of light. The soldier nestled his arm under Michael's, making sure he wouldn't fall. *Surprisingly nice of him,* he thought.

Five soldiers lounged near the entrance, drinking heavily. The air was thick with the scent of wine. "What are you doing, Titus?" one soldier asked as he wiped his chin with the back of his hand.

"Sending our friend here back home," Titus replied.

"Is he a friend of the governor?"

"No. A friend of Marcus."

The soldiers laughed. "I didn't know Marcus had any."

"Shut up," said Titus, slamming the cup out of a soldier's hand with his spear.

Titus pushed Michael through the entrance. Night had fallen but he could still see the city in the distance.

"Remember to go back the same way you came."

"I will, but I have to find my daughter first."

"Do so. But do it quickly. When you do find your daughter, take the same path home."

"Can you help me find her?"

Titus turned his back and went inside the prison. The other soldiers glared at him.

"Tell Marcus thank you!" Michael yelled.

He turned and made a run straight to the wall opening.

Leah and Elizabeth finished their prayers and began to walk silently back to the city. Each was lost in her own thoughts as Elizabeth wrestled with guilt and remorse. Leah would occasionally whisper, "Oh, Yochanan, what would you do?"

With the city wall nearby now, Elizabeth felt this was the proper time to speak. "Leah, I can't go any further. If I have to wait until morning, I will. But I have to take my chances soon at that place and ask if they can free my father. Are you sure there isn't anyone who can help us?"

Leah and Elizabeth walked a few more yards until they were inside the city. Leah looked around and saw that a couple of marketplaces were open. But the crowd that filled the streets only a couple of hours ago had dispersed. Only a few groups of people were chatting, laughing, and sharing stories of the day.

"I don't see anybody I know," she said. "I'm sorry."

Elizabeth sighed. "Then I'll have to go back."

"You mustn't."

"I don't have a choice."

"Then wait until morning," said Leah, gently rubbing Elizabeth's arm.

"Why morning?"

"The soldiers drink a lot after sundown. They can be even more vicious. It's not a safe place for women, but especially now."

"Then I'm going back to the tunnel and wait there. If he does get out, he'll surely go there first," reasoned Elizabeth.

"I will stay with you."

Elizabeth smiled slightly. "Let's go then."

They walked slowly. Elizabeth glanced up at the clear sky. *No pollution here,* she thought, admiring the clarity of the stars. The moon's light bathed the landscape in a soft glow. *So pretty.*

Suddenly they heard footsteps. Leah pulled Elizabeth around one of the market stalls and whispered, "Quiet."

The slapping of sandals and heavy gasping grew louder. A man, clearly out of breath, hurtled past them. "Dad!" Elizabeth yelled.

Michael stopped and bent over, trying to catch his breath. "Elizabeth. My God. You're okay. Oh, thank you, God."

They hugged as Leah looked on in confusion. "How did you escape?"

Michael could barely get the words out. "I didn't. One soldier helped me get my release. He was very kind to me. He told me to just go back the way we came. So, we can go home, Elizabeth!"

Leah stared at Michael, then suddenly hugged him, making him uncomfortable. "I'm so happy." But she then released her grasp. "There's something wrong."

"What do you mean?"

"They just don't let people leave there. What else did the soldier say?"

"He only said to go back the same way as I came. Why?"

Leah shook her head. "This is strange. Very strange. We should stop and talk about what happened to you," she insisted.

"I'm not stopping!" Michael said forcefully.

"Do you want to suffer the same way as Yochanan?"

"Who's Yochanan?"

Leah looked upset. "You are confusing me."

"We have to get home," Michael said impatiently. He grabbed Elizabeth's hand and began to jog. "Let's run, Elizabeth."

Leah caught up to them. "You're going to get caught," she warned.

Michael didn't pay attention. Suddenly an old man appeared in front of them. He stumbled and fell to the ground. *No time for this,*

Michael thought, sidestepping him and sprinting to the other side of the street. He could see the grates now. All six looked identical. "Which one is it?" he said frantically, kicking at each one. "Open!"

Suddenly Leah grabbed his arm and pointed down the street. "Look over there. Soldiers!" she said with distress.

Up ahead a group of soldiers had gathered. Michael glared; his body froze and his mind went blank. *What do I do now? Oh, God, my daughter.*

"Come with me," Leah urged, tugging on his shirt, as one of the soldiers gestured toward them.

But Michael still couldn't move.

"What's wrong, Dad?"

Waving his hands frantically, Michael said, "The cloth . . . the cloth . . . your shirt . . . it was him . . . it's Marcus!" Michael recognized his deep, booming voice and the piece of Elizabeth's white shirt dangling from the back of his helmet.

"What soldier? What cloth? What are you talking about? Tell me, Dad. Tell me!"

"He took a piece of your shirt."

Elizabeth looked at her long shirt. "So?"

Michael grabbed Elizabeth's hand with force and pulled her back toward Leah. "We need your help."

"I know," she said impatiently. "Come quickly."

Michael looked over at Elizabeth, who gave him an icy stare.

"Tell me!"

"Not now. We'll talk later."

Leah led the way purposefully through the maze of streets. "Stay close. We have to keep out of sight. The soldiers are everywhere."

As if on cue, two Roman soldiers strolled off a side street and headed in their direction. Leah pulled Michael and Elizabeth into a deserted, covered doorway. They pressed against the concrete wall as the soldiers strolled past. "I wonder if Marcus will get his prize soon," snickered one soldier.

"He thinks he'll get his prize tonight," said the other.

When the street was quiet again, Leah turned toward Michael.

"Why did you return to this town again? What is it that you want?"

Michael looked at her, confused. "I don't understand. I told you we just want to get home. Believe me, I don't want to stay here any longer than I have to."

Leah stared at him for a moment. "Do you want to be killed? These soldiers would love to kill you. You have to listen to me if you want to stay alive."

Michael glared at her in disbelief. "Why are there so many of them here?"

"Passover is coming, and with everyone in town for the festivities, they have come in force. But don't think that they will forget you were imprisoned with Barabbas. Now do you understand? If you love your daughter, you will listen to me."

Michael nodded. "Marcus was so nice to me. I thought I could trust him."

"You can't trust any Roman soldier. What did he say to you on the street?"

"He made some reference that he wanted to make my daughter his. I think I know what he means. But she's only fourteen. I didn't want to believe it. Tell me I'm wrong."

Leah slowly turned toward him. "Is that what he said?" she asked in a hushed voice.

"Yes."

"We need to move quickly and get back to my home."

"But we have to get back to the tunnel," Michael said. "It's where we came from."

"You need to come back to my house. I can give you some of the robes I wove to sell at market. In them you won't draw so much attention to yourself. Then maybe you will be able to get home safely. But right now, it is too dangerous."

"Hey, look, no offense, but I only know your name," Michael said with annoyance. "Why should we trust you?"

The woman took a few steps closer, studying him.

"How could you say that? You were so kind and caring to me in my time of need. I am doing the same for you."

Michael shook his head. "I . . . I . . . really don't know . . ."

"So, you don't remember? You must be careful with the friends you keep. I thought you would have known that by now."

Michael could only stare. Why did she seem to know him?

Leah led them in and out of side streets, the roads narrow and the air thick with dust. Some doorways were empty, others filled with people, their eyes roaming without any recognition. Michael noticed with a sinking feeling that Leah was leading them farther and farther from the tunnel, and the knowledge filled him with despair. He felt nearly paralyzed as she kept up a furious pace for what felt like an eternity.

Leah dropped Elizabeth's hand to straighten her veil and said, "We're almost there," smiling to reassure them. Her tone was more relaxed now that they had covered some distance. Leah reached again for Elizabeth's hand and gave it a little shake.

Elizabeth glanced down but remained silent.

Leah squeezed her hand more tightly. "You're scared. That's understandable. You've been through a lot today. We can rest, and I will get you something to eat and drink."

They turned off the road and through a front gate into a courtyard. A fig tree stood at its center, and beyond that Michael could see a simple, two-story stone house. The bottom floor was open to the courtyard and had three small rooms that reminded Michael of stalls in a barn. A lamb stood in the first one behind a metal gate. The middle stall contained many baskets along its perimeter and a smoldering pit in the center of the floor. On the far end of the last stall, a door opened to the back of the house, where a wooden ladder led to the second floor.

Leah invited them upstairs. When he climbed the ladder, Michael found himself in a large room with a window looking down onto the courtyard below. A woolen mat lay on the floor with two large, round jugs, a small pottery cup, and a covered basket upon it. Behind him were stalls similar to those below, one of which contained another ladder, which led through a hole in the ceiling up onto the roof.

Elizabeth looked around in horror and disbelief. This was like nothing she had ever seen before. There were very few furnishings, and no curtains or doors. Leah walked over to the covered basket and knelt, removing some bread from inside. She inverted the top of the basket and placed it in the center of the mat, making a simple platter. She tore the bread and placed several pieces in front of them.

"Sit, please. I'll be right back."

They watched Leah climb down the ladder before shrugging their shoulders at each other and sitting down on the mat.

"Dad, what's going on? We should get out of here," Elizabeth whispered.

Michael put two fingers over his lips. "Shh, she'll hear us."

"I don't care," Elizabeth said, her voice growing louder.

"Well, I do. She has been very helpful to us, and I think we need to listen to this woman."

"But can she help us get home?"

"I certainly hope so."

Leah returned, placing on the mat before them a tray containing two cups along with bowls of what looked like goat cheese, olives, and green onions. "Please, eat. You are my guests and I have plenty here. Take some."

Elizabeth tried to hide her distress. "I'm really not interested. I'm sorry."

Michael looked up from the food and directly into Leah's eyes. "Can you help us get back?"

"Get back where?"

"To Northport."

Leah shook her head. "I don't know where that is."

"It's on Long Island."

Leah looked puzzled.

"We need to get back to that street where we saw that soldier."

"That is much too dangerous right now. You can go if you like, but you would risk your daughter's safety."

Leah offered the food again. "Please, have something to eat."

Michael and Elizabeth tore at the bread.

"Let me give you something to drink." Leah poured wine into one of the cups, thinned it with water from the other jug, and handed it to Michael.

"Elizabeth, would you like some?" she asked, pouring a second cup.

"Excuse me?" Michael interjected.

"Your daughter is thirsty. Let me give her some wine, too."

"Really?" Elizabeth looked interested.

"Of course, you are my guest."

"Cool!"

"Not cool," Michael countered. "My daughter is too young to drink."

"Your daughter is old enough to get married," Leah said, glancing at Michael with a perplexed look. "How could she be too young to drink wine?"

"What? Me? Married?" Elizabeth asked in surprise.

"My daughter is only fourteen. She has a long time before she gets married. She hasn't even kissed a boy. Right, Liz?"

Elizabeth made a face. "Liz won't comment."

"Elizabeth?" said Leah as she offered a cup of wine.

Elizabeth looked over at her dad, who quickly shook his head. "No, thanks," she said, before muttering in his direction, "Fun killer."

Michael strummed his finger over the bridge of his thumb, mimicking the action of a bow over the strings of a violin. "She can have water."

Elizabeth smirked and rolled her eyes.

Michael took a sip from his cup. The wine was sweet but he was so thirsty he downed it quickly.

"You are still thirsty?" Leah asked.

Michael nodded. "I'll just take water this time, please."

She poured him a cup, and again he drank it quickly. Leah smiled.

Michael noticed his daughter giving him a look. "Elizabeth, are you okay?"

"Can we go now, Dad?"

"You mustn't," Leah insisted. "It's unsafe out there. The festivities will start this week and the soldiers are everywhere. Please consider staying until the morning."

Michael looked outside. It was awfully dark. *What if we get caught?* He might not be so lucky to get out the next time. He contemplated which was more dangerous: staying here in the house of a strange woman or trying to get back tonight.

Elizabeth began rubbing her eyes as a yawn escaped her lips. His decision was made. *I'm right with you, kid, I'm exhausted.*

"Okay. We'll spend the night. Thanks."

Leah left the room and returned with what looked like a rough comforter. "Here, take this bedroll over there." She handed it to Elizabeth and motioned to the small, open room on the right.

While Michael walked Elizabeth over to the little alcove, Leah cleaned up the remnants of the meal.

Elizabeth placed the bedroll on the wooden floor and lay down. "I'm scared," she whispered to her father, "but I'm so tired."

"I know," Michael replied as he stroked the top of her head. "I'm with you, sweetie. Try to close your eyes and get some rest. We'll leave in the morning."

Elizabeth studied him for a moment. He looked worn. "Dad, what happened in the prison?"

He sighed deeply, wanting to spare her the details. "It was horrible. There were bodies chained everywhere. People were in pain and I couldn't help them. They treated women like they were cattle. I'll talk to you about it more when we get back." He shook his head. "It was horrifying. Just terrible."

She nodded sleepily. He could tell that the day's events were having an effect. Michael slid down the wall and tried to find a comfortable position. He admired how easily she could sleep. He had slept like that once, too, back when Vicki was beside him.

His head rested against the textured wall as he closed his eyes, suddenly groggy. He had become a horrible sleeper since Vicki was gone, and this exhaustion surprised him. Most nights he struggled to fall asleep, his bedroom too confining to bring any peace. It was more like a shrine, a testament to a life he no longer led. His bed was always made. The living room couch became his only salvation.

Thank goodness it's only ten minutes away. Michael was late again. He needed to get to the Northport High School gym to watch a basketball game. The team had one of the best players on Long Island and he had to write a story today for his readers.

As Michael turned out of their driveway, he caught a glimpse of Elizabeth's cherubic little face giggling in the rearview mirror. She was singing along with Barney and his friends. Michael groaned inwardly. It had to be at least the hundredth time they were listening to that CD.

"Man, I'm not getting a break today," he said under his breath.

He looked back into his mirror and noticed his eyes were red and blotchy. *Maybe I'll get two hours of sleep tonight,* he thought. *That is, if I can just stop worrying about her.*

"Hey, Little Baboo. You know Daddy loves you, right? I'll always take care of you, even if I don't get any sleep." He reached back and lovingly rubbed her knee through the bulky snowsuit.

By the time he had pulled into the high school parking lot, Elizabeth had fallen asleep.

"How does she do it?" he said in wonder.

After unbuckling her from the car seat, he gently placed her in the stroller, so as not to wake her, and rolled her into the gym. Instead of trying to carry her and the stroller up into the noisy stands, he found a quiet spot for them against the wall beyond the bleachers.

"Hey, Mike!" shouted his neighbor Jim Phillips. His son Brian was on the Northport basketball team.

Michael smiled. "Hey, Mr. Phillips!" He always called him mister out of respect. "How are you feeling these days? How's the old ticker doing?"

Jim tapped at his chest twice in exuberance. "Doing well, thanks. How's your daughter?"

"She's finally asleep . . . thank goodness!"

Mr. Phillips laughed. "Good for you. You look tired. Didn't you get any sleep?"

"Oh, yeah, sure," Michael said, a grin spreading across his face. "She gives me an hour or two off, here and there."

Before long the game was under way and slowly dragging on. Michael could feel his legs straining to stay upright as he took his notes. When the third quarter began, his eyes kept blinking, so he splashed some water on his face from the fountain on the wall behind him. Instead of waking him, the water was soothing and his body began to relax.

Michael closed his eyes.

"Hey, fella! Watch what you're doing!"

A sense of panic struck him as his head jerked upright and he tried to focus his weary eyes on the court. Looking around frantically to try to clear his head, he gasped, "Elizabeth?"

"Hey, buddy!" a man screamed. "Move!"

He felt Elizabeth pulling on the leg of his jeans. She wore a huge grin. Michael smiled down at her.

"Hey, Little Baboo."

"Daddy!"

Michael looked over at the court and noticed that the basket no longer hung down but was now retracted up by the ceiling. All the players were just standing there on the court, and everyone in the crowd seemed to be staring at him. He suddenly realized with horror that he had accidentally leaned against the switch that elevated the basket.

"Oh, sorry," he muttered. Sheepishly he pushed the button to lower the basket back into place. The crowd applauded appreciatively and some rowdy fans whistled. Elizabeth giggled.

Feeling like a total fool, Michael grabbed Elizabeth and the stroller and sprinted from the gym. Out in the parking lot, he didn't know whether to cry from embarrassment or laugh as he packed Elizabeth back up in the car.

When he finally sat down behind the wheel, he turned around to look at her. She was strapped into her car seat, drinking apple juice. She waved the sippy cup in her hand and smiled.

Her happy face made his decision easy: he laughed.

We'll do okay, he reasoned. *Just two peas in a pod.*

Michael shifted uncomfortably and a few hairs on his head were caught by the stucco wall. Startled, he pulled away quickly, heaving himself up onto his knees. Elizabeth was sprawled out on the floor in front of him, her breathing even and her body relaxed. The house was quiet, although he could hear Leah in the kitchen below. After watching Elizabeth for a moment to ensure she was asleep, he stood up, but realized he had no idea where to go.

He made one uncertain step from the small room they were in and took a moment to digest the view of the room before him. Had they really eaten on that mat on the floor, with foods he never considered laid out in grand fashion? He walked over to the window and glanced out into the night sky. When was the last time he had seen a tree like that, if ever? And why did he feel this overwhelming fatigue? Where were they? Before he was aware of it, he had begun to pace silently, his face skewed in concentration.

Leah returned from below, expertly pulling herself up the ladder with a large bundle under her arm. She walked over to him, handed Michael a bedroll, and motioned to the roof. "It is warm out tonight, and the breeze should be pleasant. You will do well to make your sleeping quarters up there."

"Up there?" Michael said with a pained expression. "Outside?"

"Yes, up there." Leah looked at him with a sorrowful expression. As Michael turned to start up the ladder, he hesitated, looking back over his shoulder at Leah.

"You said you were concerned about soldiers being everywhere. I'm just really worried about that soldier who took a piece of my daughter's clothing. He said he was going to make my daughter his. Don't tell me that's what I think it means."

Leah was silent. Then she said, "The soldier is interested in taking her for his wife."

"What?"

Leah placed her fingers over her lips and pointed toward where Elizabeth lay sleeping.

"Sorry," Michael muttered.

"The soldier is interested in your daughter. It is customary for women at her age to marry and start families."

Michael's eyes widened in horror and he pointed roughly at her. "My little girl is not marrying anyone. She's just a kid."

"She is a grown woman. Enough time has passed for her to now find a husband."

"What kind of a place is this that encourages fourteen-year-olds to get married?"

Leah, looking confused, shook her head in response.

"I'm sorry, I meant no offense. But this is really surreal."

"*This* is what is expected," Leah said, her voice raised. She paused for a moment, collecting herself. "You should know that by now," she whispered.

Michael glared at her before his features softened. "I don't know anything. Believe me, I don't understand a thing about this place." He shook his head in resignation before climbing farther up the ladder. "Either way, none of this is expected from me or my daughter. And definitely not . . . *marriage*." The word tasted awful in his mouth.

Michael paused before looking at Leah curiously. "You know, I've been wondering something. Why did you take that risk and stand up for us in the courtyard?"

In the awkward silence, Michael readjusted the cumbersome bedroll under his arm as he watched her intently.

Leah took a deep breath, her eyes scanning the room. "You are a kind man," she murmured finally. She leaned over, stood slightly on her toes, and gently touched his right cheek with her lips.

Michael was mystified but decided not to pursue the subject further. He resumed his climb and called back over his shoulder, "What town are we in?"

Over the rooftop he could see the outline of the city, the flowing water moving through the aqueduct, the stars twinkling in the clear, dark sky, and hundreds of rooftops in front of him. Unlike in Northport, he could not find the bay or its boats, and from this high vantage point, nothing looked familiar.

Leah hesitated, looking up at him oddly from the bottom of the ladder. "Jerusalem, of course."

6

IN
DEFENSE

The wooden ladder shook slightly in the morning light as Michael hit the last rung without a squeak. Growing up in the Richmond Hill house, he had become a master at moving quietly to avoid drawing attention to himself.

He made his way over to Elizabeth and noticed that the top half of her bedroll was pushed up so it would serve as a pillow, and that she was sound asleep.

Not surprising; she could sleep through a hurricane. He smiled and caressed her head.

Down to the first floor he went, making only a slight creaking sound on one of the middle rungs. In the kitchen, Michael grabbed a cup hanging on the wall and tried to pour some water into it from a large jug. The water splashed out, spilling all over him and the floor.

"Shoot," he muttered, wondering if he had been too loud.

His sleeve was soaking wet and water was pooling on the stone floor. He was afraid someone would slip in it, so he tried to push the puddle around with his foot, hoping that it would evaporate faster that way. It was futile, for now the entire floor was slippery. He bent over closer to examine it.

"This will help," Leah said, placing a piece of cloth before him.

He sheepishly straightened up. "I'm so sorry."

"Why? It's just water."

Michael nodded. "Thank you."

"Can I make you some porridge?"

If we are in Jerusalem, how do I even understand what she's saying? Michael hesitated. "Ah, no, thank you, it's not necessary. I just need some water. I want to get to town and try to see if it's safe to get to the tunnel."

"The soldiers may notice you, dressed as you are. You'll be in danger. Please let me get you some clothing."

Before he could reply, Leah went upstairs, returning with a long, off-white linen robe. Michael put the garment over his sweatpants and T-shirt. The bottom of the robe touched the top of his feet.

"Better?"

"Not yet." Leah brought him a simple, woven belt and wrapped it around his waist. "Now you are done."

Michael watched Leah pour him a cup of water. "Thank you," he said, accepting it. "Can you please tell Elizabeth that I'm going back to the tunnel to see if there are any soldiers still there?"

Leah paused uncomfortably. "Would it not be better if you told her yourself what you are doing?"

"No. She'll want to come. I can't take her because of that soldier."

Leah pointed to his empty cup. "She isn't a little girl."

"No, thank you, that was enough. I know she isn't. But please, will you take care of her for me today? She's all I've got."

"I will."

Michael smiled. "I'll try to be back as soon as I can. Please tell Elizabeth I love her."

With that, he went out into the courtyard and through the gate.

The pain in Elizabeth's hip woke her. She had rolled off the bedroll and the hard, cold floor had taken its toll. She opened her eyes and sat up quickly, finding it difficult at first to comprehend the room around her. In the morning sun, the yellow stone walls were reflecting golden rays of light.

"Dad?" she called, standing. She could see the dining mat that they had sat around last night was just beyond the alcove where she had slept.

"Daddy!" Elizabeth yelled with urgency, walking out into the main room. The silence left a pit inside her stomach. She leaned over the ladder to see if anyone was visible.

"Dad? Are you down there?"

Hearing no response, Elizabeth climbed the ladder to the roof and poked her head out. She saw the empty bedroll.

"Dad?"

Elizabeth started back down the ladder, jumping off before the bottom rung to the second floor and quickly descended to the first.

Leah had left the porridge to cook over the fire and was in the courtyard praying when she heard Elizabeth on the ladder.

"Dad!"

"I am here," Leah said.

Elizabeth leaped to the floor from the middle of the ladder and turned to see Leah kneeling by the fig tree in the courtyard. "Do you know where my . . ."

Leah put two fingers over her mouth before quickly finishing her prayers. Standing, she said, "Your father is not here."

"Where is he?"

"He went to town to look for the place you came from," said Leah as she walked to the smoldering fire.

"Why didn't he wake me? Why didn't you?"

"Your father asked me not to."

"What?"

"I made you something to eat."

"I don't want to eat. I want my father!"

Leah stirred the porridge calmly. "He said he would be back soon."

"When is *soon*?"

"I don't know."

You don't know much. Elizabeth was so angry at her father, wondering how he could leave her here with this strange woman.

"Leah, we have to look for him."

"That was not what he wanted."

"Why not?"

"It's not safe."

"Not *safe*? We have to go look for him if it's not safe."

"No, it's not safe for you."

"Why?"

Leah looked at her, bewildered. "Elizabeth, you are a woman. Surely you know that there are men who would think nothing of having their way with you." Leah's gaze softened. She whispered, "They will hurt you, damage you. They would ruin you and you would never be the same."

Elizabeth scowled at Leah, her hands flailing in the air. "What are you talking about? I would never let that happen." She huffed. "My *dad* would never let that happen."

Leah carefully moved past her, retreating to the kitchen. "Your dad cannot stop them. You are a beautiful woman, Elizabeth. Perhaps you would be safe with a good man and a home."

Elizabeth reeled around and squared her shoulders. "Are you crazy? I'm just fourteen. I'm not even allowed to date." She laughed mockingly. "My father won't even allow me to kiss a guy."

"I know your father would not be happy that I spoke this way, but you must understand this is the way of our town."

"Not our town," Elizabeth shot back.

Leah remained silent.

"We still need to find my father. I can't stay here."

Leah placed her hand on Elizabeth's arm, gently stopping her from leaving through the courtyard. "If you were to go to town for your father, the soldier might remember you."

"What soldier?"

"The soldier who took the piece of your garment."

Elizabeth looked at her oversize T-shirt. She now wished she hadn't invaded her father's closet. *I wonder if this is punishment for not asking*, she thought ironically.

Leah could see the determination on Elizabeth's face. "I'll go with you."

Elizabeth's face lit up.

"But you should never wear that shirt again," Leah said, handing Elizabeth one of her own robes.

Elizabeth's smile turned to a frown. At first she just stared at it, but then put it on over her shirt.

"I'm keeping the T-shirt," she said with a bit of an edge just before heading out the door.

Out on the street, Michael looked around and didn't see any soldiers. He started moving at a brisk pace, joining the many people already at marketplaces and in the streets as they carried out their morning tasks. He passed near the courtyard area where he and Elizabeth had met Leah. It was empty.

Michael remembered that the opening of the tunnel was on the west side of the street, near a fruit and vegetable stand. He noticed a crowd of people huddled in an area about fifty yards away and wondered if that was the spot.

He could see several men and women gathered around a food cart inspecting the merchandise. His heart started to race and excitement filled his body.

It's got to be there, that's the stand.

Then, as if a wave had hit the crowd, the people dispersed as several soldiers on horses raced from the opposite direction. Their shiny golden helmets glistened in the sun, and their bright red capes flapped up and down with the speed of the horses.

Michael's stomach turned and his heart pounded. He darted out into the middle of a crowd that was moving to the other side of the street, allowing the parade of proud soldiers to whip past.

He crouched down low to avoid being spotted. Another group of soldiers was behind the initial cavalry. The crowd pushed farther back near the buildings and away from the street. He looked across the road to see if he could find the bank of sewer grates, but instead only saw another group of soldiers gathered near the stand.

He was frustrated and worried, but anxious to get back home. Michael jumped out of the crowd and ran between several men and women who were in the street. He was about twenty yards from the fruit stand now. Along the side of the wall stood about ten soldiers with long, shimmering spears, much like the weapons he and Elizabeth had seen the day before.

The sound of the soldiers' laughter made Michael nervous. He eyed each one, searching to see if Marcus or Titus was there. He moved closer to the group.

A sharp object scraped his back.

"Get away from here," a voice bellowed at him.

Michael pushed the spear away. He glared at the soldier without even thinking; he knew immediately that this was the wrong thing to do.

"We have trouble here!"

Several soldiers ran over and circled Michael.

"I'm sorry," he said, trying to back up.

"Let him go," announced another soldier as he rode across the street toward them. "He and I have a history. I'll take care of him."

While the group of soldiers retreated, Michael turned to face the man who had just spoken. He caught a glimpse of his white horse, but with the morning sunlight's glare so strong off his helmet, it was impossible to make out the soldier's face. Michael noticed, however, what he thought was a ponytail hanging out of the back of his helmet.

"Come across the street," the soldier said, motioning away from the tunnel's entrance.

Michael knew this was no time to be a hero, so he followed him blindly, squinting from the sun.

The soldier dismounted and led him through the crowd. "I helped you last night so it's time you helped me," he said over his shoulder.

"Marcus? Is that you?" Michael asked, watching the ground closely to avoid such things as squashed pomegranates in the street.

"It is me. I can get your ring back. Just tell me where the woman is and I will let you go, too."

They walked into the shadow of a building, and Michael could finally see Marcus more clearly. He noticed another scar, this one circular and ingrained on the back of his left leg where the skin was bubbled up as if it had been burned. Looking upward, Michael's eyes became glued to the back of the soldier's helmet. It wasn't a ponytail hanging there but a piece of cloth.

Michael's body froze. "I have no idea what you're talking about," he lied.

"That is unfortunate." Marcus turned to face him, taking off his helmet. The cloth that hung from it fell to the ground.

Michael picked it up, realizing that it was, indeed, a piece of his old Springsteen T-shirt, and gasped.

The soldier snatched it away. "Tell me where that woman is or I will kill you!"

"I don't know." Out of instinct, Michael reached for the cloth in Marcus' hand, ripping a piece off. He fled back around the building and out onto the street.

"Stop!"

Michael sprinted ahead, trying desperately to disappear into the crowd. He heard the sounds of horses and quickly dropped to his knees, hiding himself. He felt a burst of wind as a horse sprinted past him and then, relief.

A low rumbling could be heard over the city wall as Elizabeth and Leah approached. "What is that?" Elizabeth asked. People were milling near the entranceway as if they were waiting in line to purchase tickets to a big concert.

"It's the Romans, they're coming in more numbers now that the holiday is coming soon," Leah replied.

The crowd was eight to nine people deep on both sides. Leah squeezed past Elizabeth to guide the way through the big crowd, which was now spilling onto the streets, too. Many women and men were in the mob, some holding their children's hands. But while it looked like a modern celebration, the atmosphere was tense.

Leah and Elizabeth finally found a spot on the other side of the street and stood for a few moments. Leah rose up on the tips of her toes to look farther down the road. A massive pile of humanity was in front of her. "Let's stay here until the Romans pass," she suggested, holding Elizabeth's hand more tightly.

The staccato sound of hooves clapping the ground and whips hitting horseflesh filled the air. Elizabeth turned to her left to see the parade of soldiers crashing through the city gate. "Oh, no, they're going to get crushed!" she gasped, watching the procession of shining, armored men walking in front of a big chariot. Many people, unable to get across in time, were bowled over like pins. A woman and man fell on top of their little girl, their screams piercing the air.

"Let me help," Elizabeth cried, putting her hand out. Suddenly, she felt her body jerked back.

"Watch out!" Leah screamed as several soldiers, spears turned sideways, smashed a group of villagers into them. They both stumbled to the ground, momentarily dazed. Leah lifted Elizabeth up. Then another wave of soldiers entered through the gate. The crowd hissed and shouted angry words while Elizabeth searched the maze of people for the little girl. "Is she hurt?" asked Elizabeth, craning her neck to get a better look. But she couldn't hear Leah's answer as the procession intensified.

Elizabeth grimaced and placed her free hand over her eyes as another set of soldiers, this time armed with spiked metal balls on chains, swung their weapons toward the crowd as they passed.

Slowly Elizabeth and Leah inched their way through the crowd as several onlookers were shoved by soldiers into the throngs lining the side of the street. A loud trumpet blared up ahead, and the sound made Elizabeth cover her ears.

"Hold on," said Leah, grabbing Elizabeth's hand again and pulling her farther away from the road. A high-arching chariot, with a group of about ten Roman soldiers on either side, hurtled past, kicking up dirt that pelted people's faces. A beautiful woman sat beside a well-dressed man who looked important.

"Who is that?" Elizabeth yelled to Leah, who leaned down slightly to hear the question.

"Pontius Pilate."

Elizabeth wasn't sure what Leah said since the noise in the crowd had reached its peak level. "We have to get to the tunnel, my dad might be there," she urged Leah.

The Romans continued their march through the city gate. Elizabeth saw a man, screaming in pain and trying to stanch the flow of blood from a wound in his side, fall to the ground. Elizabeth moved forward to help him but Leah pulled her back.

"We've got to get out of here," said Leah. "It's too dangerous to try and get to where you need to go."

"But my dad!"

"We're not safe here! Let's go back home and we'll try later. He won't leave without you."

Leah expertly slipped through the crowd, making sure they were out of the parade's path. She found a slight opening near the wall, just as another group of soldiers was ready to rumble through. She and Elizabeth knifed through the small breach and moved immediately to the far left, out of harm's way as the remaining soldiers staged their grand entrance.

Michael made certain that he kept traveling in a crowd. He was unsure exactly where he was in town, but he knew if he took the right turn, he might find himself near the tunnel. But the number of people on the streets was growing.

This crowd is going to attract more soldiers, Michael thought. *I'd better get out of here.*

A beautiful woman with black curls surrounding her face stared at Michael as he searched in desperation for a safe place to go. She approached him with a quizzical look on her face. "Are you awaiting the Messiah's arrival?" she asked.

"What Messiah?" Michael countered impatiently, avoiding her stare.

"The preacher. The Messiah."

"There is no Messiah." He looked around anxiously for soldiers. "Why are there so many people here?"

"The Messiah is coming."

He stood there, stunned, but before he could say anything more, she had disappeared into the crowd. He scanned the sea of faces quickly for any sign of the strange woman but could find none.

He was jarred by the blare of a trumpet in the distance. He knew instantly that something was about to happen as the many men, women, and children stirred.

The sound of pounding hooves from an oncoming cavalry echoed from the west, prompting several in the crowd to hiss and recoil. Michael panicked and moved with them in the opposite direction, to the east, darting in and out of the crowd.

Suddenly, the buildings began to look familiar and Michael realized that he was close to where he believed the tunnel to be.

There it is!

As he hurried across the street, he wondered if he should go back and get Elizabeth or find help in Northport. But as he neared the sewer grate, people in the street surged forward against him.

The crowd grew suddenly, impairing any attempt he made to move, like standing in the path of a mass of people swelling off a subway car during rush hour. They pushed up against Michael as he tried to turn and look back to see the source of the commotion.

His view of the street was entirely obstructed. After trying in vain, he glanced around behind him until he found a discarded basket. He grabbed at it before anyone could unintentionally crush it and placed it beneath him. Standing now half a foot higher, he made out a man riding a donkey from the east. Michael could see bands of people, eight or nine at a time, dropping and bowing in front of the man, who sat motionless as he passed between them.

Shouts of *"Messiah"* came from the excited crowd. Michael froze, watching the back of the man's head as he traveled farther away. *What is this?*

As the man made his way up the street, a group of soldiers moved toward the procession. They swatted several people with the backs of their spears, knocking a child and a woman down. Despite the violence, the crowd rose up, blocking their path.

"Is that him? It can't be . . . ," Michael murmured, his gaze fixed on the scene before him.

Turning to his left, he could see the bank of sewer grates just thirty yards away, and yet, Michael found himself running toward the man on the donkey. Throngs of people were behind him as he made his way down the street. Michael weaved in and out of the crowd. He could see clearly now that many were placing palms in the man's path.

Michael was moving farther and farther away from the tunnel and closer to a group of soldiers. But the excitement of the crowd engulfed him, overshadowing his fear.

"Jesus?" The word sprang to his lips, surprising him. It was as if some part of his being could make sense of this chaos before his mind could rationalize the reason. Somehow he knew this was Palm Sunday, described so precisely, yet inadequately, in the Bible. Now that he was experiencing this moment, he knew that the Bible didn't do justice to the powerful, raw emotion of the crowds. He finally understood the act itself: Jesus' nonconfrontational response to the devastating show of force from the Romans, parading with their endless supply of gilded military might, in step with the drumbeat from the west. It began to dawn on Michael in a way that he had never fully understood how this moment truly defined Jesus' amazing character. He was so human and yet so divine in the same breath. It swept over him like a cresting wave. Before he knew it, he, too, was yelling, nearly screaming to get his voice heard above the roar of the crowd. "Jesus! Can you help me? Is Vicki okay?"

Michael found himself pushing harder between those around him. He was now within only a few yards of Jesus' humble advance.

"Halt," yelled a disconnected voice from farther down the line.

"There he is, the one who ran from me before," Marcus bellowed. Michael reeled around, recognizing the voice of the malicious Roman soldier. He was only a few yards away.

"Help me, Jesus," Michael yelled, turning away from Marcus in terror.

"I will find her!" shouted Marcus, his advance clearing a wide path through the masses. "Grab him!"

Michael opened his eyes, seeing Jerusalem swirling around him. He looked down at his hand, where the piece of Elizabeth's T-shirt was cradled. In a moment of bravery, he sprinted wildly across the street, crudely tying the cloth to the sewer grate. Not wanting to leave, but feeling exulted that he had at least left a marker for his return, he scurried back across the street and in the opposite direction of the procession. He moved swiftly, but randomly, without any purpose or knowledge of direction.

And he didn't look back.

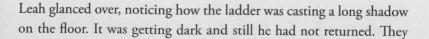

Leah glanced over, noticing how the ladder was casting a long shadow on the floor. It was getting dark and still he had not returned. They had never eaten lunch, certain that they should wait for him. But soon the sun would set. She must feed the girl and find some way to calm her.

"Elizabeth," she called out into the courtyard, "we'll set up an early dinner so that we'll be ready when your father returns."

Elizabeth turned around, looking over at her from where she had been sitting under the fig tree. "It's dinnertime already? Where is he? We should have stayed there until we found him. We have to go back and try again."

"I know. But it's not safe for you to go out alone. You saw how the soldiers treat us."

"Then come with me," Elizabeth said sharply as she walked into the house. "I won't be alone then."

Leah smiled, remembering how independent she was at Elizabeth's age. "Your father may think you are just a girl, but in many ways you are a woman."

"Then you will go with me?"

"No," Leah said, wondering where he could be.

"Could he have been at the same parade we were at?"

"I don't know. But if he was, it's over by now." Leah paused. "Your father feared for you and asked that we stay here. If he found out I let you go to town to find him, he'll be very upset."

"Why would you listen to him?" asked Elizabeth, trying to work every angle she knew. "You don't even know him."

"I don't know *you* . . . but I do care about your safety."

Elizabeth stood quietly against the wall while Leah began preparing food for dinner. She offered Elizabeth a drink of water. She accepted, turning back to go into the courtyard.

"Would you like to bring the lamb as company for you?"

"What? I guess so . . ."

Leah moved past Elizabeth, opening the gate to the lamb's corral. She handed Elizabeth a basket of grain. "The lamb is probably hungry. Can you feed her? I need her to eat as much as possible."

"Why?"

"I'm preparing the lamb for sacrifice. The Passover is coming this week, and I'm offering her up for the feast."

Elizabeth was horrified. "You want me to help fatten up the animal so you can kill and eat it? I can't do that."

Leah put her arm around Elizabeth. "I know you can. Please take care of the lamb while I finish dinner."

Holding the basket, Elizabeth reluctantly lured the lamb out to where she had been sitting before under the fig tree. Here she could see the gate to the road. She sat looking out to the road feeling apprehensive that her father was lost and would not know the house when he passed it. *Maybe I should go now? He could be waiting for me near the tunnel. What if he's been caught? Then what will I do?*

Elizabeth stared a few more moments until the lamb's cries disrupted her thoughts. She turned and faced the lamb, extending her palms. The lamb nibbled away at the grains in Elizabeth's hands while she whispered secretly to it, "Do you know where my dad is? He's been away so long."

The lamb nuzzled up against her, its soft wool brushing against her arm.

"Oh, you're so soft," she said, watching the gate for any movement. Elizabeth placed her head on the lamb's back, rubbing the animal affectionately.

She continued to stroke the lamb's back, redirecting it back to the food when it tried to turn away. "No, no, little lamb," she said through a giggle, "stay over here and eat."

Seeing Leah in the kitchen, Elizabeth called out, "Are you sure you want to kill this cute lamb?"

Leah smiled tenderly before turning toward the back wall of the house. She picked up a second basket and placed it inside the lamb's stall.

"Elizabeth, could you bring her over here, please?"

Elizabeth gingerly pulled the lamb in from the courtyard and directed her over to this new bucket filled with scraps. The lamb ate intently.

It's so cuddly, even though it's just another dinner for this woman.

"Put the gate in front of her."

Elizabeth patted the lamb on the head, whispering softly, "Let me know if you see Dad, okay?"

As she closed the gate, she asked Leah, "When are you killing her?"

"We sacrifice the animal, not kill it."

"It's the same thing," Elizabeth replied, struggling with the leather-hewn latch.

"No, it is not," Leah said, raising her voice slightly. "My husband was killed. I know when someone is killed."

Elizabeth stepped away from Leah and leaned against the wall, never taking her eyes from the lamb. "I'm sorry. I didn't know you were married."

"Yes, I was, though not at your age. In many ways I was fortunate that I wasn't able to marry then, but had to wait until my family was able to arrange it."

Leah turned back to the pot she was stirring. "Although I was older, it was a very good union, and these past two years have been difficult without him."

"How did your husband die?"

"It's not important how it happened, but it did happen."

In the awkward silence that followed, Elizabeth heard the soft breathing of the lamb, but thought she detected muffled sobs from Leah as she leaned over the pot. She couldn't tell for sure, so she looked at Leah, seeing that her hands were crossed over her heart.

"Are you praying?"

"Yes," Leah said. "I am praying for your father's safe return."

The streets were emptying, and Michael was beginning to relax. The threat of danger seemed less ominous. Before he was aware of any pain, he glanced down and saw that his sandals were torn and his heels were ripped and bleeding.

Panting, he looked around and spied what appeared to be an abandoned building. He pulled at the broken gate, walking quietly through the littered courtyard and into a dark corner in the rear of the house. Slumping down, he tugged at his sandals, but his fingers were too tired to unbuckle the straps.

On the back of his right heel, a blister had popped and a gash had developed, but this didn't concern him. He thought he might just rest for a few moments. He had barely slept the night before up on Leah's roof, and so now, without planning it, he closed his eyes.

A brisk wind pleasantly chilled his face as the ocean waves sprayed over the makeshift barriers protecting the boardwalk. He saw a tangled flag wrapped tightly around the tall metal pole in front of the vacant snack shop. Seagulls tried to navigate safe landings below as the gray winter sky threatened with a sweet smell of snow.

As he and Elizabeth walked under the pavilion, a blast of wind hit them.

"Hold up a sec, kiddo." Michael pulled Elizabeth's hood up over her head and zipped her jacket to her chin.

"I'm not a baby, Dad. I'm going to be fifteen next year."

"Yeah, well, you're always going to be my baby."

They walked down the steps to the boardwalk. "Which way are we headed today?"

"Let's keep the wind to our backs," he said, turning east.

As they strolled along the wooden planks, the whistling wind obscured the sound of their footsteps. The sea grass danced around them and carried the spray from the crashing waves up onto the shore. He pulled Elizabeth close to him.

Alone in the distance a woman was struggling to maintain her pace against the changing direction of the wind. Elizabeth shuddered when a sudden flurry of snow struck her face.

"I thought you said we were moving with the wind to our back?"

"I guess it changed. Let's keep walking anyway." His eyes were focused on the figure ahead.

As he tried to move more rapidly, the wind's power seemed to increase. He could see the woman had stopped and they were gaining on her. She looked familiar.

The fierce wind caused him to squint. Although it was difficult to see her, he was mesmerized by how the woman's scarf was dancing in the wind. It seemed to be unraveling, snapping like a snake trying to fend off a predator.

Elizabeth pulled tighter on his coat jacket. They were nearing the woman, but as they did so, the wind swirled around them, whipping at their pant legs. Elizabeth moved behind her father, burying her face into his back.

"Daddy, let's turn around."

"No, no, just a little further."

A fury of freezing air knocked them backward and propelled the lady's green-and-black scarf over their heads into the air. It dropped behind them on the ground. Elizabeth reached down instinctively and picked it up.

"The lady lost her scarf," she said, handing it to him.

Michael recognized it immediately. He brought it up to his face and took a deep breath. *It smells like home.*

He became energized as he took those final few steps toward her. He touched her shoulder gently, enchanted when she slowly turned to him.

It was Vicki. He loved the way the wind moved through her brown hair, swirling its curls back inside her hood. His eyes fell upon her soft cheeks. He had forgotten how rosy they would look during a winter walk. Her lips were parted slightly, as if she wanted to tell him something. He desperately wanted to lean over and kiss her.

He looked up into her eyes, now misty with tears. "You always had the most beautiful eyes, Vick."

With her scarf gone, he could see the gold chain around her neck.

In this cold, it had left red marks on her skin. She reached up, placing her delicate hands over the pendant hanging from it.

Michael was surprised to see how small her fingers were and how the frigid weather was making her hands raw. He reached over to touch them, but a jolt of air punched his face, causing him to wobble back against Elizabeth.

"Dad, please . . ."

He looked down at the scarf in his hand. He couldn't let go.

"I can't do this anymore." Michael looked up one last time at Vicki.

"I'm sorry. I can't help you," she whispered regretfully.

7

WARM AIR

"Elizabeth . . . *Elizabeth?*" Michael called out, staggering to his feet. His senses were foggy from the dream and he had lost all sense of time. He wasn't sure whether it was dusk or dawn. His stomach ached from hunger, and his feet were stinging. He looked down and saw his bloodstained right sandal. He flexed his legs a few times to generate some circulation.

As he fumbled his way outside, he could see the sun was climbing over the horizon, a new day—was he right to think it could be Monday?

I hope Elizabeth's okay. I have to get back . . . I gotta get back now.

Michael looked back at the vacant building. He noticed that the right side of the structure was entirely collapsed. Remnants of what he theorized were household items lay beneath the rubble; none of it was anything he would ever use back home. The feeling of complete displacement and isolation beleaguered him as he scratched at his dusty scalp. He knew he had to move forward, and finally his legs complied.

As he started down the street, still nothing seemed familiar. He could hear the ruckus of a marketplace ahead with people already noisily negotiating prices. As he drew closer, the smell of fruit surrounded him, instantly making him feel hungry and thirsty.

He reached into his pocket. "What am I thinking?" he muttered to himself. "I don't have any money."

The aroma of smoked meat soon floated in the air, making it even more difficult for Michael to maintain focus. He headed east, certain that Leah's house was in that direction. He measured his steps, moving much more slowly than on the previous day. He noted with growing impatience how long it seemed to take him to get anywhere.

Each stand of fruits and vegetables he passed seemed to multiply his hunger. He stopped in front of a stand selling bread and watched. Michael wondered if he could muster up the nerve to steal a loaf. He knew that if he got caught, he would probably face severe punishment. His sense of history gave Michael an idea of the kind of justice he would be served; if he really was in Jerusalem, it wouldn't be the kind found in Northport.

He froze again, watching an old lady grapple with her change, exchanging some of it for an enticing loaf. The storekeeper turned his back to put away the coins.

Michael inched closer to the stand. One flatbread up front was small enough to carry but big enough to appease his hunger. He drew nearer, his hand outstretched in front of him.

He stepped back in disgust. *My Lord, what am I doing?*

The storekeeper turned around and sneered. "You need something?"

"I think he does," said a bearded man behind him, slapping Michael on the shoulder. The man pulled a couple of coins from a bag and handed them to the storekeeper. "Give him whatever he needs."

"Um, thank you," Michael said, catching a glimpse of friendly brown eyes.

The man smiled. "You look like you could use a good meal."

Michael pointed to the bread in front. The storekeeper, still suspicious, cautiously handed it to him. As he did so, Michael noticed the man had departed.

"Thank you, sir!" he called out over his shoulder.

Without turning, the man put his hand up in acknowledgment.

"You can leave now," the storekeeper said in a menacing tone.

Michael nodded and started to walk south, anxious to get back to

Elizabeth. He still felt like a failure: he was no closer to getting home than he was yesterday.

Tearing at the bread, Michael looked upward and became captivated by the bright, clear blue sky dazzling above as the sun reached for its peak for the day. A small child raced past him, chasing a leaf dancing in the light breeze that seemed to glow in the morning light.

"Beautiful," Michael said under his breath as he looked over the dining room. He had chicken roasting in the oven, two candles flickering on the table, champagne poured into their wedding flutes, and Frank Sinatra's "Summer Wind" spinning in the CD player. He was ready to romance his beautiful bride.

Okay, so we're not honeymooners anymore, but we can still live like them.

Where is she? Becoming edgy, he looked over again at the clock. She took the same two trains in and out of the city each day, yet her hour-and-a-half commute never seemed to be as perfectly timed as he would like.

Michael was fretful. He had something special to share with Vicki tonight, and he wanted to talk to her right away. He thought he had set the perfect mood for the discussion, but now she was late. Sulking, he walked back and forth in front of the picture window in the living room. Just when he was ready to sit down again, he heard the sound of the key clicking in the front door.

"Vicki!" Michael shouted, a huge grin on his face.

"Hi," she said rather weakly. "Boy, I'm beat. Can we just go up to bed early and maybe watch some TV?"

Then Vicki saw the dining room. "Oops," she said with a laugh. "You've got something special planned tonight, don't you?"

Michael's smile cracked through a showy grimace. "Wow, where did you get that idea?"

"I'm sorry. I was late . . ."

"Why are you late? Why didn't you call?"

"A car got stuck on the railroad crossing in Northport. They wouldn't open the doors until we pulled completely into the station."

Michael paused slightly, crossed his arms, and dramatically rolled his eyes.

"You don't believe me? You think I have a man I keep by the cross-roads? Jealous?"

She giggled, before jumping into his arms. Her lips brushed his earlobe as she looked behind him at the table. "Thank you for setting this up so beautifully."

"I hope it's not ruined."

"It's not," she said as she gave him a peck on the cheek. "Relax."

She sat down while Michael placed a piece of chicken on her plate. "Looks great," she said. "Somehow I have a feeling we are going to talk about something serious."

Michael smiled. *She knows me.* Whenever he cooked an extravagant dinner, he had something on his mind to discuss.

"Do you need more money to invest? Oh, no, are you starting another business?" By now, Vicki was used to Michael approaching her with new, big ideas. Usually, she just held her breath.

"Nope."

"We're not going to move again, are we? We've moved four times in the last seven years."

"No."

"Well, can you blame me?"

"We . . . are . . . not . . . moving," Michael said, underscoring each word.

"Good." Vicki smiled. "Now, I'm ready for anything."

Michael was quiet, fumbling with his champagne flute. He felt the bubbles popping up to his nose as he leaned over to gain the courage to speak.

"I think I'm ready to start a family."

Vicki coughed out her champagne. "Oh, you are?"

"Yeah!"

"You do realize I'm the one who has to carry the baby for nine months, don't you?"

"Yeah."

She cut anxiously at her piece of chicken. "Honey, can you imagine how our lives would change? You know I have to keep working so that we have health care."

"So?"

"So, you would have to be the one caring for the baby while I work."

"Yes," he said sternly, "I know my role here."

After they finished the rest of the dinner in pained silence, Vicki turned to him and said, "Let's go upstairs and talk, okay? I'm really tired."

When they reached their bedroom, she motioned for him to lie down on his stomach so she could rub his back.

"Sweetie, I want a family, too. But, to be honest, I'm scared. I know you will be good at it, I just don't know if I'll be."

Michael's head shot up from the bed. "What?"

"I'm afraid."

Turning under her, Michael put his hand up to her cheek. "You will be a great mother. I know that because you are a great wife."

"That's different," she said, looking away.

"There's one thing that is the same in both situations." He placed his right hand in the middle of her chest. "This heart thumps with so much love," he whispered, reaching up and kissing her. "Believe me."

Vicki leaned over and turned out the lights, as Michael shifted back onto his stomach. He felt her soft hands massaging his shoulders again before she placed her whole body on top of his.

"I do want to have a child," she whispered to him.

"I'll be with you every step of the way."

"I know."

She rolled off him and left the room.

"Where are you going?"

"Hold on."

She walked back into the bedroom, holding two flickering candles. "These are needed up here," she said, placing them on the nightstand.

Vicki climbed into Michael's outstretched arms, resting her head on his chest. "You're really not scared?"

"No."

Lifting her head to look into his eyes, she smiled. "Thanks for giving me a push in life. I guess I needed one."

"Thanks for allowing me to push you," he replied with a short laugh.

"I know you're going to be a great dad."

"And I know you are going to be a great mommy."

"Hmmm, I like the way that sounds, 'Mommy.' " She brushed his lips with hers, in short, gentle kisses. "What should we name the baby if it's a boy?"

"I don't know," he said, laughing, "just as long as it's not after me."

"What about a name for a girl?"

"Elizabeth. I always loved that name."

"Elizabeth?"

"Yes, Elizabeth."

Awake now, Leah wandered around the second floor trying to find Elizabeth. Her face was filled with fear as she ran up the ladder leading to the roof.

"Elizabeth?"

She rushed back to the second floor, before descending to the first at a furious pace.

"Eliz—" Leah stopped as she saw Elizabeth asleep in the stall with her head resting on the back of the lamb, her cheeks stained with tears.

"Good morning, Elizabeth."

Elizabeth's puffy eyes opened slightly but she didn't respond. She was despondent, having slept poorly, distressed about her father. She had looked out the window several times during the night, finally coming down the ladder to wait for him in the courtyard. But she got scared and ran back inside to cuddle up with the lamb.

"Is my father back?" Elizabeth asked desperately. She began petting the lamb, but then with Leah watching her, stopped abruptly, feeling guilty about trying to fatten the lamb up the day before.

Leah shook her head. "I need your help."

Elizabeth let out a big sigh before turning toward the lamb. "I'll be back, Cassie."

Leah looked back in surprise as she walked over to the smoldering fire. "Cassie?"

"Yes, Cassie. Everyone has a name."

Leah shook her head. "Why don't you help me until your father returns," she said, trying to distract her. "It will be good for you."

"How do you know what's good for me?"

Leah turned around to face Elizabeth. "Do you speak that way to your mother?"

"I don't have a mother."

"What?"

"My mother isn't around." Then Elizabeth added defiantly, "But my father and I are fine, okay?"

Leah straightened up and looked Elizabeth in the eye. "I'm sorry. It must have been difficult."

Elizabeth looked away. "Sometimes."

"Who took care of you when you were young?"

"My dad . . . when he could . . ."

Leah moved a few steps closer. "Tell me what you mean."

Elizabeth sat on one of the two low stools resting near the stall. Leah pulled back a few steps, as if she recognized that the girl needed her space. "There really isn't much to say," she said, as her mind wandered back to third grade.

Elizabeth ran across the playground to play tag with Laura, screaming in delight when she finally caught up to her best friend. "Gotcha!" Then, panting, she curled down against the pole holding up one of the basketball nets.

"You win," Laura said.

Elizabeth laughed.

"You tired?"

Elizabeth nodded, trying to catch her breath. A group of girls were gathering at the far end of the playground. "Let's go see what they're doing," said Laura, jumping to her feet.

Elizabeth took another deep breath and stood up. "Is that Miss Bittner?"

"Yes! Let's go!"

The girls raced across the concrete and onto the grass where Elizabeth's class was gathering around the teacher. They could see Miss Bittner talking to the students. As Laura and Elizabeth approached, Miss Bittner put her hand up in protest.

"Hold on, girls," she said in a firm voice. "I'll be back in two minutes."

She then gestured toward Elizabeth. "Sweetie, come with me," she said as she held Elizabeth's hand.

Miss Bittner led Elizabeth inside the school and back to the classroom. "Sit here," she said, pointing to the seat closest to the door. "I have to do something, Elizabeth. But I'll be back in a couple of minutes. Okay, honey?"

Elizabeth nodded, then as Miss Bittner turned away, meekly said, "Miss Bittner, am I in trouble? Did I do something wrong?"

Miss Bittner stopped and turned quickly back toward Elizabeth. "Oh, dear, no, honey. No. Absolutely not."

The teacher bent down and gave Elizabeth a hug. "You can never do anything wrong, sweetie. I just need to take care of something outside and then I'll return."

Miss Bittner touched the top of Elizabeth's hair and weakly smiled. She stood up and briskly walked out of the classroom.

Elizabeth sat quietly, but grew anxious after a few minutes. When she heard the occasional burst of screams from the playground outside, she thought about leaving her chair. She could hear her friend Laura squealing. She walked to the window closest to the commotion. Miss Bittner was high-fiving the girls as they jumped up and down.

Elizabeth pressed her face against the window. The frown deepened when she saw a smile on Laura's face as Miss Bittner slapped her outstretched hand. When she saw her teacher and classmates make their way back into the school, Elizabeth ran back to her seat and buried her face.

The murmuring chatter of the boys and girls filled the hallway. Elizabeth wiped the tears from her face.

"Hi, Lizzie!" said Laura with a smile.

"Hi." Elizabeth eyed her friend warily. "Laura, what happened outside?"

"Nothing."

"Please tell me, Laurie, you're my best friend. We tell each other everything. Right?"

Laura sat behind Elizabeth, who turned around to face her. "C'mon."

"Shh, I'm not supposed to say. Miss Bittner would be mad."

Elizabeth smiled. "I won't tell her. Tell me. Is it a surprise for me? My birthday is next week."

Laura shook her head. "No. We're having a mother-daughter day at the park. We don't have to go to school that day!"

Elizabeth's face fell and she turned around. She placed her face in her hands. Laura got up and stood in front of her. She moved her face closer to Elizabeth. "Are you crying?"

"No!"

"Miss Bittner, Lizzie's crying." Then, in a whisper meant only for Elizabeth, Laura said, "Please don't tell her I told you."

The teacher came over to Elizabeth. "What's wrong, sweetie?"

She started to cry again. "I don't know what I did wrong."

"Did Laura say anything to you?"

Elizabeth was silent for a moment, then shook her head. "No. I want to go home."

Miss Bittner realized Elizabeth was in no mood to be consoled. She gathered Elizabeth's belongings and walked her to the office. "Elizabeth isn't feeling so good now," Miss Bittner said to Mrs. Loscalzo, the school office manager. "Can you call Mr. Stewart?"

"Don't you think you should be the one to call him this time?" asked Mrs. Loscalzo. "I don't like calling him while he's working. You know how he is."

Miss Bittner frowned. "Okay, I'll make the call next door in the nurse's office."

Elizabeth watched as Miss Bittner walked into the hallway. She returned moments later.

"Elizabeth, your dad will be by to pick you up soon." She bent down and gave her a hug. "Feel better, sweetie, okay?"

Elizabeth nodded and sat stoically in the office until her father arrived. When she saw him, her face lit up briefly. "Daddy! I want to go home."

"Are you sick, Elizabeth?" he asked, placing his hand on her forehead. He looked at Mrs. Loscalzo. "Did she throw up? Have a fever?"

"Not that I know of, Mr. Stewart. Perhaps you can give Miss Bittner a call after school."

"I don't have the time today to do that. I've got bills to pay, a mortgage, have to put oil in the tank for the winter."

"Mr. Stewart, do you want me to call Miss Bittner right now to come down to talk to you?"

"Yes."

Elizabeth squirmed in her seat and looked worriedly at her father. "Daddy, let's go. I'm not sick."

Michael sat down next to her. "Then, honey, why do you want to leave if you aren't sick?"

She hesitated. "Are you going to get mad?"

"No. What's wrong?"

Elizabeth leaned over and started whispering in Michael's ear.

Twice she pulled away, afraid to tell him, but then continued with her story. Mrs. Loscalzo, hands folded on her chin and elbows resting on the office counter, remained quiet but attentive.

Michael stood up. "Where's Miss Bittner?"

"She's on her way," Mrs. Loscalzo replied.

"Tell her I'll wait outside," he said, pointing to the doorway.

Elizabeth watched as her father walked out of the office. A few minutes later, she could hear the muted sounds of their conversation. She couldn't make out the words.

"Elizabeth, I'll be back in a moment," Mrs. Loscalzo said, picking up some mail and leaving through the back doorway linking the offices.

When Mrs. Loscalzo left, Elizabeth slipped out of the office and into the hallway. She pressed against the corner of the wall. Now she could hear them perfectly.

"So you brought my kid to tears because you excluded her?" Michael asked incredulously.

"I didn't want to hurt her feelings," Miss Bittner remarked.

"Well, that didn't work, did it?"

"Mr. Stewart, what would you suggest I do?"

"Include her."

"Mr. Stewart, when I've included her in the past, she would still end up crying. Don't you see?"

"See what?"

"Mr. Stewart, we've had mother/daughter and father/son trips or events in the past. But you never respond to them. So I didn't want your daughter to have another letdown."

Elizabeth peered around the corner. She could see her father looking down at the ground as he answered, "You have no idea how hard this all is."

"I'm sorry, Mr. Stewart, but it's not like we haven't had this conversation before."

"I'm sorry, Elizabeth," Leah said, trying to disrupt the long, awkward silence. "Is there something you want to tell me?"

"If you're so sorry, why didn't you wake me?" Elizabeth said through tears. "Where is he?"

Leah was shaken. *What have I done? What if her father was captured? He'll never get out of that prison alive now. I'll have to take care of this girl.*

"Where *is* he?"

"I am so sorry," Leah began, "but I couldn't . . . I'm worried about your father, too."

Leah tried to hug her, but Elizabeth pushed her away. "I don't need your pity," she said, wiping her tears from her cheeks. "I'm fine."

"I know you are. Let's go upstairs and eat." Leah handed Elizabeth a bowl of porridge with extra honey and led the way up the ladder.

After they ate a few moments in silence, Elizabeth asked Leah, "Do you have any children?"

Leah stopped eating.

"What's wrong?" Elizabeth asked, staring. She noticed Leah was looking at her hands in her lap. "I didn't mean to upset you."

Leah looked directly into her eyes. "We had a child. But she became ill just a few weeks after she was born. We couldn't save her."

Elizabeth put her hands over her mouth. "Oh, no . . . I'm so sorry," she said through her clasped fingers. "I don't know why I ask these things. Forgive me?"

Leah nodded, before saying, "My husband grieved for so long. I know you can't truly understand this, but when a child dies, you lose yourself . . . well, that is until he found the man who spoke about a new world."

"Who was that?"

"I'm not sure. I believe your father knows of him."

"Has my father met him?"

Leah shook her head. "I'm not sure. He's a man who talks about love and understanding. My husband would follow him and listen to him . . . when he could find him, that is. But there were many who questioned my husband's belief in this man, though he didn't care what they said. Ultimately, he was murdered."

"Who killed him?"

Leah began to cry.

"I'm sorry. Please, please, don't cry."

"Elizabeth, I just don't know what happened. I never really saw their faces. The crowd swirled around him, and I still don't know what I saw . . . if I saw anything. He had been away and I had stopped expecting him to come back.

"But then I heard him calling out to me. He was home . . . after all that time, he had finally returned! I was elated as I ran up to the roof. I only wanted to see him looking at me, after all those nights waiting up there. I rushed to the side wall, hoping to see what was going on, but the crowd was too chaotic. I was petrified, watching them swarm below. I couldn't see him."

"You didn't go out to help him?" Elizabeth asked in disbelief.

"Elizabeth, I am so ashamed. I did not know he was in trouble. I went to the roof rather than out to the well. When I realized that he was hurt, I panicked. I had been grieving and feeling isolated for so long. I just felt weak. What could I do? When I got to him, it was too late . . . *I* was too late."

The familiar front courtyard of Leah's home was about a hundred yards away. Michael was hungry, and his body felt battered. The blisters on his feet bled with each step against the dirty stone roads of Jerusalem. *This is still Monday, right?*

He approached the front gate and caught a glimpse of Elizabeth working side by side with Leah, preparing a meal in the simple kitchen. Their faces held a similar, peaceful expression.

"Elizabeth!"

"Dad?"

He could see her face breaking out in a smile.

"Dad!" She dropped a basket of grains and barreled toward him. *"Launch!"*

"No, no," he whimpered, realizing his daughter was about to run full force into his weary arms.

In her excitement, Elizabeth saw only his face but none of his wounds. She hurtled toward her father and Michael reluctantly held out his arms. Giggling, Elizabeth jumped into his arms, causing him to stagger backward onto the ground.

"Nice to see you," Michael said, before laughing himself.

As they pulled themselves to their feet, Elizabeth's mood changed suddenly and she was no longer smiling.

"Where did you go? Why did you leave me here? You left me alone! *Why?* Why did you do that? I've been so *scared*!"

"I know, I know, I'm so sorry. I have been trying to get back to you this whole time," Michael said, patting her hair. "Are you okay? I'm here now. Try to relax."

"Relax? *Relax?* How could I relax? You left me with a strange woman. You didn't tell me where you went. I was worried you were caught and back in that place."

"Remember this conversation later when I ask you where *you're* going," said Michael with a smile, trying to lighten the moment.

"Very funny," she retorted, annoyed. "This is different. You left me alone here in a strange place."

"I know. I really am sorry, Elizabeth. But I had to. I had no choice. I'm sorry." He paused. "Hey, let's go inside where we can talk more. It smells great in there. I'm really hungry."

Elizabeth stepped in front of Michael, blocking his way. "Did you find the opening?"

"Yes . . . but I got distracted . . . ," Michael said, looking away.

"What do you mean?" she shrieked. "You've been gone for nearly two days!"

"I was looking for your mother."

"What?"

"I thought I could find your mother," Michael whispered as he put his hands on Elizabeth's shoulders. "I tried . . . I tried so hard."

"You're scaring me, Dad," she replied, backing away.

"Elizabeth, I saw Jesus yesterday. I mean, I think I saw him. I don't know how it could have been him, but I ran after him. I yelled to him. He never turned around, so I'm not sure if he heard me, but I really think it was him."

Elizabeth stared at him.

"No, really, Elizabeth. I know it sounds crazy. There was this parade. You had to see it. Honest. I thought he could help us . . . you know, tell us where your mom is. Seriously, you've got to believe me. It was him."

Elizabeth shrugged her shoulders. "I was there with Leah watching a parade, Dad. I didn't see anything but Roman soldiers."

"You left with her?" Now Michael was annoyed. "I told Leah to keep you here until I came back. It's not safe where I went."

Elizabeth ignored her father's glare. "Dad, you've been gone, like, two days. I'm not sure what to believe. I don't know if we're in some kind of weird dream or what, but I don't like the idea you've been thinking about finding Mom right now. Why would she be here? We have to get home. And now you're saying you saw Jesus? Come on. Let's not get crazy now."

"It can't be a dream, Elizabeth. I know what I saw. I know what I heard. I can smell food and taste it. I thought maybe Jesus could help us get Mom back."

He raised his arms out to his sides, indicating the scene around them. "Elizabeth, c'mon, who would have believed any of this was possible? Jeez, after all those years in church, I don't think I even believed that half those stories were real. And yet, look where we are. Seriously, do you really think this is some sort of dream?"

Elizabeth slapped at his arm in frustration. "Maybe it is a dream."

"No, really. I know what I saw and it makes no sense. But if this place is possible, anything could be, right? Even your mother . . ."

"Whatever." Elizabeth dropped her hands to her sides. "Can you just get us home?"

Michael winced, realizing how stupid he must sound to her. *Why can't I just let go?*

He wrapped his arms around Elizabeth. "You're right. This is just crazy talk. I'm sorry. I'm so hungry and thirsty . . . maybe I was seeing things? You know, lost out in the desert and all?"

"Lost in the desert . . . ? "

He grimaced at her, his eyes wide. "I got a little loco, I guess. Don't worry; I'll get us back tomorrow. Let me just get some water and food, okay?" Michael started to limp forward through the front gate.

Elizabeth saw the blood on his sandals; he really was in bad shape. Leah, who had been watching from the courtyard, noticed as well. She ran outside to help him, but Elizabeth immediately intervened and nudged her away.

"My father needs *me*," she said pointedly.

Later they were sitting around the dining mat when Leah said, "We have some fresh bread, which Elizabeth helped make."

"Really?" Michael said, looking at his daughter with surprise.

Elizabeth looked up and gave her dad a playful glance.

Leah laughed. "You sound surprised. Is that so hard to believe?"

"No, no, of course not," he said with some pride in his voice. "I'm just still surprised we can even understand each other."

"What do you mean?" Leah inquired.

"Well, we're from Northport and you're here in Jerusalem. Shouldn't we be speaking different languages?"

"I'm speaking the language I've always spoken . . . and so are you."

"English?"

"Pardon?"

"This can't be," he muttered under his breath, turning to Elizabeth wide-eyed.

Leah paused for a moment. "You know, Elizabeth was a big help to me while you were gone. She was very brave here all by herself. You should be proud of her."

"I am," Michael said, leaning in closer to touch Elizabeth's hand.

Leah poured some water into their cups and they began to eat. "So you were able to find your way through the city?"

"Yes," Michael said in between bites.

"Did you see that soldier?" Leah asked.

Michael hesitated. "No, never saw him."

Leah looked at Michael. She leaned over and poured some more water in his cup, searching his face for an answer. "You're sure?"

"I'm sure."

Michael tried to change the subject by describing to Elizabeth the marketplaces and buildings he had seen. He avoided any stories about the pain or tension he faced during his encounters with soldiers or civilians. He wondered if he should continue to discuss his theory on seeing Jesus.

That's madness . . . this is all madness.

Elizabeth put down her cup and rubbed her eyes. "I'm not sleeping alone tonight," she said through a yawn. "I've done that two nights in a row and you keep disappearing. Tonight, you're staying with me. I need to keep an eye on you."

Elizabeth pulled him up from the mat and brought him over to her bedroll, laid out in the small alcove she had tried to sleep in the night before. Dragging him down next to her, she whispered, "Don't ever leave me again."

He was quiet, sobered by the intense grip his daughter had on his arm. He began to rub her head. "Always remember I love you."

She smiled, but the fatigue from her previous poor night of sleep coupled with all her anxiety regarding her father's absence was too much. While looking into Michael's face, she began to blink her eyes up and down several times.

"Close them, Baboo," Michael said. "I'm here, and I'm not going anywhere without you."

"I'm right *here* . . . Elizabeth, you're okay."

Her crying wouldn't stop despite distracting sounds from the television, the radio, and even the stereo. The stroller was now against a wall in the living room, discarded there after he had unsuccessfully tried to calm her by pushing her around the house. Even his grand attempt to play "Silent Night" on a flute, an artifact he'd unearthed dating back to his grade-school days, failed to pacify her. So he stood there, two-year-old Elizabeth screaming under one arm with an old, tarnished flute anchored beneath the other.

Oh, Vick. What more do I have to do?

Anguished, Michael walked from room to room, searching for anything that would stop her screaming. He opened up drawers, showing their contents to Elizabeth. But the tears and wailing continued.

Back in his room, he noticed something caught in the bottom drawer of his dresser. It was where he kept the last few items of Vicki's clothes. Wincing, he pulled it open and immediately saw her old blow-dryer. On cold nights, Vicki used to rub his back and warm him up by directing the hot air from the blow-dryer to his feet.

Michael pulled out the old dryer before placing Elizabeth down on the bed. She was squirming now, arms flailing and mouth wide-open with screams. Michael plugged in the blow-dryer and turned it on.

Initially, the hum of the dryer drowned out her screams. But as he rubbed Elizabeth's forehead while carefully directing the hot air toward her little, exposed feet, she finally calmed down. Elizabeth reached over and grabbed his thumb. She gripped it tightly and closed her eyes.

Exhausted, Michael looked up toward the ceiling. "Thanks."

Michael was distracted by the feeling that someone was watching him. Realizing it was Leah, he immediately glanced up.

"I'm sorry," Leah whispered, looking away, "but are you sure you didn't see the soldier?"

He glanced back at Elizabeth to make sure she was sound asleep. "Actually, I did."

Leah put her hands over her mouth.

"It's okay. He doesn't know where we are."

"You have to be more careful! He will be looking for you again."

"I know, but I'll be okay." He rubbed his eyes and shifted under her glare.

"But what about your daughter?"

"What about her?" Michael countered defensively.

"She can't lose you," Leah said, fixing his stare. "She would be all alone then. You don't want that."

"She told you about Vicki?"

Leah was silent for a brief moment. "She did . . . I'm sorry. I wish you had told me sooner."

"I don't need you to be sorry. We're just fine."

"But your daughter wasn't fine today or yesterday without you. I hope you understand that."

"I do."

"Good," Leah said gently, turning to leave.

Michael glanced at Elizabeth, who was peacefully sleeping now. "Excuse me, Leah? Thank you for taking care of my daughter."

Leah nodded and smiled at him, leaving Michael to wonder once again, who was this woman?

8

A WOMAN'S TOUCH

The smell of smoldering wood greeted Michael in the early morning, and he could hear Leah moving around downstairs. Elizabeth had finally released her grip on his arm. He stood up slowly and quietly, so as not to wake her.

He crept down the ladder. He could see Leah kneeling, her hair tied up in the back, her mouth moving in silence.

Is she praying? Michael wondered as he moved closer to listen. But as he took a few more steps, Leah stood up.

"Oh, I didn't know you were there," she said.

"I'm sorry," he stammered, "I was just wondering what you were doing."

"I was saying my morning prayers. Would you like to join me?"

"Um, hmm, no thank you. We really have to get back to town."

Leah noticed the dried blood on his right foot. "Go outside where the light is better and wait for me. We should clean and dress the wounds on your feet."

Michael hesitated momentarily, but decided she was right. He walked out into the bright morning sun, coming to rest underneath the fig tree, which provided him with some welcome shade.

Leah returned with a small bottle, cloth, and a shallow bowl of water. She knelt down to look more closely at his wounds, causing him to pull his feet away in embarrassment.

Looking up into his eyes, she gently placed his feet closer to her. After removing his sandals, she soaked a cloth in water and used it to carefully wipe away the crusted blood. Once the cuts were clean, Leah poured the ointment into her hands and began massaging it into his wounds.

Her hands feel soft, Michael thought, remembering how long it had been since a woman had touched him. He closed his eyes.

"Boy, that feels good," he said, resting his head against the bark of the tree.

"Good. Just don't move."

"Dad?" a voice called out from the edge of the courtyard. Moving out into the full morning light, Elizabeth caught a glimpse of Michael and Leah under the tree.

"Dad!"

Michael stood up quickly, knocking over the bowl of water and jostling the ointment bottle from Leah's hand. Elizabeth ran back into the house, climbing the ladder in haste.

"Let me get breakfast," Leah said, retrieving the bottle before walking briskly back into the kitchen.

"Elizabeth!" Michael called as he hurried back to the ladder leading up to the second floor. He raced over to her bedroll, where she was sitting with her back to him.

"Elizabeth, are you okay?" he asked, gently touching her shoulder. She flinched.

"I'm here. I told you I wouldn't leave you again."

She winced. "What were you doing with Leah?"

Michael slid down the wall to be near her and wrapped his arms around her shoulders. "She was helping me. My feet hurt so much when I woke up. They were bleeding. Leah offered to put some medicine on them."

Michael pulled Elizabeth to her feet, guiding her gently to the dining mat.

She was quiet for a moment before asking, "Okay, so when are we leaving?"

Leah entered the room, averting her eyes. She was carrying what looked like pancakes in a shallow bowl. She poured some honey on top and handed it to Elizabeth.

"I know you like honey," she said with a smile before walking away.

"Aren't you going to eat with us?" Elizabeth asked, sitting with Michael on the dining mat.

"No. I should get the water," Leah said awkwardly while climbing down the ladder.

After she left, Elizabeth picked up a pancake and offered one to Michael. "These are pretty good."

"Really?" he asked with an incredulous smile. "Her cooking is that good?"

Elizabeth saw where this conversation was going. "No one cooks better than you, Dad."

"Now, *that's* my girl," Michael said with a laugh.

"Let's leave!" Elizabeth suddenly said with a burst of energy.

"Not so fast! We have to be careful. We need to talk to Leah about what time is best to leave."

"Why?"

"She knows the town. I want to talk to her first about it."

"Well, when are you going to talk to *me* about it?" Elizabeth demanded, bolting to her feet.

"Sit down. We *are* talking."

A loud noise echoed below, startling both Michael and Elizabeth. They ran over to the small upstairs window overlooking the courtyard. Leah had fallen. She lay on the ground, holding her ankle and groaning. The jug had rolled over and was leaking water.

"Leah!" Michael shouted out the window. "Are you okay?"

She didn't answer.

Michael hurtled down the ladder and ran out to the courtyard. When he reached her, he fell down beside her onto his knees. "Are you hurt?"

"I think it's my foot."

Michael pulled the jug upright before he lifted Leah from the ground. "Put your arm up over my shoulder," he said, wrapping his arm around her waist.

Leah stared into Michael's eyes. Her green eyes gleamed brightly in the sunlight. "Thank you."

"No problem," he murmured.

From the second-floor window, Elizabeth saw him wink at Leah. Elizabeth disappeared quickly, reappearing momentarily in the courtyard beside them.

"Hey, Dad, come check out Cassie!"

"Not now, Elizabeth. Honey, can't you see Leah is hurt?"

"Yeah, I can see . . ."

Michael helped Leah onto the stool in the kitchen before bringing the water jug in from the courtyard.

Catching his eye, she said quietly, "Thank you."

Michael was embarrassed. "It was nothing. Anytime."

Elizabeth came in closer, pulling on her father's arm. "Aren't we leaving?"

"Yes, of course."

Leah stood up, wincing. "No, you mustn't go now."

"We are going," Elizabeth interjected.

"Hold on, Elizabeth. What do you mean, Leah?"

She pointed outside. "While I was out getting the water, some neighbors told me of a man destroying the Temple. I think you may know of whom I speak. Yes?"

Michael shook his head, confused.

"Well, there are soldiers everywhere now. The Romans are upset."

"Why do they care about a Jewish temple being destroyed?"

Leah took a deep breath as she sat to rub her ankle. "Because the man defiled the Temple built for us by the Romans."

"You aren't going to listen to this, are you?" Elizabeth asked, shocked that her father was just standing there pondering what Leah had said. "We have to get back now."

Michael motioned to Elizabeth to walk with him out into the courtyard.

"What, Dad?"

"Come over here."

Elizabeth obediently followed her father to the fig tree.

"Sit down."

Elizabeth glared at her father. "Why are we sitting here talking when we could be getting back to the tunnel?"

"First, I need you to calm down."

"I'm calm!"

"*This* is calm?"

Elizabeth sighed. "I'm calm, see?" she said, flashing a forced smile.

"I told you I thought I saw Jesus. He was on a donkey and people were placing palms in front of him. Yes, I know I couldn't see his face because there were so many soldiers. But I saw the back of him. I could swear it was him."

"No, Dad, not again," Elizabeth said in a harsh tone, holding up her hand in protest. "We need to get back to the tunnel."

"I know we do, but really, Elizabeth, if you had seen him riding through the crowd . . ."

Elizabeth shook her head, interrupting him. "You stopped to watch a man on a donkey?"

"I know what I did. But don't you get it? We're in Jerusalem. We got here through a tunnel. Isn't this crazy? Look at the buildings, the Roman soldiers in the street."

"You thought they were in a play."

"Yes, yes, I did at first . . . but that doesn't make any sense."

"And saying you saw Jesus does?" she asked, dramatically raising her eyebrows.

Michael stood up and paced back and forth in front of the fig tree a couple of times. "I know it sounds out of this world. I know I'm the last person you think would believe it. But I thought I saw him. I thought I was at Palm Sunday."

Elizabeth rose to her feet and hugged him. "I didn't see it. We're both confused. I just want to get home. That's all I want. Why can't we just leave now?"

Michael shook his head. "Oh, Elizabeth . . . we just can't."

Elizabeth pulled away from him, her body trembling with frustration.

"Come on," he whispered, trying to soothe her. "I just can't take that chance right now. I'm worried about these soldiers everywhere."

After another moment, Michael decided to be totally honest with her. "Actually, Elizabeth, I'm just really worried about that one soldier from the other day."

"So it *is* true what Leah said?"

Michael's eyes widened. "What did she tell you?"

"She told me the soldier could take me and force me to marry him. Could he really?"

He waved his hands in the air, shaking his head several times. "No, no, no. I won't let that happen. If he took you, I would have no way to get you back. I can't lose you. I can't."

Elizabeth was terrified now. Michael could see her body stiffen, her hands clenched at her sides. He wrapped his arms around her.

"Remember this, Baboo: no one will ever take you. I won't let it happen." Michael kissed the top of her head. "Come on. Show me this Cassie," he said, smiling, as he led her back across the courtyard to the lamb.

Elizabeth kept her arm around him as they headed toward the tree. "You know, if we are stuck here for a bit, maybe we should look for Mom."

Michael pulled away and held her at arm's length. "Elizabeth, you know I want that more than anything in the world. But your safety is more important. Let's just see what happens, okay?"

She nodded before leaving him to walk ahead.

Following her, he stepped into a puddle. "Man, there's so much water on the ground." Michael began moving his right foot back and forth across the muddied ground, trying to spread it out so it would dry faster.

"Dad, what are you doing? It's just from the jug that Leah dropped before. It's no big deal. It'll dry up."

"Hey, Sammie, come down, let's play!" he called upstairs while watching the rain pelt the casement window. His younger sister was a gullible little girl who loved to be the center of attention, which meant he knew how to manipulate her.

She dropped her Curious George coloring book on the kitchen table and headed downstairs to join him. "Okay," she said in her sweet, innocent voice, "what do you want to play?"

"Go upstairs and get a loaf of bread," Michael said quietly, "and don't let Mom see. I'm going to show you a new game."

Samantha was excited: her older brother was going to play with her. She recognized the enormity of this event and quickly sprinted up the stairs. She peeked around the corner to the living room. Rebecca was nowhere in sight. Jetting through the hallway and into the kitchen, Samantha hopped up on a chair and grabbed the loaf of Wonder bread from the top of the refrigerator.

Back in the basement, Michael set the bread down next to him. He took a worn Bible from the bookcase and draped an old tablecloth around his body. After covering the rusty metal table between them with some stained red, white, and blue napkins left over from the Fourth of July, he found a discarded plastic cup behind the couch and rinsed it in the utility sink in the corner. Michael filled it with water and carried it carefully to the table. Then he pulled out several slices of bread and tore them into small pieces. Placing them on the napkins, he looked up toward the ceiling.

"What are you doing?"

"Shh," Michael said quietly, "we're at mass."

"No, we're not."

"Pretend we are."

Samantha shrugged, gazing innocently at her big brother. "Okay, I guess. What should I do?"

"Just be quiet for now. If you're good, I'll let you have Communion. But don't tell Mom: you're too young to eat it."

Samantha smiled, thinking that this was getting good. "Okay, I won't tell," she promised solemnly, adding, "I won't get you in trouble."

"Good." Michael looked up at the ceiling again and made the sign of the cross. As he tore another slice into pieces he whispered, "This is my body, do this in memory of me . . ."

He held the cup of water over his head. "This is my blood, do this in memory of me." Michael looked down into the cup to see if the water had changed to wine.

"Ew, gross. Let me see!" Samantha grabbed his arm, throwing him off-balance and spilling the water on the floor. She watched as the water pooled toward the edge of their mother's favorite old rug, soaking the tassels. "Mommy's rug!" She added in a voice only he could hear, "Oooh, are you in trouble!"

"What's going on down there?" Rebecca shouted from above.

Michael could hear the annoyance in her voice and felt the familiar knot growing in his stomach. "Nothing!"

He turned sharply toward his sister and hissed, *"Shut up."*

Samantha took a dramatic breath but Michael covered her mouth with his hand. "Cut it out and I'll let you have some of the bread now."

She nodded happily as Michael offered her a small piece. She shook her head. "I want a bigger one."

"Okay, okay, here's a big piece."

Samantha swallowed it seriously while holding her tiny hands together just as she had seen her mommy and daddy do at Sunday mass. "I wish I had a hat like Mommy wears."

"You don't need one."

Then Michael offered her a sip of the water.

"Yuck, I'm not drinking from that," she said, making a face, "you drank from it."

"Just drink it, Sammie. Remember, you have to pretend it's wine, so only take a little sip."

His little sister perked up. She was able to be a grown-up while playing with her brother. She nodded and reached for the cup. It slipped from her hands and clattered on the tiled floor.

Michael froze in horror.

"Now look what you did!" Samantha yelled. "You made me spill it."

"I did not. You dropped it!"

Samantha started to cry and Michael heard angry footsteps. Their mother was coming down the staircase. From where they sat, he could already see the bottom of her shoes.

"What's going on down there?"

"Nothing," Michael said, praying that she wouldn't come down any farther. He knew it was no use. *Nothing* always meant "something" in the Stewart house.

Thump, thump, thump. Three more steps and she was able to peer over at them in the corner. He watched her take it all in—the water on the floor, the mangled bread on the table. She swiftly came down the rest of the stairs and towered over them.

"What's going on here?" she asked quietly.

Michael hated the quiet voice. It was worse than the shouting because he knew what was coming.

"Look at this mess. Who did this?"

She noticed his sleeve was wet, and her voice grew even more calm and frightening. "Did you do this, Michael?"

Michael remained absolutely still, silent.

"Are you going to answer?"

More silence.

"I'd better get an answer or you'll be in the house for the rest of the summer." Rebecca crossed her arms. "And your father will have to deal with you."

Neither one answered. His mom's face became even angrier. Her hands were clenched. Michael kept his head down slightly and stared at her brown loafers. Sears Roebuck.

"Fine, you can stand down here all day long. Just wait till he gets home."

Samantha began to sob. Her best friend's birthday party was tomorrow and she knew her dad wouldn't let her go. She cracked.

"I did it."

Michael's jaw dropped. *Was she stupid?*

Rebecca's eyes narrowed. "Michael, upstairs!"

Michael looked over at Samantha, remaining perfectly still.

"Get upstairs now, I said!"

He reached the top of the stairs but lingered in the doorway. He hoped because his sister was small and young that she would just be sent to her room. But he was wrong.

Whack! He jumped. His sister's scream went through him like a knife in his stomach. *Whack, whack, whack.* He started to cry.

It's all my fault, he thought.

Michael turned and raced through the hallway and up the second flight of stairs to his bedroom, covering his ears. It was such a small house that even conversations in the basement could be heard through the heating vents.

Whack!

Today was no different.

Michael curled into a tight ball on his bed even though he knew it was over. After a minute, he sat up, wiping his face with the bottom of his T-shirt.

Someone was coming upstairs. Michael jumped off his bed and ran to the hallway. Sammie stood near the top of the stairs. Her face was splotchy from crying, and he could see the marks on her arm. They looked at each other for a moment. Her blue eyes filled with tears.

"I'm so sorry, Sammie," Michael said as his voice started to break. "If you can't go to the birthday party tomorrow, I'll play with you . . . whatever you want to play, even dolls."

Samantha nodded and tried to smile. She turned and headed down the hall to her room.

Michael followed her, making sure she got there safely.

9

FALLING BACK UP

Elizabeth joined Michael on the rooftop that evening while Leah remained downstairs. The previous day's events had left them exhausted both emotionally and physically. For a while they sat in silence, enjoying the peaceful view before them.

Michael was the first to break the silence. "It's so beautiful here at night." He caught Elizabeth studying him thoughtfully. "What are you looking at?"

"Nothing." When he refused to look away, she shrugged. "It's just rare that I see you"—she hunted for the word—"smile."

"I smile!"

"No, Dad, you don't."

Michael thought a moment, then shook his head. "I don't, do I?"

"Nope."

He sighed. "I guess I haven't had much to smile about over the years." After an awkward moment of silence, he added, "I miss your mom."

Elizabeth shifted nervously and tried to change the subject. "Look at those stars, Dad." She pointed to a cluster in the sky.

Michael stared at his daughter. "Elizabeth, you always change the subject when I talk about Mom. Why?"

She looked away. "No reason."

"There's got to be some reason."

"There's no reason, Dad, okay?" Elizabeth edged away slightly, still focusing on a group of stars in the clear, dark sky. "So pretty," she tried to say, but the words got stuck in her throat.

"Oh, honey, I'm sorry. I don't mean to upset you. It's not easy for me to talk about Mom either. I just felt this was a good time."

Elizabeth cried harder, and Michael wrapped his arms around her. "Talk to me, sweetie."

She turned to look at him, eyes red and watery. "Do you really want to know how I feel about Mom?"

"I think so, but we really haven't talked much about her."

Elizabeth tried to wipe away her tears. "I feel terrible. I feel horrible. I get so upset when you mention her."

"Why? Why would you get upset? Haven't I told you how much we wanted you? How excited we were when we found out it was going to be you?"

She nodded weakly.

"Then why do you feel so horrible when I talk about her?"

Elizabeth leaned against him and sobbed heavily. "Because she died when I was born."

Michael held her tightly and rubbed her back. "Oh, honey, oh, honey. You don't think she would have lived if you weren't born?"

"I don't know," she said, trying to catch her breath.

"No!" he said emphatically, cutting her off. "I can't believe you ever thought that. Why would you ever think that?"

"I don't know. We haven't spoken much about that night."

"Well, but I think you can understand why I don't like to talk about it, right?"

Elizabeth nodded again.

"You know, Elizabeth, I have never been able to forget that night for many reasons. First, I lost my best friend. Second, I feel responsible."

"Responsible?"

Michael hung his head. "If I had just stopped her . . ." His voice trembled and then trailed off.

"There's nothing you could have done, Daddy."

They sat there quietly for several minutes, gazing upward at the night sky in all its heavenly glory. Suddenly Elizabeth cleared her throat. "Have you ever thought about finding someone else?" she blurted out.

He paused a moment before answering, "I have. Then I wonder what your mom would think. Would she be okay about it?"

Elizabeth looked at him questioningly so he attempted to lighten the mood. "Or would she be waiting for me at the pearly gates, ready to scold me?"

Elizabeth giggled weakly, and he continued, "I haven't really met many women over the years."

"Leah seems to know you."

Michael sat back. "I don't know why. I've never seen her. Not even back in Northport."

"I know. But she keeps on saying she knows you." Elizabeth dropped her voice. "Do you think she's crazy? She told me she lost her husband."

He shrugged. "Maybe she's just confused because she's still grieving. I remember after your mom passed away I would be walking down Main Street and I would think I had seen her." Michael shook his head. "Once I even ran up to some poor woman on the street. The back of her head looked just like your mom. I felt so bad. I scared her when I started yelling your mom's name until she turned around."

Elizabeth started to tear up again and he quickly backtracked. "Oh, I'm sorry, I'm talking about your mom again."

"No. It's okay, Dad."

"Then why are you crying?"

"Because even though it was impossible, I was hoping you were going to tell me that it really was her."

He had absolutely nothing to say to that because he'd wished the same thing a million times himself.

Michael awoke well rested the next day. His feet were starting to scab over and he felt more energetic. Elizabeth was still sound asleep, exhausted from the chores she shared with Leah and her rooftop talk. Her long brown hair was nestled underneath a woolen blanket. She looked so grown-up yet oddly vulnerable. Michael was still amazed at how well Elizabeth had handled the lamb the day before.

He smiled and gave her a gentle kiss on the forehead. She rolled over slightly, alarming Michael, since he wanted her to sleep in so that she was fully rested for their trip into town to find the tunnel. Yesterday had been reassuring, and he felt it was time to go back, but he didn't want to wake her too soon.

He backed away quietly, looking out through the second-floor window. Although it was dark outside, the early-morning light was about to appear. He walked past the alcove where he knew Leah was still sleeping, having heard her quiet, shallow breathing. He tiptoed to the ladder and gingerly descended.

Michael walked into the kitchen area and began searching through covered baskets for something to make for breakfast. He thought maybe this could be the day he would repay Leah for her help.

Why not prepare breakfast?

It was dark in the kitchen except for the last few embers still gleaming in the fire. He took some wood out of a basket and added it to the hearth. When he started to blow on it, black smoke engulfed him.

Oh, no, what have I done? He kicked off a large piece of smoldering wood. He grabbed some kindling and looked for a hot spot to place it. When he did, it seemed to ignite a flame.

Michael threw some grains from a nearby basket into a pot and poured water over them. He was impressed with himself. This was just like making oatmeal at home.

I'm not working with a Viking oven, but I'm certainly no Viking.

As he placed the pot over the fire, he felt a burning sensation near his right knee. "Oh, no," he gasped. Michael's garment had caught fire from his leaning in too close to the flames. He swung his hands wildly, trying to put out the flame.

Turning quickly to grab the jug of water, Michael stumbled slightly and bumped into the simmering pot, which came crashing down. He dropped to the stone floor, attempting to catch the fallen bowl. The water and grains spilled all over him, extinguishing the fire and completely soaking him.

"Oh, my!" Leah exclaimed, jumping from the bottom rung of the ladder. She began waving her hands back and forth in front of her face to clear some of the black smoke. "What happened?"

"Ah . . . I was trying to help," he said sheepishly. "I was preparing breakfast."

"Oh. Is that what you call this?"

Michael was stunned and embarrassed, but then he detected the smallest smile on Leah's face. *Oh, she's teasing.*

He started to chuckle. "I'm really sorry. You have done so much I just wanted to help you, too."

"Help like this I cannot use." She began to giggle, surprising herself.

Michael was even more shocked by her laughter, spurring him to laugh harder.

Between laughs, Leah gasped, "What a mess!"

"I can help you with that."

Leah laughed even louder. "No, no, please!"

Surprised by Leah's sense of humor, he decided to egg her on, just as her fits of laughter were slowing. "You sit, I will cook and clean, and then you can clean up after me," he said, straight-faced.

Leah's smile widened, and once again she erupted into uncontrolled giggles. She pushed back her hair again. "Ooh, that's enough for me!"

Embarrassed, she looked down at her feet, but when she did so, she noticed the burned hole in his robe. "Oh, what happened there?"

"I was cooking?"

"Hmm, of course. I have more robes upstairs. Stay here. I will be right back."

Leah climbed up the ladder, and Michael could hear her rustling through some baskets. When she came down, she handed him a clean garment.

"You need to clean yourself up. Taking you to the baths is not advisable at this hour with so many soldiers in Jerusalem right now. Instead, go behind the house where there is water. I will take care of breakfast."

Michael walked around the ladder and through the door at the back of the house. The area outside was about fourteen feet long and five feet wide. It was walled off so he was unable to see any of the other houses nearby. In the far corner was the door leading to the crude latrine that they had been using.

They've got an amazing drainage system back here, Michael thought, *better than any of those facilities we use when we go camping.*

He had definitely used worse.

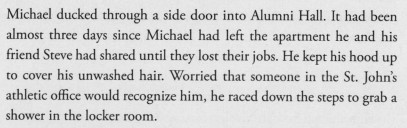

Michael ducked through a side door into Alumni Hall. It had been almost three days since Michael had left the apartment he and his friend Steve had shared until they lost their jobs. He kept his hood up to cover his unwashed hair. Worried that someone in the St. John's athletic office would recognize him, he raced down the steps to grab a shower in the locker room.

As he turned the corner in the basement, he found sinks and shower rods outside the entryway. *Oh, no. What's going on?*

He peered in where the showers were. A construction worker in a yellow plastic hard hat spun around as he was dismantling a shower stall. "You need something?"

"Yeah, a shower. I just worked out."

"Not today."

Michael sighed. "What about tomorrow?"

The heavyset man laughed. "We're just starting. Come back when school starts again."

The St. John's students were on holiday break. It would be another two weeks before classes would begin. Michael looked at the mirror on the wall. *Just great. Look at me: a college graduate only six months ago. Lot of good it did me.*

The sight of his unshaven face reflected in the mirror only made his self-pity grow. He rubbed his torn gloves across his face, but they, too, were filthy from wear.

He walked down the adjacent hallway toward the job board hanging in one of the unused display cases, but grew ashamed. *Why am I even looking? I can't even find a way to get a shower.*

His despondency slowly turned to anger, both at himself and those who ever doubted him. *I'll show them. I'll get a shower and then go door-to-door looking for a job.* He decided to go clean up in one of the upstairs bathrooms.

Quietly, he navigated inconspicuously through the hallways and back up the stairs near the basketball office. The bathroom was located directly across from where many of his friends worked, the same people with whom he had shared road trips while watching some of the greatest St. John's basketball teams play. His heart was skipping as his mind raced for a plausible excuse for his appearance should he be spotted. He opened the hallway door slightly, peeking through to see if anyone was around. The hall was clear.

Michael dashed up the five steps to the bathroom door, which he struck with such force that it slammed against the concrete wall, sending a big echo through the six-thousand-seat arena. *Darn, I hope no one comes out and looks.*

Inside he remained silent for a few seconds, listening for any movement. When he heard none, his body relaxed slightly as he pulled off his hood. *What a mess.* He removed his tattered gloves and stuffed them into his pockets, squishing a piece of stale pretzel and a package of soup crackers he had picked up in the subway two nights ago.

The crunching sound frustrated him. "Can anything else happen?" he muttered.

He rammed the soap dispenser a few times, eking out a few miserable drops. He pressed the faucet down, but only a brief spurt of water trickled through. *Oh, great, one of these.*

The idea of shoving the faucet and then quickly cupping his hands underneath it to capture a pitiful amount of water irritated him. He snickered to himself: funny how in all these years it had never before bothered him.

He was splashing the first handful of water on his face when the door opened behind him. He spun away from the sink as St. John's wildly popular basketball coach walked in.

"Stewy! How the heck are you?" He met Michael with a huge smile on his face.

Every time until this exact moment, a smile from the coach would make Michael feel like gold. Today, he felt like dirt.

"Um, fine, how are you?" Michael replied, tugging up his hood.

"How's life after college? You still writing? I always said you had a good pen."

Michael sighed. "Everything's fine, Coach."

"What are you doing?" the coach asked, glancing at the dirty collar of Michael's coat before looking back at him. "Where are you working?"

Michael put his gloves back on and tucked them inside his faded jeans pockets. "Doing a few things, got some job interviews. Everything is really going well, Coach."

The coach finished up his business and washed his hands. Grabbing a paper towel, he flashed another huge grin. "Well, don't be a stranger. Stop by the office anytime."

He gave Michael a hearty slap on the back and walked out. Michael walked quietly behind him, let the door close, and looked around. *Please, don't let anyone else come in.*

He returned to the sink and removed his hood and gloves again. *I've got to wash my hair quickly.* It was flat and greasy. His light brown hair looked nearly black. *Disgusting. How do I go for a job interview looking like this?*

He heard some footsteps outside the door. He walked quickly to the far-end stall and opened it. He locked the door and kept silent.

Another man walked in. *Oh, boy. Now I'm going to have to wait even longer. Terrific.*

He sat on top of the toilet and waited. Moments later the bathroom was empty again. Michael opened the stall door slightly to see if the area was clear. He closed and locked the door again.

This is embarrassing. He looked at the toilet. *It's clean.* He turned back toward the door before refocusing his thoughts on the task at hand. *I can be at any job interview in two hours if I just get cleaned up.*

Michael started pulling several yards of toilet paper from the roll. He began wiping the outer and inner edges of the toilet. He flushed, watching the paper twirl down and thinking it was an appropriate metaphor for his life.

He stared for several seconds, gazing at the still water in the white, round ceramic bowl. *It's clean, it's clean,* he tried to convince himself. He listened intently to hear if anyone was coming. *Just go ahead and do it. Yeah, no one will know.*

He got down on his knees, pulled back the toilet seat, and removed a plastic bag from his coat filled with some soap he had lifted from a train-station dispenser. Michael let the pink soap slowly drip out from the bag into his right hand. When the bag was almost empty, he leaned his head into the toilet, moistening the top of his head. *Yuck.*

He quickly soaped up his scalp before plunging the top of his head back into the toilet, cleaning most of the soap away. He furiously pawed at the toilet paper, sending bits and pieces to the ground while drying his hair with gobs of it.

With his hair nearly dry, he leaned back on the toilet and stared at the blue-painted door. He took a deep breath before standing up. Michael opened the door, his eyes catching his reflection in the mirror. Head slumped, he watched the sink catch some of his tears. He quickly looked up and wiped the remaining moisture off his face with his hands.

Michael walked back inside the house, placing his burnt robe in an empty basket just inside the door. He noticed Elizabeth standing on the last rung of the ladder.

"Dad," Elizabeth said, running over to him, "you showering?"

"Yes," he said, adding with a laugh, "you got anything to make me smell better?"

"I think I have something like that for you," Leah interjected from where she stood in the kitchen.

"You have what?"

Leah reached toward a small shelf containing an assortment of bottles. She scanned it briefly, her hand lingering over the one gap in the line before selecting a small, light blue jar. She handed it to Michael.

"This?" he asked. "Didn't you use this on my feet?"

"This is different. Try it."

Michael uncorked the bottle and poured the oil into his cupped hand. It was musky but still pleasant smelling. He winked at Elizabeth before rubbing it onto his chest and under his arms.

Then they went upstairs to eat breakfast. The feast included goat cheese, bread, and water. When they were nearly done eating and had already begun cleaning up, Elizabeth smiled at Michael.

"Dad, let's go see Cassie."

Michael nodded, looking up at Leah.

"In all the rush this morning I didn't have time to say my prayers and bathe," Leah said, taking the last bowls from the floor. "Please excuse me."

"Okay," Michael replied. "We'll be fine."

Leah went to the back of the house while Elizabeth led Cassie out from behind the gate.

"Say good morning to her, Dad," she said over the braying of the lamb.

"Ah, hello, Cassie," he said with a laugh, "can you help us get home?"

"Dad!" Elizabeth said when she noticed his feet were no longer bleeding.

"What's wrong?"

"Nothing's wrong"—she pointed to his feet—"it looks like everything is right!"

"Yeah, they don't hurt so much. Leah's medicine really worked wonders!"

"Okay," Elizabeth said with reservation. She looked at him for a brief moment. "We can go now then, right?"

"Well, I guess we can."

Leah walked in with her hair wet, wiping her forehead dry. In the morning sunlight, her light brown hair glistened around her. Michael was enchanted by her and couldn't help but watch Leah as he continued speaking with Elizabeth.

"Um, we can't run out right now though . . . we must figure out a plan, you know, the best time to leave."

While Elizabeth looked at her father suspiciously, Leah selected a bottle of oil from the shelf and started rubbing some on her hands. When she realized Michael was watching her, Leah blushed and retreated upstairs.

"Dad? When are we going to talk? I think we should leave now."

"We can't, not right now. We have to make sure that we're safe, and then we can make an attempt."

Leah returned downstairs with her hair beautifully plaited down her back. She looked at Michael briefly before heading to the kitchen.

Calling out to her from the courtyard, Michael inquired, "Leah, how's the ankle? Do you need us to do anything?"

"My ankle is fine," she said with slight amazement, "but I should get water."

"I'll do that," said Elizabeth, rationalizing that by pitching in with the chores, they would be able to leave sooner.

"No. Let me. It's too heavy for you."

"Dad, I'm not a child. I can help."

Michael's eyebrows shot up. "Oh, really?"

"She's very strong and hardworking," Leah interjected.

Michael was silent for a moment. "I guess I'm outvoted. But what about other villagers seeing her and wondering who she is? What about all the soldiers around? Elizabeth, what if that soldier sees you . . . and I'm not there?"

Leah was quiet at first, but then said, "There are so many soldiers, but the soldier you speak of is likely waiting to find you by your tunnel. What are the chances that *that* soldier will be by the well?"

Leah left them to think about this while she went upstairs, returning with two veils: one white, one black.

"Put this on, no one will notice you." She handed Elizabeth the white one.

"Okay, Dad?"

"Hmm . . . okay."

With a jug in each hand, Leah and Elizabeth headed outside into the courtyard and through the gate onto the road. Michael went back upstairs and leaned against the wall, laying his head gently down on Elizabeth's bedroll.

Leah has such beautiful green eyes. It had been so long since he had had such thoughts of a woman.

Responding to Miss Voet's call, Michael entered the school, expertly acquiring his visitor pass from the front office. Embarrassed that the ladies knew him by first name, Michael shyly said hello.

"Oh, Michael, is your daughter sick again?" asked Virginia, one of the school secretaries, winking at him.

"Hmm, yes," he said sheepishly. "Thanks again for your help."

Waiting in the hallway for the first-grade teacher while Elizabeth sat inside the nurse's office, Michael wondered if this was the fourth or fifth time he had been summoned to the school. At the beginning of the school year, he would rush up to Woodside Elementary to take Elizabeth to the doctor every time she called home sick. Miraculously, she would get a clean bill of health from the pediatrician and would develop an appetite for cookies and candy by the time they got home. It was obvious to him now that his daughter had become quite calculating: for some reason, he was the carrot and she was holding the string to which it was attached.

"Mr. Stewart," Miss Voet said, extending her hand. "It's so nice to meet you."

He stood up. "Miss Voet."

"Please call me Melissa."

She had black hair and brown eyes and wore a pretty black dress with dark brown high-heeled shoes and small hoop earrings. He noticed she wasn't wearing any rings.

"We have a problem, Mr. Stewart," she murmured to him.

"Call me Mike."

She smiled. "Mike, we have an issue with Elizabeth: she's sick."

"Really?"

"Not sick the way we normally think about it. She's homesick. We have to do something about this because she is distracting the class with her groans."

"Groans?"

"Yes," Melissa said through a smile. "Your daughter is dramatic. She really wants me to know that she's unhappy. She grabs her stomach and groans. Some kids laugh, some kids are scared. Either way, it's a distraction."

Michael couldn't help but laugh. He saw Melissa roll her eyes and sigh.

"I'm sorry," he said. "I really am. I didn't know this, though I thought she might be faking this stuff. I'll talk to her about it and try to make her understand she can't do this anymore."

Melissa smiled again.

What a beautiful smile, Michael thought before he could catch himself.

"Do you want to schedule our parent/teacher meeting now?"

"Um, ah . . . I don't know. Can't this count as the meeting?" Michael saw Elizabeth through the hallway window into the nurse's office. He waved to her to come out.

Melissa frowned slightly. "Well, it can, if you want," she said as Elizabeth opened the door, "but I was looking forward to talking to you more." She smiled at him again.

Is she interested in me? Michael wondered as he took Elizabeth's backpack.

"Hi, Daddy!"

"Ah, hi."

He was flustered. "Okay," he said to the teacher as he grabbed Elizabeth's hand and started to walk away.

Melissa stood there in the hallway, wondering whether that was a yes or a no. Little did she know then that Michael would never schedule that appointment or any other for the rest of the year.

"Leah! We haven't seen much of you. How are you?" the woman called to them when Elizabeth and Leah were nearly finished filling the first jug of water.

Leah straightened up before slowly turning to greet the woman. "Rachel! Good to see you. I've been very busy."

Rachel looked at Elizabeth quizzically.

"Oh, this is my cousin's daughter, Elizabeth. They are here to celebrate the Passover festivities with me."

Elizabeth slowly turned and nodded meekly to Rachel from behind the veil.

A commotion erupted nearby as soldiers descended upon the area. Leah tried to focus on the faces of the ones on horses nearing the well.

She thought there was one with a piece of cloth in his helmet, but she couldn't be sure.

"Oh, dear!"

"What's wrong?" asked Rachel.

"I've got to go," Leah said, grabbing Elizabeth's hand and squeezing it hard.

"What's going on?" Elizabeth asked as Leah handed her an empty jug.

"I think it's that soldier," Leah whispered, directing them toward the house.

Elizabeth quickened her pace and felt her insides go numb. She dropped her head low so her face would be better covered by the veil.

"Not too fast," said Leah. "They will be suspicious if we walk too quickly in this hot sun."

They safely made it through the gate into the courtyard, although they felt little peace until they were back in the kitchen. Leah's face was flushed as she put the water jugs away. Elizabeth carried one over to her but then slumped back against the wall in the kitchen.

Realizing that Leah was staring at her, Elizabeth finally asked, "What?"

"I'm so sorry. I don't know why I said you would be fine with me. I was so foolish, and you could have been badly hurt. Please forgive me."

Michael heard them downstairs and swiftly descended the ladder. But when he reached the bottom, both Elizabeth and Leah just looked at him. There was a tense silence. He waited for one of them to speak.

"What was all the noise about?"

Elizabeth and Leah looked at each other, although Leah quickly turned away.

"We broke a jug out by the well, that's all," Elizabeth lied.

Leah's head shot up as she looked at Elizabeth in astonishment.

"Oh, I thought you might have seen some soldiers, given the way you two have been acting."

"No, no, Dad. We didn't see any."

The three ate lunch in silence. They had salted and buttered cakes of crushed, malted grains. Elizabeth nibbled on some raisins but avoided the mulberries and nuts. Michael ate heartily while Leah barely touched a thing.

"I am going to get more water," Leah said, watching Elizabeth's eyes widen. "We need water."

"I thought you had already gotten the water," Michael said.

Leah didn't answer. Michael and Elizabeth looked up from their bowls to watch her as she quickly descended the ladder.

"Are you ready to go today?" Michael asked Elizabeth, but she didn't answer. "Hello? Elizabeth?"

"Yes, Dad, I'm ready."

"It doesn't sound like you're ready. Everything okay?"

"I'm not sure . . . there were soldiers at the well."

Michael stood up. "You said there were none," he replied, raising his voice and staring at her. Without warning he turned and ran up the ladder. As he reached the roof, he lay on his stomach and began to crawl its length. With barely a sound he made it to the far side and peered over the edge, looking toward the well.

Leah had followed curiously behind him. She looked at him from the top of the ladder. "What are you doing?"

"Shh. There he is," Michael whispered, motioning for her to be quiet. "Or at least I think that's him. It's hard to tell. But I see a soldier over there talking to one of your neighbors."

"What?"

Before Leah could finish her sentence, Michael put one finger to his mouth. "Quiet, I'm trying to listen."

He slid his body another few inches forward and raised his head slightly. Leah could hear some muted voices, but she could tell by Michael's rigid form that he could hear every word. Once he was sure that the soldier had left, Michael gestured for her to go back downstairs.

"What's wrong?"

"Go down," he whispered as he began to crawl back toward the ladder.

Elizabeth was waiting at the bottom. "Dad, what's wrong?" she asked worriedly.

"In a minute, Elizabeth. I have to ask Leah something."

He grabbed Leah's arm and guided her into the first room of the house. "The soldier was asking questions about me and Elizabeth," he said urgently. "Your neighbor told the soldier that she was a relative."

Leah nodded. "This is fine. Don't worry. They won't bother you then, knowing that you're a relative. It will make sense to the soldier, knowing the festivities are taking place this week."

Michael shook his head. "How many soldiers did you see outside by the well?"

"There were some but I couldn't tell how many."

"Great," Michael muttered, then added in resignation, "Well, we have to stay for now."

"I'm sorry. If I had known it would cause any danger to you or Elizabeth, I would have never asked her to come with me."

Michael rubbed his temples wearily. "Just give me some time to think."

"Can you ever forgive me?"

Michael took a deep breath and looked into her eyes. "Yes, yes, of course."

"Thank you," she said in a whisper, her voice faltering a bit, before leaving him to climb back to the second floor.

Michael leaned against the wall and watched Cassie stand to stretch. "Sometimes I wish I were you, Cassie. No worries about your daughter, no worries about keeping her safe . . . no worries at all."

He stood there quietly for several minutes, pondering his next move. Was it safer to remain or more dangerous now?

His train of thought was broken by the sounds of Leah talking to

Elizabeth upstairs about weaving, asking her if she would like to try to make her own basket. Michael strained to hear his daughter, who wondered aloud if she would really be able to learn how.

"Of course," Leah replied.

The lamb was braying to be let out of its stall, so Michael unhinged the gate, poked his head out cautiously, and followed it out into the courtyard. Sitting in the shade beneath the tree, he could hear Elizabeth and Leah giggling upstairs. Something about Leah's teaching Elizabeth to weave made him feel both peaceful and restless.

"Now watch me, Elizabeth," Michael could hear Leah calmly instruct. "First soak it . . . now pull it up tight . . . no, no . . . good . . . oh, good, Elizabeth . . ."

"How is she doing up there?" Michael shouted to them from outside. He could hear Elizabeth giggling.

Through laughter, Leah called back down, "Good! It's just that the reed keeps hitting her in the face when she tries to bend it!"

Michael relaxed slightly, then smiled to himself, listening to them for a while. Leah's voice was so calm and smooth. He found it mesmerizing.

"Dad," Elizabeth called from the window, "come and see what I've done!"

Michael stood up, brushed off some dust, and went up to the second floor. His daughter was waiting for him at the top of the ladder, holding a small, unfinished woven basket. Despite some gaps in her weaving, it was spectacular.

"See?"

"Beautiful, Elizabeth!"

Leah smiled, catching Michael's eyes. "Would you like to try?"

"No, no. Boys don't do that sort of thing."

"But you tried to cook," Leah said. "Boys don't do that here either."

"You called that cooking?" asked Michael, laughing.

"No, I was just being polite," she replied with a smile.

Since Elizabeth was enjoying weaving with Leah, Michael decided to go back downstairs and sit under the fig tree again. Cassie wandered nearby, eating some grain from a basket left near the wall. Seeing Elizabeth so happy with Leah lifted his spirits. He wondered if Leah could ever be part of their future.

He shook his head and fretted about the new night approaching. Life now seemed so simple in Northport when Vicki was around.

Michael loved walking after a good swim. The weeks following Labor Day were always the best time of year on the beach because it was quiet and empty. The sand was still warm, and the sun's heat soothed his shirtless chest while the waves caressed his toes.

Michael saw the Connecticut shoreline across Long Island Sound. He smiled, watching the scenery around him: a father teaching his son how to fly a kite, seagulls wrestling for a piece of bread tossed to them by an old lady sitting on a bench, a girl throwing a stick for her dog to chase, and a few boys playing football near the basketball courts.

But his favorite scene was the beautiful woman with green eyes lounging on a blanket about twenty feet ahead. She was watching him, smiling.

"Excuse me, young lady. Is there room on this blanket for me?"

The woman smiled back demurely. "Of course, young man." She started to laugh. "Are you trying to pick me up?"

"Of course."

Vicki was lying on her back, sipping white wine, and giggling. Her hair was tousled slightly from the ocean breeze.

Michael dropped down next to her on the blanket. "Look who's here."

Vicki rolled over to him, staring into his eyes. "What would you do if I wasn't here?"

Usually it was Michael who started these kinds of conversations. But not now; it was much too beautiful today.

"Not here? Where are you going?"

"Come on, I'm serious. I'm so happy I found you. I know I couldn't live without you."

"Yes, you could. You could have anyone you want."

She became quiet, openly upset that he wasn't taking her seriously.

"Oh, you know I would be remarried in a month or two," he kidded.

"Really?"

"Yes."

"Hmm . . . would you remarry someone who looked like me?"

"Not sure. I like blondes. You know, the Christie Brinkley type?"

Vicki whacked him on his shoulder. "Oh? Maybe I should rethink who I might remarry."

"You have someone in mind?" asked Michael as he grabbed her arm gently.

"Yes, I do," she said with a sly smile. "I like a tall man. Maybe Brad Pitt?"

"So, you're looking for a man with looks *and* money?"

"And Christie Brinkley doesn't have money?" Vicki countered.

They both laughed.

"You really like blondes?"

"Yeah, but she has to have a nice tan, too."

"I'm not talking to you," Vicki said, turning her head.

"Then I will kiss you since your mouth will be shut," said Michael with a laugh. He peppered her with several kisses on the top of her forehead, behind her neck, the sides of her cheeks, and a few on her nose.

She giggled at him. "Okay, okay! I'll dye my hair for you."

"Good. And you can call me Brad."

"You!" She pushed him over onto his back, staring down into his eyes. "Oh, you know you'd miss me."

"Dad?" Elizabeth said, crouched down next to him. "Dad, you fell asleep. Did you have a bad dream?"

"No, Baboo. I actually had a great dream. It was about your mom." He stood up, pulling her up with him into a hug. "I miss your mother so much."

"I know, Dad," she replied, feeling uneasy from the seriousness of his tone.

"I've tried to do the best for you, Elizabeth. I'm sorry I haven't gotten us home. I really have tried."

"I know. I know you tried."

"But it's never been enough. I don't know why I've been such a jerk. I've been so upset about losing your mother. I've made so many stupid mistakes. I could've done so many things differently.

"I should have let you roller-skate with the kids on the block but I was afraid you would hit your head. I should have let you go swimming with your friends at Jones Beach but I was scared a wave would drown you.

"I should have let you go shopping at the mall with your friends but I was worried about strangers. I can't bear the thought of losing you."

Michael's body began shaking as he held her tightly.

"It's okay, Dad."

"No, no, it's not okay, Elizabeth. There were times parents would call and ask me to set up play dates. And I would never respond because I was so worried you would just drift out of my life."

Michael released his hug and threw his hands in the air. "I didn't let you have ice cream. *Ice cream.* Can you believe that? Looking back on it now, I can't believe it.

"Elizabeth, I can never let anyone take you away from me. I will never let anyone hurt you. When I see you, I see your mother. Without her, you are the only reason why I have any energy to live.

"Understand this: you are the greatest gift I have in this world."

Michael pulled her closer to him. "I'm afraid of losing you."

Elizabeth nodded. "Please don't be afraid because when you're scared, I am, too."

"I won't. See?" His face lit up and he grinned, prompting Elizabeth to giggle.

Michael glanced up and saw Leah watching them from the upstairs window, smiling.

10

PAINFUL REMINDERS

Elizabeth fell asleep easily after a lovely yet quiet dinner that night. Michael was reclining next to her, but still wide-awake. From across the room, Leah whispered to him, asking if they were comfortable. Michael nodded, although he realized immediately how restless he felt.

"Hey, do you want to go up on the roof to look at the stars?" he whispered back.

Leah hesitated. A look of concern etched across her face. It had been a long time since she sat on the roof, almost two years. "Yes."

They climbed up the ladder. The sky was so clear that the illumination from the stars cast a soft blue light on Leah's face. She shivered.

"Hold on." Michael went down the ladder and returned with the blanket from his bedroll. He placed it over her.

"Thank you."

The roof slanted slightly to the right and was surrounded by a three-foot balustrade on which they sat. The sky was glistening with stars—*like a mosaic of beauty*, Michael thought. A tranquil breeze danced off Leah's hair, and the light from the moon was reflected in her green eyes. She looked more serious than usual.

"I used to spend a lot of time up here with Yochanan. We would talk about our dreams. But the last time I was here . . ." Leah bowed her head.

"Oh, your husband? I can see why you would come up here a lot." He took a panoramic view of the town. "It's so peaceful and beautiful. The sky is really pretty."

She remained silent, catching Michael by surprise. "It is pretty up here, right?"

But Leah didn't answer. She was lost in thought.

Several soldiers chased after the brown-haired man. Leah stood frozen, staring down at Yochanan's face, which was covered with blood.

The biggest Roman soldier towered over him, grinning. "Bring me back the other rebel," his voice boomed as three soldiers joined the pursuit. "Rebels like you will be punished." Then he spat at Yochanan, striking him in the side of the face. "Peasant! Jew!"

"Get away from him," screamed Leah from the rooftop. She ran to the ladder and half slid, half fell to the bottom. Then she grabbed a cloth from the kitchen and raced to the well, where she collapsed to the ground next to Yochanan.

"Is this your husband?" the soldier demanded.

"Yes!" She spat the word through her tears.

"Your husband deserves to die. Rebels should die."

Leah glared, her chest heaving. "He is not a rebel. He is a good man. A peaceful man."

"Let him die in the dirt, fitting for such a man."

Ignoring him, Leah bent over and wiped some blood off Yochanan's forehead. "Yochanan, can you hear me?"

There was no response.

She stood up and went to the well to pull up a bucket of water. Dipping the cloth in it, she went back and gently began to cleanse his wounds.

"Let him die!" the soldier said as he slapped her hand away.

Instinctively, Leah jumped to her feet and pushed the soldier away, slamming her hand hard against his metal armor. The soldier laughed as he saw her wince in pain. "Woman, you are weak."

She swung angrily at the side of his head, surprising him with the force of the blow.

"Never touch a Roman soldier," he bellowed as he whipped his spear against the back of her head. She fell forward, landing partly on Yochanan, who groaned.

She got to her knees immediately, overjoyed that he had made a sound. "Yochanan, how do you feel?" She poured some more water on the cloth and gently pressed it on his head.

A few soldiers had joined their leader near the well and were talking. "Did you catch the other rebel?"

"There are still some after him."

"Is he caught?"

The soldiers looked at each other and shrugged.

The Roman soldier growled. "We must get him. Move!"

Together they turned and moved away, back toward the city. Leah pulled Yochanan's head gently onto her lap. "The soldiers have gone, Yochanan," she said softly, fighting back tears. "We are safe now. You are safe. Please, please speak."

His eyes were glassy and some of the blood on his forehead had trickled into his eyebrows. Furiously she wiped it away. "What happened, Yochanan? Why did this happen?"

He weakly touched her hand. "I am fine. How is my friend? Is he safe?"

Leah wasn't sure how to answer Yochanan without worrying him. "I am confused about this friend you speak of."

"He was with me when we were chased," Yochanan mumbled. "Did he get home?"

She nodded vigorously to reassure him. "Yes, he went home, Yochanan. He is safe."

He smiled. "He is a good man."

Leah shook her head, confused. She continued to try to stem the flow of blood from his wounds. It just wouldn't stop. "How do you feel? Can you walk?"

"My legs . . . ," he whispered. "I cannot move them."

Leah's tears dripped onto Yochanan's face as she cradled him in her arms. His eyes began to close and she held on more tightly. "Do not close your eyes, Yochanan!" she begged. "Please!"

"Leah, come close," he said faintly. He managed to reach up with his arm and pulled her head down, closer to his mouth. Gently Yochanan touched her cheek and then her lips. "You are mine, always."

"Always," she whispered, her body shaking.

His hand fell back to the ground and she pulled away to look down at his face. Gently she began to rock back and forth, whispering over and over through her tears, "Yochanan, do not go. Do not go. You are mine, always. Always. Do not go."

Leah stood up and walked to the other side of the roof. "Come here," she said. Michael joined her. "Look over there." She pointed at a mountain in the distance. "Do you see?"

Michael nodded.

"One time Yochanan took me there. Did you know that?"

"I'm sorry?"

She glanced back at him, her eyes upturned and searching. "I always thought you knew him so well," she whispered.

Michael was baffled, but she continued before he could answer. "We spent the whole day there, talking and enjoying the beauty of the mountain. There was a babbling stream we walked in that we followed all the way down to the valley. It was the most perfect day. He held me so tightly that night. The stars were so bright that we could see our reflections in the stream."

She paused. "I miss Yochanan so much. It's been so long, don't you think?"

"What do you mean?"

"My world has never been the same. And never will be."

Michael could see her eyes were misty. "I'm sorry. Let's go back down."

"No, I am fine. Yochanan would call me silly for not coming up here."

She returned to her seat on the balustrade. "It is beautiful up here, isn't it?"

Michael followed her back and sat next to her.

She took a deep breath and pulled the blanket tightly around her. "Yochanan kept me safe before he died. He would wrap his big arms around me whenever I would be afraid."

Michael nodded. "Vicki was much the same way for me. I think I drove her nuts with my fears." He laughed, then grew silent.

After a few moments, Michael quietly asked, "What happened to Yochanan?"

Leah sighed. "Do you mean how I saw it?"

"Sure."

Leah folded her arms tightly across her chest. "There is much violence in our world. But I never expected it to come to my doorstep. I never expected that a man with his message could anger people. The Romans are a ruthless people, Michael. You stay in your place to be safe. But Yochanan needed to find peace and comfort in his life. For some reason I couldn't give him that. I wish I had done something sooner. But I didn't know what to do.

"We always live with some danger, but it is our way. I never thought it would end in death . . . but it did, and so randomly. One moment he was there and then, what?"

Leah faced him in earnest. "Michael, I am asking you what happened." Her tone was urgent and unrelenting. "Why was it necessary?"

Michael shrugged. "Leah, I can't say. I'm having a hard time myself understanding why my Vicki had to die the way she did." He was anxious, worried that he wouldn't be able to find the words of comfort that she so obviously needed. He paused. "Perhaps I can help if you tell me more about what happened."

She hesitated. "I was grieving myself when everything happened. . . ." She took another deep breath and looked away from Michael. "After we lost our daughter."

"Oh. I didn't know you had a daughter. I'm so sorry."

Leah looked at him in disbelief.

Michael added in a whisper to her, "I can't imagine the pain of losing a child."

Leah touched his arm. "We were so happy when she was born. She was a great gift to us. Yochanan smiled every day she was here. He would hold her in his big arms and walk her around. Yochanan would bathe her and sing to her. I never saw him so happy. She was everything to us. Two weeks later, we had lost our whole world. She got very warm, much too warm. And she wouldn't eat. It all happened so fast. And there was nothing. Looking back, I know I lost both of them that horrible day."

Michael gently rubbed her shoulder as she began to weep. After a moment, he offered her the sleeve of his garment to wipe the tears away from her cheeks.

Leah took another deep breath and looked down at her hands, resting now in her lap. "He spent many days away from me. He wouldn't talk much. He wouldn't let me hold him anymore. He was angry at times, and so sad and quiet at other times. Maybe it was my fault. Maybe I didn't do enough to help him through it. But I was having a hard time myself."

She paused a brief moment. "He would go away for days at time, leaving me alone for so many hours. He sought out that preacher. He told me he found peace when he listened to him.

"I wanted to help him but he wouldn't let me. I tried everything to reach him but he only wanted to talk about what he had heard. I didn't listen. I couldn't listen.

"He had been gone for several days when it happened. I heard men yelling outside. As much as I didn't want to think it was him, I knew it was. I was afraid. I went up to the roof of the house thinking I would safely see who was there. When I looked down, I saw him lying down on the ground, bleeding from his head."

She wiped her tears away with her own garment this time. "He died the next morning."

Michael grimaced.

"I'm sorry," she said, looking up at Michael. "I haven't cried much since Yochanan died. When word of his death went around the village, no one came by to talk to me."

"Why?"

"Because of his battle with the Romans! The soldiers remained nearby for many days."

"Looking for who?"

Leah shook her head. "For you." Her eyes searched his for meaning.

Michael stared at her before shaking his head. "I really don't know what you're talking about."

Leah sighed, then continued, "We were both so lost in our pain that even in this small house, it was as if we could never find each other. Yochanan spent much time away with that group, listening to them talk about a world of peace and love. Yet he died so violently. Is that peace and love to you? Is it?"

Michael looked into Leah's eyes and shook his head. "I don't know how it can be," he whispered to her. "I can't imagine living in this world you live in. In prison, it was just horrible." His voice trailed off.

"What happened?"

"There were some things I could see, other moments I could only hear." Michael squirmed a bit. He grimaced. "This woman, she must have been the prisoner's wife. The prison guard seemed nice at first, allowing her to bring her husband some food. I heard the guard tell the man and woman he was going to let him go. I saw him unlock the gate, and as the man went to hug his wife, the guard stabbed him in the heart."

Leah gave no reaction. She just stared at Michael.

"I started to scream for help. But he came over and swung his spear at me. So I backed up against the wall. The woman was bent over her husband, screaming and crying. She was hugging him. I could tell he wasn't dead yet, just bleeding from his chest. The guard came back and grabbed her. I could see the blood was all over his hands and face. And he laughed. He just laughed."

Leah gently stroked the top of Michael's head. He looked up at her and continued, "He pushed her into the cell. I couldn't see anything then. I just heard her clothes ripping and her screams. It was sickening. And the poor guy, I could see him taking his last few breaths, watching his wife get beaten and abused. And I couldn't do anything."

Leah remained silent.

Michael looked at her. "Why are you so quiet? Do you believe me?"

Leah nodded. "I do. Yochanan was imprisoned at Antonia for a short time. I thought I would never see him again. Days went by and I would wait near the front of the prison, hoping someone would tell me what was going on. I heard the screams, too, Michael. I saw many bodies carried out of there, dumped like trash by the gate for the families to find. Yochanan told me later that these were the lucky ones; some of the dead were just left in chains, to terrify the other prisoners."

"What a terrible world you live in," Michael said angrily.

"And what makes your world better? Do they have a greater reverence for life where you live? If so, I would like to see it."

Her words hit home. "My town is pretty safe," he said thoughtfully, "but, no, there are parts of my world that are no better. I can't say we've come very far in the 'respect life' category." He paused briefly to measure his words properly. "There are many men who talk of peace, yet send many men to kill others in faraway places."

The night air was getting cool, and Michael could see the stars were shining more brightly in the crisp evening air. "You know, my wife, Vicki, showered me with love and it was the only peace I ever found."

He paused and looked at Leah. "We're more similar than you think. When she died, I thought I lost everything. But I didn't. Maybe you didn't either. You know, for the longest time I didn't think I was worthy of anyone's love."

Leah's eyes widened. She turned directly to face him.

"Everyone is worthy of love. You just need to be open to others, and it will seek you out. It has taken me a long time to learn that."

They sat there in silence, watching the shooting stars dance across the sky.

"It's so peaceful up here," he sighed. "So peaceful." Michael slid down the side of the balustrade. "Come here."

Leah gazed at him a moment before joining him on the ground.

"Look." He pointed up at the stars.

"What?" she asked, looking up, her hair grazing his shoulder.

"That's the Big Dipper."

"Do you mean the *North Star*? It's how the fishermen always find their way home."

11

LIZZIE HAD A LITTLE LAMB

The sun glistened over the horizon, directing its soothing morning rays onto Michael's face. Feeling the warmth, he awoke, rubbing his eyes and instinctively putting his hand out on the ground next to him to see if she was still there. He felt nothing.

Hmm, he thought while opening his eyes, *where is she?*

Surprised by his initial reaction, he stood up quickly. *She wouldn't be here; she's not like that.*

Michael gathered up the bedroll and quietly walked down the ladder to the second floor. He crept into Elizabeth's room and watched her sleep peacefully. He touched her shoulder, planting a gentle kiss on her forehead. Then he started down the ladder leading to the first floor, noticing Leah preparing breakfast in the kitchen.

"Let me try to cook for you again," he said eagerly.

Leah looked up at him. "Do you really think that's best?"

Michael pressed his lips together before saying, "I'm not sure, but I figure it's worth a shot."

In response, she put her hand over her mouth and laughed nervously. When she heard Michael chuckle slightly, she burst out in laughter.

"Okay, okay . . . I get the message. My cooking days here are finished."

"No, please, I'm sorry." She waved her arms, trying to calm herself.

"Why don't I try to show you how to make some porridge? It's the easiest to cook."

"Oh, maybe you have the book *Cooking for Dummies* for me?" he said with a smile.

Leah's face went blank, puzzled by the reference.

"Oh, sorry . . . it's a joke between me and Elizabeth. Sorry, again."

She laughed. "Sometimes you talk strangely."

Michael nodded. "I can understand why you would say that."

She pulled out a basket of grains, ready to begin her lesson. After dropping a handful of grain into the bowl, she said, "Pour some water into this."

Michael did as he was told.

When Leah picked up a spoon to stir the porridge, Michael reached for it, touching her hand. "May I?"

She looked at him. "Of course," she said softly, handing him the spoon.

Michael began stirring, slowly dragging the spoon through the watered grains and mashing them against the outer rim of the pot. As he worked toward the center, he caught her looking at him and smiled.

"Do you ever cook for anyone but yourself?" Michael asked.

Leah's eyebrows lifted. "And why do you ask that?"

He was quiet for a few seconds. "No reason. Just making conversation."

"Hmm . . . keep stirring but a little quicker. Good, very good." She took the bowl and placed it above the fire. "Okay, it's ready to cook."

"Do you want me to help with the fire?"

Leah gave him an incredulous look.

He laughed. "Okay, I get the message."

The smell of porridge and the crackling of fire awakened Elizabeth.

"Morning, Dad," she said as she climbed down the final rungs of the first-floor ladder. "Hey, Leah."

"Good morning, Baboo."

"Daddy, launch!"

Michael quickly pointed at Leah. "Not now, Elizabeth. How about a hug?"

"Okay," she said, falling into his arms.

Michael looked over at Leah, who was laughing at the sight of them. "Are you hungry?" he asked Elizabeth.

"Yes!"

"Extra honey this morning?" Leah asked.

"Yes! Thank you."

Leah handed Elizabeth a bowl. "Go upstairs, we will join you."

Smiling, Elizabeth turned and headed back up to the dining mat on the second floor.

After Elizabeth had left, Leah turned to Michael. "What are your plans today?"

"I'm not sure yet. I have to speak with Elizabeth."

"Michael, today begins Passover. I have to go to town to prepare for the meal . . . which means I also have to take the lamb to the Temple to be sacrificed."

"Oh! Is it really necessary to kill the lamb?"

Leah hesitated. "We sacrifice the lamb, Michael."

"Oops. Sorry."

"I know Elizabeth is fond of the lamb, but it is our tradition to sacrifice on this night. The lamb is my sacrifice."

Looking out to the courtyard at the fig tree, Michael said, "I'm not sure how Elizabeth is going to handle this."

He paused, not sure if he should continue. "If you're going near the Temple, can you check the tunnel for us? I want to leave later tonight, but I'm concerned about the soldiers." He stopped and looked at her. "Is this too much to ask?"

"No. I want to help you find your way home, Michael. It's by the courtyard, right?"

Michael grasped her hands in excitement. "Yes! I marked the grate with that piece from Elizabeth's shirt. If it's all clear, we can leave tonight!"

Leah glanced at him, wide-eyed. Michael realized that he was holding her hands tightly. Embarrassed, he squeezed once gently before dropping them.

"Leah, can I feed Cassie again today?" Elizabeth called from upstairs. "Leah?"

Leah smiled tenderly, her eyes downcast. "Yes, Elizabeth, you may," she called back.

Leah gathered the food onto a woven tray and ascended the ladder. Michael followed her, bringing a second tray of bowls.

"Oh, hey!" Elizabeth squealed as they reached the second floor. "Leah, after breakfast should I put together some more grains for Cassie?"

At this, Leah looked away while Michael sighed.

"What's wrong?" Elizabeth asked.

When Leah remained silent, Michael quietly said to Elizabeth, "We'll talk about this later."

After they had finished eating, Leah rose uneasily to her feet. "I have to go to town to pick up some fruits and vegetables." She looked at Elizabeth again kindly, then turned to Michael.

Catching her eye, Michael whispered to Elizabeth, "I'll be right back, honey."

He followed Leah down the ladder, noticing at the bottom that she was holding her head.

Leah turned to face him. "Michael, I'm really sorry. I'm worried about Elizabeth."

He recognized the strain in her face. "Leah, please, she's going to be fine. I'll speak to her this morning while you are at the market. Plus, she'll be really relieved when I tell her you're going to scout out the tunnel."

After watching Leah leave through the front gate, Michael took a deep breath and reentered the house. "Elizabeth?"

She came downstairs with the bowls from breakfast.

"What's up, Dad? Where's Leah?" she asked, depositing the bowls in a pail of water near the fire.

Michael forced a smile before turning to Elizabeth. "Honey, Leah's going to the tunnel for us! She's checking it out to make sure there aren't any soldiers. We could leave in a few hours, maybe."

"That's awesome!" Elizabeth exclaimed. "Wow, I should feed Cassie quick so that we're ready to go when Leah gets back."

Michael winced uncomfortably. "Honey, I don't know if you should worry about that."

"Are you kidding? I want to feed her one last meal before I go."

Michael reached over, touching her cheek gently. "Elizabeth, I want to be honest with you. You know, today starts Leah's religious holiday. You're old enough for me to tell you things like this now: the lamb is going to be taken to Temple this afternoon."

"For what?"

"The lamb is part of Leah's tradition. It will be offered up for sacrifice."

Elizabeth covered her face with her hands. "You mean Cassie is *really* going to be killed? I just thought that after Leah saw how much I liked her—how much I *love* her—that it would be different."

"She's a lamb, and here a lamb is—"

"You mean *Cassie,* right, Dad? You can say her name."

Michael nodded.

"Let me see her," she said, storming off past Michael out to the front yard where Cassie was grazing. She hugged the lamb, then started to run toward the front gate.

"Elizabeth, please . . . get back in here!"

"No! If we're leaving, why can't we just take her?" She ran a few steps, stopped, ran a few more steps, and stopped again. Each time she paused, she looked back at the lamb, frustrated that Cassie wasn't following.

Michael ran to her, pulling Elizabeth gently into his chest. "It'll be okay."

"Yeah, sure," she mumbled, "but why did I have to know?"

The maze of streets was bustling with activity. Many women were out anxiously buying the proper foods for the evening's feast. A few neighbors acknowledged Leah, who glided past at a brisk pace, basket in hand as she respectfully nodded her salutations.

The excitement of the festivities was bittersweet for Leah; images of Yochanan occupied her thoughts. It seemed like only yesterday that he had been with her, inspecting honey pots and dried roots, smiling at her and her ballooning pregnant belly that even her long robe could no longer conceal. He had offered every item of produce he had selected to her for final approval. Back then, he was the one easily shouldering the ungainly basket that was now weighing her down. These memories, combined with the growing anxiety of trying to help Michael and Elizabeth, sent Leah's emotions spiraling in every direction.

Although she had gathered everything she needed, Leah was overwhelmed by a sense that something was still missing. Of course, the leafy lettuces, handful of nuts for the charoset, and spicy roots were sufficient. Mentally, she knew her list was complete. Yet something felt just beyond her grasp, waiting in the mist of her thoughts to be plucked out and examined. She decided to circle the market stands again, hoping the walk would jar her out of this odd reverie.

As she worked her way around the jostling, frenzied crowd, she suddenly realized with startling clarity what was troubling her. Yochanan might be everywhere today, but for her, the thought of him was now tied to someone else, another man: Michael.

She stopped abruptly and immediately felt a woman's hand on her back. They apologized to each other silently, a raised hand in forgiveness, a concerned smile. But all of it made Leah feel guilt and remorse. It was easier to focus on Elizabeth, and in doing so, she decided to pursue one more purchase.

She cut into the current of the crowd and headed toward a stand of plump melons. She felt sympathy for Elizabeth, abandoned in this world, a sensation that Leah understood all too well. Now with the sacrifice of the lamb—the name *Cassie* came to mind, but Leah fought to repress it—Elizabeth would be even more isolated. Leah picked up a melon in the front, purposefully concentrating on everything else but how Yochanan would thump them with his thumb. She settled on a medium-size one. She guessed it was eight or nine pounds, bigger than the usual. *I've got more mouths to feed this year.*

Her mind turned back to Michael, and the task that lay ahead. From the afternoon of their first encounter, she remembered where the tunnel was and mentally charted a course to it. As each step brought her closer, she found herself wondering what it would mean to have them leave. She had certainly felt the anxiety of harboring people who some would consider outlaws or even possible criminals. And Michael's physical nearness had at times made her feel uncomfortable. Yet there was no denying that they had given her a new mission, a goal that provided her solace for the first time in years. If they could freely leave her, then where would it actually *leave* her?

She walked the remaining three hundred yards until she was at the corner of the alley on which the tunnel was located. She slowed, instantly alert to any signs of soldiers. She drew nearer to the building on the corner and peered around its facade. After a few moments of waiting for the crowd to thin, she was finally able to spy the series of grates. A white cloth was tied on the arching bars over one near the center. *There it is, like he said!*

But then she realized a soldier was to the left of the tunnel's opening. He was leaning comfortably in the shade of the stucco wall, perfectly at ease, with the appearance of a man waiting for a friend. She wondered if this was the man Michael feared: he was dressed in the traditional uniform, yet he could have been anyone. But then on the ground next to him she saw his helmet with a remnant of Elizabeth's shirt still affixed to it and knew he was the one.

As she stared at him, another feeling coursed through her, one that she couldn't decipher. Something about him resonated with her, but still, every soldier was a threat. As she tried to shake off her unease, she noticed another soldier walking toward her, his eyes thankfully averted. Leah stepped back, ducking into the darkness of a recessed doorway, pinning her back against its interior wall. She let the basket slip down her frame, coming to rest on the ground. Sheltered from view, she listened with keen interest as people passed by, failing to notice her slim shadow projected obliquely on the opposite wall.

Through the din of the crowd, Leah could hear the two soldiers greeting each other. Being part of the military, they were gallant and loud, their voices carrying over the rumble in a way that no villager would ever dare to emulate. They were complaining about Passover and how the need for surveillance brought them back again to this city. They obviously abhorred this duty, and their annoyance was tangible. As they spoke, a clanging, rhythmic sound of metal hitting the cobblestones cut through the air. Leah shivered. The blunt end of one of their deadly spears was repeatedly striking the ground, as if in boredom. She concentrated in earnest, trying to filter their speech through the metallic sound.

"Yes, I've been waiting here for a few nights now," said one man.

The other man laughed. "How long do you plan to stay?"

The clink of metal striking stone obscured the man's response. Then the noise stopped, as if something else had drawn their attention; Leah prayed it wasn't her.

"I'll find that woman." The first man's tone was even and dry.

The other man snorted. "You always do."

They both chuckled in unison. "You know me too well, my comrade."

Something in the voice was eerily familiar to Leah, and she felt a rush of panic. It was as if a door were opening from within while she struggled to hold it closed.

She slid away from the wall and took a quick glance out into the street. Their backs were to her. The first soldier was holding the spear, turning it into the mortar between two paving stones. He raised it nearly a foot before letting it drop through his hand to the cobblestones below, catching the shaft again when it rebounded upward. It had a sharper sound this time.

"I'll find that woman by finding that man," said the first soldier. "Are you with me?"

"Of course," the other soldier replied. "I owe you a favor, Marcus."

"That's right," the voice echoed back.

It is him. Leah's knees buckled and her stomach lurched as she felt transported back. She remembered the view from her rooftop, her excitement tangible at Yochanan's return, then cut short by the horrific scene that played out before her: Yochanan slumped in the street, blood everywhere. The soldier before him that night with the crimson-tipped spear was the same jovial one leaning by the grate before her now. She vomited on the ground in front of her, fearing that they would hear her retch. As she pulled her body back, only one thing shook her: *How can Michael not recognize him?*

Leah grabbed her basket from the ground and stepped over the puddle of vomit. She edged to the corner, determined to make her escape. As she did, the one she now knew as "Marcus" glared right at her. She bowed her head in respect but, with her heart pounding, stepped out too quickly in her attempt to blend in with the crowd. She glanced back quickly and saw Marcus pointing at her, his head bent in speech toward the other soldier. She forced a smile again, then joined a group of women walking in the opposite direction, toward the city wall. She tried in earnest to engage them, all the while her mind racing.

Yet only one thought remained constant: *He's coming after me now!*

Elizabeth spent the entire morning petting the lamb and fingering its tightly wound curls. At times, she would place her head against the back of the lamb's neck, her face mixed with both anger and hopelessness.

Watching Elizabeth, Michael once again felt helpless in this other world, unable to save the lamb and ease his daughter's pain. He thought about kidnapping the lamb and telling Elizabeth to make a run for the tunnel. But he knew this was reckless and disrespectful to Leah, particularly after the risk she was taking at the moment to help them.

How can I not say good-bye to her?

Michael walked over to Elizabeth and gently rubbed her back. "I'm sorry, sweetie."

"Can you tell Leah to stop this? She'll listen to you."

"I tried, Elizabeth. I really did. It's a special holy day for her. And this is how they celebrate, much like we celebrate by eating turkey on Thanksgiving."

Elizabeth frowned. "Daddy, I love Cassie. Would it be so bad if we just took her with us?"

Michael leaned over to hug Elizabeth. "I know Cassie means a lot to you but she belongs here, and it's not our place to interfere." He stroked her back, noticing a tear roll down her cheek. "Please, don't get upset. You know how it upsets me when you cry."

She pulled away. "Sometimes, Dad, I just need to cry. Is that okay?"

"Yes, yes, it's okay," he whispered in her ear, reaching down to hold her hand.

Michael knew something was terribly wrong when he saw Leah crouched directly behind the front wall, watching the gate intently. Leah's face was drawn, and her eyes wide with fright. When he started toward her, she flailed one hand in the air, waving him back toward the house. She listened for one long moment before spryly leaping to her feet, surprising Michael with her agility. She met him at the kitchen, but when he reached for the basket she was carrying, he was startled to see that her hands were shaking.

"What happened?" he whispered, taking the basket from her. "Are you okay?"

"Michael, the soldier was there, waiting for you. Where's Elizabeth?"

"She's upstairs. You saw Marcus? Did he follow you?"

"No. I don't believe so. But go tell her to stay there. Please don't scare her. Give me a moment and I'll bring you both lunch."

"I don't care about eating. Just come up where it's safe." Michael climbed the steps quickly, trying not to look concerned. But instead of stopping at the second floor, he hurried up the ladder leading to the roof. He peeked out and looked around in a circular motion. *No one out there. Thank God.*

When he descended back down to the dining area, he saw Elizabeth smiling. "What's going on?" she asked curiously.

"Um . . . nothing." *I've told Elizabeth too much already.*

She gave him a look of disbelief, noticing her father's face was milky white.

The awkward silence was broken as Leah began preparations for lunch. She removed the lettuce, herbs, and horseradish root from the basket before following him. As she reached the top of the ladder, she called out sweetly, "I got you some watermelon, Elizabeth."

Despite her grief, Elizabeth didn't want to offend Leah. She rose from her bedroll and joined them at the dinner mat, where she and Michael had already set out bowls of cheese, almonds, and cucumber.

Upon seeing the simple yet elegant lunch, Leah whispered to them, "Thank you."

Michael smiled. "I'm sorry, but I couldn't find any bread."

"There isn't any in the house because of the seder. This is just perfect." Her breathing became more even as she ate.

"So was he waiting at the tunnel?" Elizabeth asked, adding a piece of watermelon to her plate.

Leah nodded.

Elizabeth frowned, looking at her father. "So what does that mean?"

"It means we're not leaving yet," Michael murmured.

Elizabeth quietly ate three slices of watermelon, each bite precise and deliberate. Leah and Michael chewed on nuts, enduring Elizabeth's stoic silence.

Finally Elizabeth asked quietly, "Why do you have to kill Cassie?"

"Elizabeth, please?" Michael begged.

"No, it's fine, Michael." Leah raised her hand. "Elizabeth, this is the tradition of our people. Each year a lamb is sacrificed to show our devotion. Our people have done it for a very long time."

After a moment of thought, she added, "Don't you have traditions where you come from?"

Elizabeth sighed. "My father doesn't believe in traditions."

Michael grinned uncomfortably. "She's right."

"Can I be excused?" Elizabeth asked.

"Yes, yes," Michael said anxiously. "Just stay out of the courtyard."

Elizabeth looked away and went down the ladder, avoiding eye contact with them. They heard her outside Cassie's stall.

"She's not taking this well," Michael said to Leah, moving to the upstairs window to watch Elizabeth playing with Cassie below.

"I know." Leah quietly removed the cups and plates from the mat before starting down the ladder.

Michael followed her downstairs to the kitchen, where he watched Leah. She was puttering around the room, cleaning and moving plates to different parts of the tiny kitchen.

Why is she lingering?

After a moment, he finally asked, "Can I help you?"

"No, no, no. I just need some time."

Michael watched Elizabeth continue to pet the lamb. He was fixated on his daughter, but soon realized that Leah was intently watching too. When Michael's eyes met Leah's, she turned away from him.

"I need to speak with you about something."

"What is it?" Michael asked.

Leah hesitated as she covered her head with the veil and took a short length of rope from the wall behind her. She moved toward Cassie's stall. "It should wait," she said, nodding in Elizabeth's direction. "It's time for me to take Cassie to the Temple, Elizabeth."

"Are you sure you should go?" Michael asked urgently.

"Yes, I think I just panicked before." Leah smiled at him.

Elizabeth looked up into Leah's face and solemnly nodded. She hugged Cassie one last time, then slowly stood. "Bye, Cassie."

Leah tied the rope loosely around the lamb's neck and gently guided it out of the courtyard. Michael watched the front gate close behind them before he turned to look at Elizabeth. She was standing alone, under the fig tree, without a single tear in her eye—something that made Michael feel as if his heart would burst.

Michael sat against the wall in Cassie's stall, watching Elizabeth. "Honey, we have to think about getting back."

Elizabeth looked at her father. Her eyes were now red and puffy from saying good-bye to Cassie. "I just want to get back home to my friends. I don't like it here."

Michael nodded in understanding. "I know. I want to leave, too, but until that soldier leaves, it's impossible."

Elizabeth shrugged in agreement. She picked up a piece of straw from the ground. "Dad, do you believe in life after death? Do you think there's a heaven?"

He was surprised by his daughter's question. He had dwelled on the subject quite a bit over the past fourteen years. "Honey, you're so young, why are you worrying about this right now?"

"Because I think of Mom a lot, especially around her birthday. Can we do something together on her birthday next week?"

Michael's head dropped. "It's a tough day for me, Elizabeth. I don't feel much like doing anything on that day."

"I know." Every year for as long as she could remember, her father had shut the blinds in the house on April 17 and sat in his dark bedroom.

She looked at him searchingly. "If that man you saw really was Jesus, do you think he could bring Mom back somehow?"

The question hung in the air. Michael had no idea how to answer. He had been sure of what he'd seen on Palm Sunday, and somehow, on that day, he'd felt something stir within him. Was it faith? Hope? Whatever it was, it had been fleeting but genuine. But now, in the practical light of day, that possibility seemed ridiculous. The last thing he wanted to do was alarm his daughter with some far-fetched idea, all because he couldn't find it in his heart to let go of the past.

"Elizabeth, I think what I saw was amazing," he said slowly. "But I really doubt Jesus, God, or anyone else could bring back Mom."

"Why not? Jesus was supposed to work miracles. Why couldn't we try to find him?" Elizabeth leaned forward in excitement. "Why couldn't we ask him for a miracle?"

Michael shook his head. This was getting out of hand. "No, Elizabeth. It's dangerous enough already for us here. The last thing I want to do is jeopardize your safety. I've already lost your mother. I couldn't bear to lose you, too."

She glared at him. "You're always using me as an excuse. You just don't want to try."

He didn't bother answering. He reasoned that she wouldn't, or couldn't, fully understand until she was a parent. He didn't have the energy to explain that he tried all the time. To be a good father. To be supportive. To fill two parents' shoes instead of just his own.

They sat in silence. Finally Elizabeth asked with a sidelong glance, "Dad, what do you think of Leah?"

"Hmm . . . I don't know. I don't know her well enough to say." He looked at his daughter; to him, she had matured so much over this past week.

Elizabeth snapped the piece of straw between her finger and thumb. She scowled in frustration. "Ugh, I hate waiting here. We should be back at the tunnel by now."

"Yeah, me, too. I'd do anything to get rid of that soldier. Leah thinks it won't be safe until after sundown."

Elizabeth gave a look of displeasure. "Now you're talking like her."

Michael walked over to Elizabeth and sat down. He put his arms around her.

"Elizabeth, the only thing I want right now is to get you home safely so you can be happy."

She rested her head on his shoulder. "That sounds nice."

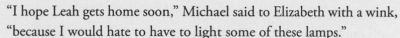

"I hope Leah gets home soon," Michael said to Elizabeth with a wink, "because I would hate to have to light some of these lamps."

She just stared at him, motionless.

Michael grew restless. Night fell quickly here, and they needed to get home.

Suddenly, he heard heavy footsteps on the road. Elizabeth wanted to investigate, but Michael motioned for her to stay down.

"Shh," he said, putting a finger over his lips.

Panic seized him. *It's a soldier! Is it Marcus? Leah* was *followed!* Fear spread through him as he leaned near the window, trying to look outside. The noises grew louder and were coming from near the courtyard now.

He grabbed Elizabeth and pointed upstairs. "Go, go to the roof. Quickly!"

When they got up to the second floor, Michael pushed Elizabeth over to the roof ladder. "Up!"

Elizabeth stumbled. "Ouch!"

"Quiet," Michael whispered to her. "Go to the other side of the roof!"

Elizabeth looked at him in horror.

"Whatever happens . . . I love you," he said.

Elizabeth mouthed, *I love you, too.*

Hearing the front gate screech, Michael spun back, frantically trying to find a weapon. He pushed over a group of baskets near the far wall. Out fell balls of yarn and a couple of four-inch metal weaving pins. Michael crouched down, grabbing one.

He inched his way back to the ladder that led to the first floor and peered down nervously. Footsteps echoed from the kitchen beneath him. Someone was moving toward the ladder. Michael clutched the metal pin tightly. He raised his arm, ready to strike whoever tried to take Elizabeth.

"Michael?" a soft voice called out.

Michael's heart stopped. He dropped the pin. *Clink. Clink. Clink.* The pin bounced several times off the ladder and to the ground where he could see Leah standing.

"Leah?"

She glanced at the metal object, then looked up at Michael. Her face went blank, and she slumped back against the wall below. After a moment of complete silence, she walked back to the opening.

"Michael, you scared me so. What are you doing?"

A lamb began braying below.

"Cassie?" Michael asked.

"Cassie!?" Elizabeth yelled from the rooftop, looking down at her father.

Michael looked up at her gleaming face. "It's okay, Elizabeth! You have a special visitor."

Elizabeth scurried down the ladder, barely stepping on each rung. The little lamb's ears perked up. "Baa, baa."

"Cassie!" Elizabeth leaped from the ladder to the kitchen and fell to the ground, where she embraced the lamb.

Leah stood nearby, waiting for Michael to join them. He looked at Leah and saw her eyes were moist and red.

"Cassie, oh, Cassie," Elizabeth squealed. "I love you, my little lamb.

"Thank you, Leah, thank you!" she cried as she ran over to Leah to hug her. Elizabeth fell into her, pushing Leah back against the wall. "Thank you, thank you!"

Shocked, Leah slowly placed her arms around Elizabeth and held her.

While Elizabeth and Leah hugged, Michael continued to stare into Leah's eyes. *Thank you,* he mouthed to her.

For a moment she made no reply, but then smiled at him. "No, thank *you*," she whispered, her hand coming to rest on Elizabeth's shoulder.

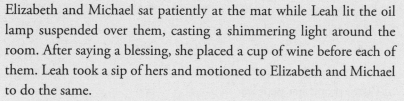

Elizabeth and Michael sat patiently at the mat while Leah lit the oil lamp suspended over them, casting a shimmering light around the room. After saying a blessing, she placed a cup of wine before each of them. Leah took a sip of hers and motioned to Elizabeth and Michael to do the same.

"Can I, Dad?"

Michael hesitated. He looked at Leah and remembered what had occurred during the last few hours with Cassie. "Well, why not? It's a good day to celebrate a little."

Elizabeth reached for her cup, watching the wine swirl inside when she picked it up. Even after Leah had thinned the wine with water, it was still thicker than eggnog. Elizabeth could smell its sweetness and slowly brought the cup to her lips. The wine reminded her of the kind they used at mass, but this was far darker in color, and when she tasted it, she liked it.

"Hmm . . . good."

Michael smiled. "Sip it slowly, please."

"Okay, Dad."

Leah placed a bowl of water down on the mat and washed her hands. "Please, join me." She gave them leaves of lettuce. She dipped hers into a bowl containing a lumpy mixture; Michael and Elizabeth followed suit.

"Mmm," Elizabeth said, "this is good. What is this, Leah?"

"I made it especially for you, Elizabeth. It's charoset. You make it from honey and crushed nuts."

"Thank you," Elizabeth said, dipping another piece of lettuce into the bowl.

"This *is* good," Michael agreed. "Thanks, Leah."

Leah, who was happy to see them enjoying this special meal, indicated the plate covered by a cloth on the center of the mat. She removed the cloth to reveal three matzos, the middle of which she broke into two, hiding the larger piece back under the cloth.

"I know you are hungry," she said, giving Michael a wink.

"Do you have any questions about this holiday?" Leah asked Elizabeth, who was flustered from the few sips of wine she had taken.

"Um, well, what makes this night so special?"

Leah smiled at her as she began to tell them about the rich history of Passover and her people.

As she retold the story in the same precise and methodical way it had originally been told to her, Michael became captivated by how the lamp's glow illuminated her rosy cheeks and green eyes.

Wonder how old she is? He found her so beautiful and her tone reassuring. He tried to pay attention to what she was saying but her voice was like an elixir, easing all the physical and mental stress he had endured over the past few days.

Occasionally, Leah would reach over and touch his hands when making a point about the holiday. Her touch was magnetic; he moved closer to her. When Leah would brush her hair from her face to regroup her thoughts, his heart seemed to pound harder.

When Leah finished, Michael glanced over at Elizabeth and noticed how relaxed she seemed. She was smiling, too.

Leah placed another cup of wine in front of them. "Your second cup of wine."

"Oh my," Michael said. "How many cups of wine do we get?"

"I am supposed to set out four."

"Thank you!" Elizabeth squealed.

"Hey, Baboo, just take one sip from the rest of them, okay?"

Leah washed her hands in the bowl again, encouraging Michael and Elizabeth to do the same. Lifting the two matzos plus the half from the third, Leah recited a blessing, then divided the bread among them. She showed them how to dip a leaf of lettuce into the charoset before placing it in the center of matzo pieces to form a sandwich. She ate hers, encouraging Michael and Elizabeth to do likewise.

Leah looked pleased with them when she uncovered the remaining bowls on the mat, revealing a feast of cheese, nuts, and fish.

"We're not having lamb tonight," she said, looking at Elizabeth.

"Hurray!"

"I hope you don't mind the fish," Leah said to Michael.

Michael smiled. "Fish is great tonight, thank you."

After they ate from the bowls, Leah brought out the hidden matzo half as dessert. She then placed another cup of wine in front of them.

"Oh, jeez," Michael said, looking over at Elizabeth, who had fallen asleep. Smiling at Leah, he asked, "What about her?"

"Perhaps I shouldn't have made the charoset?"

"Why?"

"Because there's wine in it."

Michael looked over at Elizabeth. "Oh, no!"

He glared at Leah, pretending to be shocked, but then began to laugh. "Well, it doesn't look like we're getting back to the tunnel tonight. I can't carry her."

"I am glad. I was worried. I didn't want to say it before, but with everyone celebrating Passover, the streets will be empty except for soldiers. You can hide in a crowd from them, but you're at their mercy when you're alone."

Michael nodded. "I guess you're right. Let me make Elizabeth more comfortable. C'mon, sweetie, get up." He tucked his arm underneath Elizabeth's to lift her. She felt heavy to him as he staggered over to her bedroll.

Placing her down gently, he whispered, "Sleep well, Baboo." He brushed her hair from her eyes and kissed her forehead before turning to leave.

"Night, Daddy," Elizabeth mumbled as she rubbed her face into the blanket.

Leah watched from the other room, but when Michael returned to the dining area, she sat down quickly at the mat. He sat facing her. Leah placed the final cup of wine in front of him.

"If I must," he said, smiling, picking it up and taking a sip. He was enjoying this time with her, and the wine was sweet and smooth in his mouth. "This is really good," he said, leaning on his right elbow, reclining closer to Leah. "Do you mind?"

"No, I don't mind," she said, watching him closely. "You know, I have enjoyed my time with Elizabeth. She has been a pleasure to me."

"Yeah, she's a great kid. She's a lot like her mother: so friendly and happy. I'm not like that at all. I wish I were. I'm just an old guy who pushes people away."

"No, I don't think you're like that."

"You don't?" he said, rather pleased. "What do you think I'm like?"

"Well . . . what can I say?"

"Oh, c'mon, you can tell me." Michael sat up, moving closer to her and adding with a smile, "I can take it."

Leah placed her cup of wine down.

"You're very strong, Michael, but you are kind, too, and loving, especially with Elizabeth . . . and what a cook you are!"

Leah smiled at him, which drew his attention to her soft lips, and he leaned over slightly without thinking. She looked into his eyes, her hair falling in front of her face. She brushed it back behind her ear.

"You make me believe," she whispered to him.

Something snapped in Michael's head and he recoiled quickly, standing up. "I've got to go."

"Michael?"

"I need some air."

Michael started climbing down the ladder, but stopped abruptly to glance back at Elizabeth. "I'm sorry, can you please watch over her?"

"Of course, of course, but where are you going?"

He didn't answer. He was already in the courtyard heading for the gate.

12

BLOOD MONEY

The slapping of his sandals on the hard stone road echoed throughout the empty streets of Jerusalem. Michael walked around aimlessly, almost unaware of how deserted the streets were.

What am I doing out here? What about the soldiers? What if I get caught? They'll surely kill me this time.

He stopped in the middle of the street and looked around. *Where am I? I've got to get Elizabeth out of here. How could I have been so stupid? Why did I let it go this far?*

Remorse built up inside his mind, disabling his eyes as they stayed transfixed on the unusual structures of the city. His stare was disrupted when he heard someone approaching. Michael turned and noticed a bald man wearing a purple belt around his waist. Thankful he wasn't a soldier, Michael relaxed slightly.

"Excuse me," he said, "I've lost my way."

"Then it's best you find it," the man responded. "For a man like you, this is not a night to be out."

"Why?"

The man looked at him with pity. "Roman soldiers will be in the streets very soon. You would be wise to be away from here before they come."

"But there's nobody out here," Michael said, looking around at the vacant streets.

"There will be."

"What do you mean?"

"It doesn't concern you. Move on!"

"You're right," Michael agreed quickly, trying to quiet him. He glanced over his shoulder, fearful that the man would draw attention to them—the kind of attention Roman soldiers would notice.

The man nodded approvingly. "You are wise to think that way. Now go home."

Michael saw two Roman soldiers moving toward them at a slow, leisurely pace. He nodded farewell to the bald man and walked to the other side of the street. The soldiers quickened their step, trotting past him as they caught up with the bald man.

As he watched them, fear gripped him. *Are they talking about me? I'm not waiting to find out.* He frantically looked around, but there was nowhere to hide, so he sprinted to a darkened alley.

Wham! He ran into someone.

"Watch out!" a man shouted angrily. He stooped to retrieve the the bag he had dropped.

"I'm sorry, sir," Michael replied, bending down to help. He picked up a couple of coins. As the bearded man stood up, Michael recognized him. "Oh, it's you," he said in surprise. "You helped me in the marketplace the other day."

The man glanced at him, then turned quickly, looking nervously around. "What are you doing out tonight?"

Still hazy from the wine, Michael recklessly blurted out, "Maybe I'm looking for Jesus. You know where the garden is?"

"What do you mean?" the man asked, frowning.

"Well, maybe I'm wrong—heck, maybe I'm even dreaming."

"Friend, you're not dreaming. Go home."

"Buddy, I don't know where home is."

"Then go back to where you came from. It is dangerous. Everyone out here is dangerous tonight. Believe me, you don't know who your friends are."

Michael noticed how closely the man was holding the pouch to his chest.

"Go now," said the man. Suddenly he broke into a run, the bag swinging from his hand.

Stunned, Michael watched as the man's figure retreated. "Wait!" he called, holding up the coins. "You forgot your money." He began to run, too. "Stop! You forgot your money!"

Knowing it was probably a bad idea to follow him, but too drunk to care, Michael continued to pursue the man. Rounding the corner, he caught a glimpse of him about twenty yards ahead, darting to the left into an alleyway.

These streets! It's like running through a maze, and I'm the rat.

When he came to the end of the alley, Michael saw the man reach the wall surrounding the city and run through a gate into the dark night. He was gone.

Michael stopped, trying to catch his breath. "Oh, I don't believe this."

Exhausted from the chase, he slumped down against the wall. As Michael did so, he felt the stones slice a gash in his back.

"Oh, great!" he gasped, reaching back to feel the torn skin. He looked down at his hand, now covered in blood. "Wonderful. A great way to top off the evening."

Michael leaned harder against the concrete wall, his chest heaving, and his head pounding. *Why am I doing this?*

But as he rested there a moment, Michael heard footsteps approaching. *Soldiers?* he thought, starting to panic. He looked around and noticed a gate farther down the wall. He jumped up and ducked through it into another quiet courtyard, then crouched down. He could tell he was in someone's yard. A house was across the courtyard, similar in design to Leah's. Lamps were burning brightly on the second floor, but he couldn't hear any voices.

All the thoughts that he'd tried so hard to dispel these last few days with logic and lagging faith now came rushing back to haunt him. This was it. If these events were truly unfolding—and he was here to bear witness—could this be the night of the Last Supper? And if so, would it be some form of blasphemy to consider warning Jesus? What would happen if he altered anything, assuming he even could at this point? Would fate, or perhaps something more divine, simply lead the soldiers to Jesus some other time? Would they still crucify him? What if he could find Judas and stop him? Should he?

Most important, he could no longer avoid the biggest question of all: if Jesus didn't die tomorrow, what would it all mean for everyone?

A high-pitched voice engaged in whispered conversation broke his concentration. Michael waited a moment until the sounds of shuffling feet had receded before cautiously making his way back through the gate and onto the road. He could see a group of men walking about thirty yards ahead. As he followed them at a safe distance, Michael soon recognized the bald man talking to his bearded friend from the market. Surrounding them were about twenty soldiers dressed in purple cloaks, walking in twos. They were carrying sharp spears and lit torches.

It was an odd procession, but Michael felt as if he'd seen it before. Slowly the realization dawned on him, though he tried desperately to find another answer or excuse. The whole scene felt like a reenactment of one of the most terrifying stories in the Bible. He looked more closely at the bearded man. *Oh, no, not him.*

The bearded man led the soldiers through the gate of a walled garden. Michael kept his distance but followed closely enough so as not to lose them. When they abruptly stopped, he hid behind a tree that was rooted just outside the stone wall enclosing the garden. From there he could see the man draw near someone kneeling in prayer at the foot of a tree. He watched in horror, knowing what was coming.

The bearded man approached Jesus, then kissed him on the cheek.

An explosion of activity erupted as the soldiers began to shout, brandishing their spears. In response, the apostles leaped to their feet, flanking Jesus. Their fists were raised and Michael found Judas mes-merizing—he was moving toward them, as if to join their ranks. Then Michael saw Jesus put his hand up as a sign of peace. All eyes in the crowd instinctively followed him. Then he stretched his hands before him in a gesture of surrender. The soldiers immediately surrounded him and began to lead him from the garden.

Jesus is coming my way! Michael thought as the group approached. He leaned back farther into the shadows behind the tree. *I can try and stop this. I can fix this. This isn't how this has to go down. He doesn't have to die. Not this way. I should do something now. He doesn't have to die.*

But as Jesus drew near, Michael was too terrified to move. He was paralyzed by indecision, unable to even call out to him. He covered his face with his hands until they passed.

When he could no longer hear them, he stood up, dazed. He started to run in the opposite direction but slammed into one of the soldiers.

"Out of my way!" the soldier shouted, shoving Michael to the ground and pressing a spear to his chest. "Do you want to live?"

"Yes," Michael gasped.

The soldier kept his spear near Michael's racing heart. "Were you in the garden with that rebel?"

Michael was silent.

"Are you one of his followers?"

Michael felt the spear scratch against his skin, knowing it was leaving a mark. He slowly looked down. "No."

The man withdrew the spear. "Get out of here!" he growled.

Michael rolled to his side, hiding his face. He lingered for a mo-ment, stunned with the knowledge that he now possessed. *I'm no better than Peter.*

From the corner of his eye, he saw Judas running out of the gar-den. Anger flared through his own humiliation, propelling him to his feet.

Michael sprinted after Judas into a deserted field just beyond the garden walls. He slowed to a jog as he watched Judas collapse near a large rock. He put his hands to his face, his body heaving with cries of sorrow. His wrenching sobs were heartbreaking.

Watching Judas, Michael felt the fury that had raged within him only a few moments ago evaporate. He had not only just watched the greatest betrayal in mankind's history take place, but had even played a part in it himself. With that realization came pity, despair, and a surprising sense of mercy.

Judas continued to weep as Michael slowly approached. The sound of his sandals alerted Judas, who raised his head to look at Michael, his face red. "Are you here to stone me?"

"I was."

"Then do it now." Judas fixed his gaze, searching Michael for a reason. "If it's the money you want, you can have it." He pulled the satchel from his belt and threw it to him, hitting Michael squarely in the chest. The bag dropped to the ground with a loud thud, spilling its contents in a pool at his feet.

Michael flinched with disgust. "I don't want your money."

"Then what do you want from me?"

"An answer."

Judas looked away. "I have nothing for you then."

Michael stepped over the fallen money and stood above him. "Why did you do it?"

Judas pulled himself upright to look Michael in the face. "The others will come for me soon. You should go."

"Tell me why you did it and I'll leave."

Judas wiped his eyes with the sleeve of his robe. "Why would I betray him, my friend, my rabbi? Why would I hurt him when my life has only been about me doing whatever he willed?" Judas glanced up into the night sky, a bitter smile curving his lips. "Maybe I'm the devil?"

Michael felt his skin crawl as Judas' smile spread across his face. He stepped back and shivered involuntarily.

Judas' smile vanished, replaced with a pained sneer. "Maybe I am.

I feel like I am." His eyes filled with fresh tears. "It wasn't supposed to be like this."

"What do you mean?"

Judas jerked to his feet. "I mean, he wasn't supposed to let them take him. I thought he and the others would fight back. Finally, it was time for him to fight, to defeat them, to stop the Romans. To rise up and defeat our oppressors!"

Michael shifted uneasily. "Did you really think he would?"

Judas hunched his shoulders and didn't reply.

Michael continued, "Look, I'm the last person to preach, believe me. But I do know that Jesus' teachings always seemed so nonconfrontational, so selfless, so kind. He was all about love and peace, not violence and hate. He's not someone to use a sword."

Judas glared back. "You don't know him like I do. I saw him do things that no other man could do. Things that were impossible to believe, and yet I did and so many of us did. He said he was the Son of God, the King of Kings! He's more powerful than anyone, anything. Everything bad can be changed. Every wrong righted. He is the Son of God. Or I thought he was."

"But now you're not sure?"

"He went without a fight! He surrendered! They're just going to kill him. He won't rise up now and defeat anyone. They will beat him, destroy him. The crowd will only see him as weak. No one will stand up for him. No one is that brave."

Judas paused a moment, then continued in a whisper. "We can't stop them from killing him." His head dropped into his outstretched hands, and he began to weep again. "I've killed my friend."

Michael grabbed him by the shoulder, shaking him. "Come back with me, Judas! It's not too late. We can give the money back. Tell them you've made a mistake. He isn't the one. Tell them he isn't claiming to be the Son of God. Just tell the soldiers he isn't the one."

Judas glanced at Michael with sorrow. "You don't understand. He *is* the one." Judas' shoulders rounded as he sank to the ground.

Michael fell to his knees frantically, pulling at Judas. "Stop it! It's not too late. We can still do something about this! Get up and at least try!"

Michael seized him by the arm, but Judas pulled away from his grasp. "Stop your crying! We've got to do something. We just can't let this happen." Michael snatched at him again, but still Judas would not budge.

"Just go," Judas mumbled. He lifted his head to look at Michael. "The others are coming for me. You will be in jeopardy. I am nothing. Worse than that: I just betrayed my friend."

"Don't say you're nothing. You helped me when I was in need. Let me help you."

Judas was resigned. "I'm about to feel God's wrath. It's best I face this alone."

"The God I believe in loves everyone. I thought you said you believed?"

Judas stood up. "My faith has never wavered. I believe in my whole heart. He is who he says he is."

"All right, let's go back then."

Judas laughed harshly. "It's too late. I have nothing to live for. I have lost everything, by my own hand."

He suddenly began to tear at the hem of his robe, glancing around. As he started toward a nearby tree, Michael grabbed his arm.

"I'm not going to let you do that."

Judas slapped at Michael's hand, but caught him instead on the cheek and freed himself. Michael fell back, bewildered. "Leave me. Be my friend or become my last enemy." Judas continued on, stopping under the tree, its gnarled branches arching over them. He started to reach up with the torn piece from his robe. Michael raced over and tackled him to the ground.

"Even your life is important."

The two wrestled in the dirt, each struggling to gain an advantage. Finally, Michael pinned his knee on Judas' chest.

Judas looked up at him, pleading, "Please, go. You know you will lose your life."

A loud noise in the distance startled them. Michael rolled off as they both looked toward the commotion, listening intently.

Judas pulled himself up on his elbows. "See? You're going to get killed if you don't leave."

"Well, I'm not—"

Whack. Dazed and with pain searing from the base of his skull, Michael was thrown forward on his hands and knees and collapsed in the dirt.

The screens that covered the porch were tearing, and their flapping had become a constant distraction to his daily meditation. Trying to find a reprieve, he moved out to the small, thin cement stoop in front of the shabby three-story house. Michael tried to focus but his mind was overwhelmed with new problems.

Usually he closed his eyes and allowed himself to drift off to a boat bobbing on a calm ocean during a hot summer day. He tried several times to place himself on that familiar sailboat, but each time he opened his eyes, anxious, angry, and bitter.

Michael watched the kids swat at a Wiffle ball up and down 191st Avenue. He smiled, then closed his eyes once more. Almost instantly he heard the *bang,* followed by a screeching, cyclical *whir.* The alarm on the Stewarts' blue Chevy pierced the Richmond Hill neighborhood in World War II fashion. *Oh, jeez.*

Glaring at the kids who were giggling, he stormed over to the 1975 model and cracked the side of the passenger door with his foot. The noise waffled to a halt. He sighed and sat down again.

The kids continued to play. *Whack.* The street's biggest kid belted a drive off a tree that careened off the top of Michael's head. A burst of laughter erupted from the other kids.

Michael opened his eyes. He looked at Ian, who had his hands over his mouth, waiting for a reaction. Usually he would joke and play sports with Ian and his friends. Today he was in no mood.

"Do you want to hit?" Ian asked, rubbing the top of his crew cut nervously back and forth with his hand.

"Not today, Ian," Michael replied sternly.

"Hey, kids, I'll play for Mr. Grouchy," said a voice from down the block. It was Michael's friend Chuck, who lived on the far end of the street. He tossed the ball to Ian, then pulled at the tips of his own hair, exaggerating its spiky appearance. Ian smiled.

Chuck could always do that to the kids. His big smile and gracious demeanor endeared him to the youngsters. "I'll be with you guys in a second," he shouted.

He sat down next to Michael. "Hey, how's everything?"

"Just wonderful."

"I'm guessing things aren't wonderful."

"You guess right."

Chuck squirmed unconsciously before changing course. "Hey, I thought you were going to the club in the Rockaways to meet my sister last night."

Michael looked skyward. "Oh, God . . . I forgot."

Chuck's sister, Jeanette, was the cutest thing in the neighborhood. She loved sports and was one of the few girls on the block who was close to Michael's age. He had liked Jeanette for a long time but could never muster up the nerve to ask her out. But when she finally sent him a cryptic message to meet her at a club, he had blown it.

"She's a little confused," Chuck said. "My sister waited for you."

Michael took a deep breath. He picked up a rock from the grassless garden behind him and flung it across the street. "I'm sorry. I couldn't do anything about it. I feel terrible."

"What happened?"

"My mom."

"Again?"

"Yeah. She went back to the hospital last night. My father brought her home this morning."

"How is she?"

Michael shook his head.

Before Chuck could respond, the screen door behind them slammed. "Michael, go upstairs and spend some time with your mother for a while," his father ordered.

"Got to go, Chuck."

"I'll be around if you need to talk. Let me know if you need anything."

Michael gave his friend a playful pat on the shoulder before scurrying up the peeling, wooden steps. He walked gingerly into the house and even more cautiously up the stairs to the second floor.

He cracked the door and peered in to see if his mom was awake. Rebecca was silent, lying on her back. Michael moved a few steps closer and settled his body near the windowsill, watching her, wondering what had happened in such a short time.

He knew she had a beautiful heart—he knew this with absolute certainty—but as she lay motionless in front of him, that seemed to be the only thing about her that had remained untouched. Trying not to disturb her, Michael walked quietly over to her bed. Who would have expected that it would be this quick? Drawing nearer, he rested his hand on her knee for a moment before recoiling in horror. Through the heavy blankets, he could only feel bone—no muscle, no fat, no softness—just bone.

He wondered where all her beauty had gone. The thick brown hair that was her trademark was gone, replaced now with bare skin and clusters of radiation burns by her brow. Her once muscular arms were withered and small. Worst of all were her eyes. Those luminous hazel eyes were dull, her eyesight nearly gone. His sister Sam had said that she might recover her sight, but staring down at her now, he knew that was just wishful thinking.

She was still sleeping, and for a moment Michael considered how easy it would be to leave undetected. This wasn't what he wanted.

Watching her waste away ripped his insides apart. But something pulled him closer to her and he sat gently at the foot of her bed. Michael cleared his throat quietly, so as not to startle her. Leaning down, he whispered into her ear, "Mom, I'm here. It's Mike."

His mother opened her eyes, a faint smile registering across her face.

He began again. "Hey, what happened here? You were walking around just two weeks ago."

"God is asking me to leave, Michael," she said softly, before he could finish.

"No. No, I prayed, Mom. I asked God to stop the sickness. Every night I did. It's not time. You just have to keep going, keep fighting. This is only your fifth inning. We've got more baseball games to go to . . . this isn't the end."

"Mike, I wish it were up to me now. You know—"

"Mom, who am I going to go to baseball games with?" His voice trailed off the instant he felt a wet tear spill onto his cheek.

"I don't have the strength anymore."

He couldn't stand her talking like this: resolved, giving up. He stood up abruptly, walking over to the St. Jude statue she kept on her bureau. He wanted to break it in half.

I can't believe I didn't see this coming. "Is this the way God wants you to leave, Mom? Look at what he has allowed to happen."

"A lot happened in this house, didn't it? I'm sorry, Michael."

Michael glanced back over his shoulder at her, his eyes catching the cross hanging over her bed. "We have to do something. We've got to get you back to the hospital. Now." He walked over to her, reaching down to lift her up.

Rebecca started to groan. Her face tightened as Michael wedged his hands under her legs. "Michael, no . . . no . . . no . . . Please don't. I'm in so much pain. Please."

He fell to his knees beside her, his head coming to rest on the edge of the bed. He could feel her fingers straining to touch his hair. He lowered his head slightly so she could reach him, but then heard her soft sobs. He lifted his head to look into her eyes, seeing the tears that dripped to the sides of her cheeks. He reached for a tissue on the nightstand to wipe them away.

"Mom, I really need you to stay. You have to fight. I need you here."

Michael touched her thin fingers. He leaned over to whisper in her ear, "Mom, I've got to do something, I just can't sit here and watch you die like this."

Rebecca's sobs grew more defined.

"Oh, Mom, I'm sorry."

"I'm sorry, too. I'm sorry for doing this to you."

He looked at his mother in amazement, before closing his eyes and bringing his head down close to hers so that their foreheads met. "Why are you sorry? Why? You have nothing to be sorry about."

Rebecca moaned and jerked her head sideways.

"What's wrong, Mom?"

"The pain, Michael . . . the pain . . . it's so bad . . . please do something . . . please . . ."

"What? What can I do?"

"Take the pillow, Michael . . ."

"Do you want me to put another under your head? Under your feet?" he asked as he grabbed a pillow from the far end of the bed.

"No. No. Please end my pain." Rebecca squirmed. Her ravaged face tightened as another wave of pain engulfed her fragile frame.

"I don't know what you mean."

"Put the pillow over my face and hold me."

"What?"

She groaned again. "I can't take this anymore. Please do it."

Michael stood up, horrified. "I can't. Let me take you to the hospital, get you some painkillers."

"No. No, please, no more hospitals."

Rebecca thrust her hand out toward him, struggling to find him. Losing strength, Michael crumpled down beside her, taking her hand gingerly into his own.

"Please, Michael, let me go to God without any more pain."

"God, Mom. Why don't you ask Dad? I can't . . ."

"He would never do it. Oh, please, I can't bear this anymore." She squeezed his hand in a halfhearted attempt to underscore her feelings.

"Oh, Mom, I don't want you to be in pain anymore but . . ."

"Hold me when you do it. I'll go straight from your hands to God's."

He leaned again near her left ear. "I love you, Mom. You'll see, someday we'll be together in heaven. We'll both be there with Jesus."

Michael stood up. He looked down and memories of his mother flooded his mind: her gleaming smile that outshone his beautiful red bike that Christmas morning, her favorite chocolate-crunch bars she filled their Easter baskets with, his surprise and complete delight at hearing her guttural cheer when Billy Martin returned to the Yankees on Old-Timers' Day, her peaceful countenance that greeted him when he stepped off the stage at his Molloy High School graduation, and the colorful birthday cakes she baked for him the first of each March.

His body trembled and shook. He held the pillow in both hands and tried to compose himself. He watched as his mom fended off another round of piercing pain. Michael buried his face in the pillow to silence his sobs.

He removed the pillow from his face to look at her. He edged forward. As he lowered his arms, the door flung open.

His father stopped abruptly, scowling at him. "What are you doing?"

Michael was unable to speak. His father ran at him, and he suddenly relaxed, allowing himself to be pushed against the wall.

"What were you doing!?" his father demanded.

Michael dropped the pillow and pushed his father away. "I was trying to help her. She's in a lot of pain."

His father spoke in a hushed, direct tone. "You don't think I know that? Don't you think I'm trying my best here?"

Rebecca moaned. His father instinctively dropped his grip from Michael's arm and moved quickly to her side.

"Please, Jim, I'm in so much pain," she whimpered.

"Okay, honey, we'll get you back to the hospital."

With the receiver to his ear, Michael was already dialing 9 on the rotary phone.

The throbbing in his head mimicked the rhythmic beat of a phone dial, reminding him first of those late mornings after a night spent at one of the university bars. But the smell of death was what fully roused him. Rolling onto his back, Michael found himself in the shadow of a tree, his lungs heavy with dust. Unsure of himself, he looked around slowly trying to remember where he was.

The distant sound of crickets chirping their love song across the mountainside was his only response. The sound seemed to sear through his skull, resonating far too deeply in his ears. He winced as his fingers found the raised bump on the back of his head.

Then he broke from his reverie, finally remembering the circumstances of his meeting with Judas. Michael struggled to sit up. He tried to take a deep breath, but a spasm of dry coughs overwhelmed him. The full moon cast a perplexing shadow on the ground before him. Looking up, he immediately recognized the limp, motionless body of Judas, suspended from a tree branch, his head hanging at a grotesque angle.

"Oh, Lord, no," he moaned.

Michael stumbled to his feet, tripping twice on the rocky ground. He felt drawn to Judas, but as he neared, his body seemed to slow in reverence. "Why did you do it?" he pleaded, now standing close enough to touch Judas' bare foot. "Why? We could have stopped this."

Michael stepped back from the body, trying to determine how to get Judas down. He felt repulsed by the body, yet somehow obligated to help him. The torn cloth he was hanging from had been thrown over the branch, its ends tied to form the noose. Michael would only be able to get the body down if he either cut the rope or untied the knot from around Judas' neck. The former seemed implausible, the latter, inexcusable. He looked on the ground around him for something sharp. About ten feet away, his eyes noticed the open bag of coins, gleaming like knives in the moonlight.

He heard a commotion from the top of the hill and saw the outline of a group of seven or eight men in the distance. Michael staggered toward the coins, as if to hide the evidence of his friend's betrayal. He grabbed at the bag, but the pouch had split along its seam, allowing coins to scatter on the ground below.

"Is that him?" he heard a man shout.

"I don't know," cried another. "It's too dark to see."

A stone whizzed by Michael's head, striking a branch behind him, cracking the night's silence. He wrapped the bag in his hands, holding it tightly as he ran up a short, steep hill. At the top, he hid behind the craggy trunk of a towering tree. He watched as the men gathered under the dangling corpse.

"Why did you do it?" howled one man, jabbing awkwardly at Judas' leg like a boxer before a punching bag. "You didn't have to do it! Why? Why? God have pity on you . . . on all of us!" Another from the group moved closer, pinning the man's arms behind him.

Michael watched, eyes brimming with tears. Unconsciously, he leaned his head against the tree for support. As he did this, he caught their attention.

"Look! Somebody's up there." The man pointed toward Michael.

"Leave him be," said another.

Michael started backing up, carefully keeping his frame behind the tree, tightening his grip on the pouch of money.

"I'm going to get him," the man said in reply. He started to sprint up the hill.

Michael turned on one foot, running off blindly into the night. He moved like a wild beast, thrashing through whatever lay in his path. He looped back, down past the far wall of the garden, and once again onto the serpentine streets within the city walls. He kept one eye out for danger, but the other for someone else: the bald man.

I'll just give the money back, he thought again and again.

Leah knelt on the mat, stunned by Michael's sudden departure. The glow from the waning lamps suddenly felt too intense, too intrusive. She wondered if she appeared as foolish as she felt. The bowls and cups that had held such promise throughout the meal now were empty; sitting there alone, she felt solidarity with them.

"Oh, Michael," she sighed softly.

Pulling herself smoothly to her feet, she looked out through the open window. Even with the moonlight, she saw little, which was exactly what she expected. The best view of the road was from her roof.

Resigned, Leah crept quietly to the ladder, glancing at the sleeping Elizabeth as she passed. She knew it was finally time to look, yet she struggled to find footing on the bottom rung. It had been so much easier with Michael here; she had felt almost drawn the other night. Tonight, every muscle fought her, and even her normally obedient hands needed extra guidance.

Instead of throwing her leg up onto the roof at the top of the ladder, Leah slid to her knees. She prayed silently for strength before rising to her feet. Her attention focused not on the balustrade to her right, or to the far side where she had shown Michael the view of the mountains, but to a spot immediately behind her. Then, as if in a trance, she glided there, stopping mere inches from the roof's edge.

Her body grew still but her mind whirled, flooding her with images that she had long ago discarded. Over the past two years, she had refused to see the scene in its entirety. Glancing down now, she saw everything: the road, the spear, the soldier standing over his motionless body. Closing her eyes, she could hear the blood spill into his throat, so that his call for her was not muffled or breathy, but instead gurgled out of him.

But now with Yochanan everywhere around her, beneath her, and within her, her mind focused on the one thing that she had most feared. By letting it all come back to her, the chasm was open and she could recognize everything for what it was. No longer could she forget, no longer could she imagine. If everything has a beginning, middle, and end, what happens when the middle plays again?

How can I let Michael be here?

Elizabeth awoke with a mild headache and found her attempts to go back to sleep futile. She was thirsty and got to her feet to find a cup of water. "Leah?" she called, spying the glow from the lamps still lit on the dining mat beyond her.

With no light emanating from the kitchen below, and the courtyard dark and silent, Elizabeth climbed up the ladder to the roof. At first she thought it was deserted, but when she turned her head at the top, she saw Leah standing with her back toward her. "Leah?" she called softly.

Leah shivered once, her arms pulled tightly to her sides. She spun back, alarmed. "Yes?" she whispered breathlessly.

"What are you doing?"

Leah shook her head gently, her expression locked into a grimace. "Nothing." She stepped toward Elizabeth. "Is your father back?"

Having pulled herself partially up onto the roof, Elizabeth stopped abruptly. "What? Where'd he go?" She scowled at Leah.

Leah hesitated. "Let me explain." She walked to Elizabeth, offering a hand to help her up to the roof. They made their way to the balustrade, where Leah sat immediately; Elizabeth lingered a moment before sitting down next to her.

"Okay, now tell me what happened."

Leah looked out into the night sky. "He left right after dinner, soon after he had moved you to your bedroll. We started talking and then he ran."

"What did you say to him?"

Leah rubbed at her temples. "I don't remember exactly. It seems very foolish now. I think I told him that he made me believe . . . although now I am no longer certain *what in*."

Elizabeth frowned. "And he didn't say where he was going?"

Leah shook her head.

"Oh, great," Elizabeth said worriedly. "We've got to find him. It's pitch-black out there. He could be lost."

"I know," Leah sighed. "It is not safe out there for him. But it is also not safe for us, especially you."

"I don't care about my safety," replied Elizabeth, standing. "You should probably stay anyway—he is *my* father. I bet he went into the city. He seems confused—he told me he wanted to find my mom here somehow. He misses Mom so much."

Leah was skeptical. "Why would she be here? How is Michael going to find her?"

"It would take too long to explain. But he believes someone he thought he saw could help him. To tell you the truth, I don't know if he did or not. But he believes he did." Elizabeth started toward the ladder.

Leah was unconvinced, but threw her hands up weakly in protest. "Elizabeth?"

"I'm going," Elizabeth said as she stepped down onto the first rung, "even if it means I try this alone."

Leah nervously fingered her robe, pressing it down around her knees. She sighed. "I will come with you, though. I do care about both of you."

Elizabeth glanced over her shoulder, a smile spreading across her face. "Thank you," she said gratefully.

Michael first saw the undulating heat waves, wafting high in the sky, before he could make out the crowded fire pit below. As he drew near the edge of the sunken courtyard, he felt an enormous sense of relief: apparently, the man pursuing him had given up. His eyes focused on those lounging around the roaring flames: soldiers and villagers alike, seeking warmth in the night.

A cluster of soldiers were sipping some kind of hot brew while others were huddled together, whispering. Michael was aware that the darkness fully shielded him, yet he was worried about the inherent dangers of the crowd. These soldiers seemed almost tranquil, but he knew that could change in a second. He was strategizing how to get back to Leah's when he felt the weight in his hand, realizing he still had Judas' purse.

Oh, no, I've got the money! I've got to give this back. His mind whirled.

The soldiers stood abruptly, forming a tight pack as if an unheard signal had been sounded. They retreated back into the streets from the opposite side of the courtyard, leaving just a few villagers around the fire. Michael became determined to get rid of the silver, hoping one of them knew where he could find the bald man. He strolled quickly into the courtyard, stopping next to a man in a muddied robe, his hood covering the top of his head and the sides of his face.

"Excuse me, sir," Michael said quietly. "I'm trying to find a man I met earlier. He was bald and wearing a purple sash."

"Why are you asking me?" the man asked roughly.

"Well," Michael stammered, "I have some money from one of the Rabbi's followers."

"You *what?*"

"Shh," said Michael, sitting quickly next to the man, their shoulders now touching.

Two townspeople swiftly moved to them. "What's the problem here?" asked one.

"Nothing," the hooded man replied.

One of the villagers looked at Michael and then at the man. He pushed the hood off the man's head, exposing his face and neck. Judging by the dark circles under his eyes, the man hadn't slept in days.

"Weren't you the man seen with Jesus?" the villager asked suspiciously.

"No." The man shook his head in earnest.

"Are you sure you aren't one of his followers? I thought I saw you with him."

The man rose to his feet, his frame large and imposing. "I am not that person. I have never seen that man."

Michael grew anxious. Fearing a confrontation, he quickly got to his feet and took off into the night. Only several seconds later, Michael recognized the screeching cock's crowing as if it were an alarm. He let the weight fall from his grasp, the split pouch of coins cascading onto the stone ground below, ricocheting in every direction.

The pebbles on the road felt like tacks through his worn sandals, but he didn't stop. He looked for the easiest path back to Leah's and slowed only when he was sure no one was near.

"I'm lost again," he gasped through heaving breaths.

In the silence, Michael heard someone calling his name. He stood motionless. The voice grew clearer as he saw two familiar figures up ahead.

"Michael? Michael, is that you?" Leah called softly.

He walked quickly toward them and whispered loudly, "Yes, I'm here!"

"Are you all right, Dad? Leah said you ran out."

"I know, I'm sorry." He wrapped Elizabeth in a big hug. "I got lost. Where are we?"

Leah pointed to his right. "My home is over there. We're not too far away." She noticed blood on his clothes. "Are you hurt?"

"I'm okay." Michael stopped, turning toward her.

"Is everything okay, Dad?" Elizabeth asked.

He paused. "No, actually nothing is 'okay.' Elizabeth, should we be doing something to make this all stop?"

Elizabeth stared at him. "What do you mean?"

"I saw Judas die, and Jesus being led away. Peter denied him. And I did nothing. *Nothing!*"

"But, Dad," Elizabeth said, shaking him by the shoulders, "what could you have done?"

They walked back to Leah's house in silence. As they entered through the front gate, Michael finally felt a sense of peace.

13

BURDENS

Michael awoke with a throbbing headache. But as he rubbed his eyes, he felt relieved that the air was cool and dark. When he stood up, he noticed that he had an extra blanket wrapped around him. He saw two flickering lamps in the distance still burning from the night before.

It's time to go. We don't belong here. There's nothing more we can do.

His aching legs carried him across the rooftop as he measured each step so he wouldn't fall. He staggered near the head of the ladder but made his way down safely. He saw no one on the second floor so he proceeded down to the first. Leah was in the kitchen by the fire while Elizabeth was in the next stall, petting Cassie.

Leah looked up at Michael. "How are you? How do you feel?"

He gingerly rubbed his head. "I've been better, but we really have to get going."

"Of course. Breakfast soon will be ready," Leah said.

"No, we've got to leave now. Elizabeth, get your things."

"Okay, Dad," she said as she passed Leah in the kitchen on her way to the ladder.

Leah gave him a puzzled look. "Why now?"

"It's Good Friday. This is the day they will crucify Jesus. There'll probably be no one on the streets. They'll all be in the courtyard. With everything going on today, it's the best time."

"Let me get my veil." Leah looked at Michael sadly. "Drink some water before you go," she said as she proceeded upstairs.

Elizabeth appeared with a fresh robe tucked under her arm. Michael met her at the foot of the ladder.

"Listen, I want to talk about last night."

"Dad, you don't have to."

"No, I want to," he said, following her. "I got lost when I was out. I saw Judas. I spoke to him. I asked him why he did it, and he said he thought Jesus would rise up against the Romans."

Elizabeth's eyes widened. "Are you sure?"

"I'm sure. He told me just before he . . ." Michael paused. "Well, before he killed himself. I tried to stop him. I tried to convince him to give the money back and stop it all. But he wouldn't listen to me. He must have hit me hard. When I woke up . . . oh, it was awful. His body was hanging from a tree."

Elizabeth gasped. "Oh, Dad!"

"Today's the crucifixion."

"How can you be so *sure*?"

"I saw everything in that garden last night when they handed Jesus over to the Romans."

"What?"

"Yeah, it was unreal. But think about it: we've been here a week, and each day when we wake up, another event is happening. It was Palm Sunday five days ago. Last night was the Last Supper. I literally saw him being handed over to the soldiers. I heard him tell the apostles to put down their swords! Today has to be Good Friday. We've got to go now while we can."

Elizabeth hesitated, weighing what he was saying, but then turned to him. "But we can help him! We can stop them from killing Jesus!"

Michael wrapped his arms around her. "I tried to help him last night. I had a chance, but I froze when I saw the soldiers taking him from the garden. I tried to convince Judas to come back with me, but I couldn't save him either. I'm not going to try again today, knowing that you may never get back, knowing that it will do no good. Last night the streets were empty with just a few soldiers around. Today there will be hundreds more. And there will be angry crowds. I can't lose you."

Elizabeth pulled away. "But we could *try*. We *have* to try."

Michael exhaled slowly. His voice trembled. "But *should* we? If we change this, Elizabeth, if we stop it or even just slow it down, what does it mean for everybody else? They always told us growing up that his crucifixion was part of this great plan for the world, and heaven. 'God sent his only son' for this to happen, right?"

Elizabeth stared at him accusingly. "You always told me to help other people, and yet, *once again,* you're backing away. Can't we try?" She rattled Cassie's gate. "Daddy, please."

Michael stretched his arms out resignedly and Elizabeth hugged him.

"Okay, we'll go," she agreed quietly. "What about the soldier who's looking for me? He's going to be after us, right?"

Michael nodded. "I know. He's frightening, but I believe that today all the soldiers will be there with Jesus. There's a good chance that the soldier won't be near the tunnel."

Leah came down the ladder carrying a white veil. "Put this on," she said, motioning to Elizabeth. Her face grew worried as she watched Elizabeth wrap the veil around herself.

When they passed through the front gate, Michael stopped to close it behind them. He looked at the quiet, vacant house.

"Thank you," he said to Leah, touching her arm.

Leah moved expertly through the maze of streets, her brisk pace never slowing. Although it was eerily quiet when they first left Leah's, a distant roar soon pierced the morning solitude.

Michael felt worn down, racked with guilt over his actions the night before. *I'm sorry, Jesus, I should have helped last night. I couldn't and now I can't help today. I'm sorry.*

"Dad! Look!"

Michael realized that they were just outside the courtyard where they had met Leah. From the road, he could see Jesus standing on the big marble steps in front of hundreds of people.

"Oh, no," he said under his breath.

Turning back to the road, Michael saw in the distance the alley leading to the tunnel. *It's right there! We can leave right now. It's safe.* But when he looked over and saw Jesus in front of the angry mob, he felt drawn. He knew he couldn't leave. Not like this.

"Elizabeth. Come on."

They walked slowly through the massive gates into the courtyard. They were quickly surrounded as more people swarmed in. The crowd seemed angry, even ravenous.

"Daddy, I'm scared," Elizabeth whispered under her breath.

Leah grabbed her hand and looked deeply into her eyes. "I'm here. I won't leave you."

Elizabeth tightened her grip on Leah's hand and let herself be led farther into the courtyard.

The noise around them escalated to a fever pitch when a new man, not the high priest but a noble-looking man—a true Roman—strolled out before them. He was escorted by several soldiers to the edge of the stairs, where he stood, surveying the scene. He watched as more soldiers came marching in from the right, their spears and armor gleaming in the early-morning sunlight. The crowd parted quickly for the soldiers, who quickly surrounded Jesus.

"What crime has this man committed?" the Roman shouted to the crowd of soldiers.

"He has claimed to be the Son of God," one of them replied.

Michael grabbed Leah's arm tightly. "Leah, is that man at the top of the stairs named Pontius Pilate?"

Leah nodded.

"He's the man we saw at the parade on Palm Sunday, Dad," said Elizabeth.

Michael reached down to hold Leah's hand, and she grabbed it tightly. Pilate called out to the crowd, asking them which prisoner should be released as a gift from the Romans. Michael stood trans-fixed, horrified at the cries around him.

"Barabbas," they cried. "Barabbas!"

Elizabeth looked at her father in disbelief. He rubbed her back quickly to reassure her. The atmosphere was chaotic and confusing, making it hard for them to follow the proceedings.

The crowd began to shout again. *"Crucify him, crucify him!"*

Leah turned to Michael and whispered fiercely, "This is unbear-able."

Stunned by the scene, Elizabeth leaned her head against Leah's shoulder.

Michael looked at them. "Elizabeth, you must stay with Leah at all times. If we get split up, go back to the house."

Elizabeth and Leah nodded as the crowd grew louder, swelling up closer to the stairs.

"Would you crucify this man who has done nothing wrong?" Pilate asked the crowd again. "Shouldn't he be the one set free?"

"Barabbas! Release Barabbas!"

Pilate motioned to his guards, who brought Barabbas out to the cheering crowd. Their howling overwhelmed Pilate, and he relented by freeing Barabbas. Then Jesus, with his hands tied, his legs badly bruised, and bloodstains on his torn clothes, was led down the stairs into the courtyard.

"Go now," Michael urged.

But swarms of people had entered after them, blocking their exit. Michael could feel the thrust of the crowd propelling him backward. He heard the soldiers taunting Jesus with lewd cries—*"Our king, our king!"*—but Michael was unable to see what they were doing.

A Roman soldier stood on the marble stairs to the far right with a whip in his hand. Michael realized with horror that the soldier was stretching, loosening his shoulders much the way a baseball player does in an on-deck circle. A moment later, Michael saw the soldier run down the stairs to join the others beating Jesus.

The sickening sounds of leather striking flesh knifed through his ears. Elizabeth was openly sobbing under her veil while Leah held her. It seemed to go on and on. Michael couldn't imagine how anyone could endure it.

"No more! Please!" Elizabeth screamed before Leah could push her face back into her chest.

The smell of blood was thick around them.

"Stop! Please!" Michael howled.

A soldier ran through the crowd toward Michael. When he was near, he thrust his spear toward Michael's stomach. He fell backward into the crowd, his head slamming against the stone ground.

"Be quiet!" the soldier shouted.

Elizabeth and Leah helped Michael back to his feet. He was dazed.

"It's too dangerous here," he said to them. "Go!"

"Dad, I'm not leaving you. Are you okay?"

Michael nodded weakly. "Yes. Please, you need to go. I'll be right behind you. Please."

But just then the beating stopped, and the soldiers broke into the crowd, creating a path. One of the soldiers brushed against Michael.

Looking out behind them as they passed, he could see Jesus' limp body lying by the stairs on the ground. Michael turned away, covering Elizabeth's face with his hands.

"Don't look!"

Michael watched the soldiers pull Jesus to his feet before placing a big wooden crossbar on his back. They began to push him forward.

"Stop!" Michael screamed.

Jesus staggered a few steps, unable to keep his balance, and tumbled back to the stone pavement. The beam bounded off the ground and lay at his side while the soldiers surrounded him, laughing maliciously.

"Stop this!" Elizabeth yelled.

"Take her home," Michael pleaded over his shoulder to Leah. But Leah pushed forward with the crowd, trying to get a look at Jesus.

"Who will help him?" shouted a soldier.

Leah released her hand from Elizabeth and stepped forward. "I will!"

"No!" Michael yelled. He yanked her back toward Elizabeth, but she resisted. "You can't do this. They'll hurt you if you fall. Let me do it."

He paused, grabbing her shoulder to make her look into his eyes. "Your place is with my daughter," he said to her.

Leah stared back at him, her face blank. She leaned forward and kissed his cheek while Elizabeth grabbed Leah's arm. Michael turned from them and stepped out from the crowd toward the soldiers, his hand raised.

"Pick it up!" one of them commanded.

Michael bent down on one knee, bracing himself to pick up the heavy crossbar. As he tried to get a grip on it, he looked over and saw Jesus on his knees. Their eyes met. Michael wanted to look away but couldn't.

"Are you here to lift your burden or to help me with mine?" Jesus whispered to him.

Michael stared.

"Get up!" a soldier commanded.

Michael looked at the crossbar and then again directly into Jesus' eyes. The other man stared back with total understanding and empathy, and Michael was dumbfounded. How could Jesus be worrying about him—about Michael Stewart—at a moment like this? The sudden realization made him weep.

Jesus looked at him forlornly. "Heartbreak is necessary for one to understand how great God's gift of time truly is."

Michael's body heaved a couple of times as he tried to regain his composure.

"Don't look too far, Michael. Your daughter can lift your burden," Jesus said.

The soldier grew impatient. "I said, *get up!*" He kicked hard into the softness of Michael's back.

The blow rattled him, throwing him off-balance. But he quickly planted his feet again and lifted the heavy beam. It was rough in his hands and he felt tiny splinters dig into his skin as he hoisted it up onto his shoulder. His knees buckled but he regained his footing and walked slowly out of the courtyard. Michael could hear Jesus as he, too, was kicked to his feet. But with the crossbar so heavy and the crowd so tight around them, Michael couldn't turn to see him.

"Follow me!" the soldier demanded, leading them out onto the road.

Michael wasn't sure if it was a drop of rain that hit the top of his head or a tear from heaven.

"I'll stop when I want to stop," Vicki teased, looking at him with a smile.

Michael looked straight ahead, occasionally wiping the front of the car window as he identified the Queens storefronts they passed. Just after the movie theater, he said, "Okay, slow down now and park on the next block."

"There?"

"Yes, in front of that little hill."

Vicki found the curbside vacant. "This is easy," she said as she parked the car underneath a streetlamp in front of a baseball field.

"Come on. Let me show you this statue."

"Here?" Vicki looked outside. The rain was pelting the top of her windshield, which had fogged up again. She wiped it clean and looked out. "It's pouring out there. Can't you just tell me what the statue looks like?"

Michael was frustrated. "No, I need you to come out and see it with me. It's fantastic."

Vicki looked at Michael as if he were crazy. "Is this going to make you happy?"

"It could."

"Well, if I'm going to get soaked on a baseball field looking at some dumb statue, you better be happy." She laughed again, flipping her hair off her shoulder with exaggerated flair. "I hope you understand I don't do this for every boyfriend."

"Oh, you have others?"

"I may," Vicki said with a sly smile as she reached for the door handle, "but today you will do."

Michael opened the passenger-side door, leaping over a huge puddle before meeting her by the front of the car. "Come on," he said, grabbing her hand and pulling her up the slippery grass over the hill.

Vicki glanced around through the pouring rain. "So where is it?"

He pulled her toward second base. "It's way out there," he said, indicating center field.

"I can't see it!" Rain was dripping off her hair into her eyes. Vicki took a few steps but felt Michael pulling her back.

"Mike?" she said, turning to look at him curiously.

Michael's face was peering up at her and he was on one knee. He reached into his pocket and pulled out a ring.

"Vicki, you make me happy and you make me believe in love. Will you marry me?"

Vicki stood stunned with her mouth wide-open.

"Hey, Vick, I'm getting drenched here, so I'm going to need an answer soon," he said with a laugh.

"This is it? This is really it?"

"Vicki, this is definitely it," Michael said. "So, will you marry me?"

"Yes!"

Michael stood up, and Vicki jumped into his arms.

"Let me do this right." He got back on his knee and placed the ring on her finger.

Vicki dropped to her knees and hugged him, knocking them both over. They lay there on their backs near second base, watching the falling rain glisten in the streetlights illuminating the field.

After a few moments, Vicki began waving her hands in the ground over her head.

Michael laughed, watching her. "What are you doing?"

"I'm making a mud angel," she said, laughing.

"Cool." Michael replied, before making his own.

Vicki rolled over to Michael, resting her head on his shoulder. "Mrs. Michael Stewart. Wow."

She held her ring above them through the pouring rain. Michael thought it looked like a star in the sky. Catching him watching it, she rolled over and kissed him.

"Keep me safe," she whispered.

"I will," he promised. "I will."

Was that a raindrop?

He looked up at the sky. The sun was bright overhead. Michael's right shoulder ached with the weight of the crossbar. They had only traveled about twenty to thirty yards.

"Move!" one of the soldiers yelled to Michael when he briefly stopped to shift the beam on his shoulder. His knees buckled again.

"Over there!" yelled another soldier.

Michael could see a hill in the distance with three huge wooden posts planted vertically in the ground. But as he began to walk again, the crossbar skidded awkwardly behind him, catching on the uneven stone road. Its weight vibrated through his shoulder, slowing him down.

As he neared the hill, Michael heard a commotion behind him. Two soldiers grabbed the crossbar off his shoulder and pushed him away.

"Go now," one soldier ordered him.

Michael looked behind him. The soldiers had grabbed Jesus and were tearing off his bloody cloak. Then they pushed Jesus down. Michael leaned forward to try to catch him, but the guard blocked his way. He saw Jesus' head slam against the ground.

Michael was pushed back into the small crowd that had assembled on the hill. Many women were softly crying under their veils. Grief overwhelmed him.

What have I done?

The clink of nail hitting bone shook him. In horror, he saw the soldiers huddled over Jesus. He didn't need to see what was happening. Michael turned away. The sobs grew louder around him. He could hear the crossbar bearing Jesus being anchored to the post.

Michael turned in time to see the soldiers placing Jesus' feet one over the other and nailing them to the wood. His face, battered and bruised, sloped downward. Blood dripped from the crown of thorns around his head, falling to the ground.

Looking up at the cross, Michael went numb. *What have I done? Oh, Lord, I'm so sorry.* He fell to his knees and started to wail.

A wooden decoration depicting Jesus, his father, and his mother sat atop the Christmas tree. It nearly touched the ten-foot ceiling. Presents were piled all around, with glitter and gold ribbon wrapping several big boxes. A bright blue bicycle, with shiny black tires and a sparkling bell on the handlebar, stood nearby. On the stairway leading up to the second floor, garlands and poinsettias circled the wooden banister, and Christmas cards were strung through the railing. The aroma of a roasting turkey filled the air.

Michael sat in the living room with his eyes closed, just letting his senses drift.

"You okay, sweetie?" Vicki asked as she rubbed his shoulder.

"How could I not be?"

"What were you thinking about?"

"I was thinking one thing," he said, placing his hand on her belly and smiling. "It's perfect, so perfect."

Vicki gently touched Michael's wedding ring and he felt a rush of love.

"Okay, lovebirds," Samantha said as she walked in from the kitchen. "Time to break it up. Ken's almost done with dinner. He's making it extraspecial for the future Miss Stewart."

"That's Elizabeth Stewart," Michael proudly boasted.

Samantha looked into Vicki's eyes. When Vicki nodded, Samantha squealed, "Oh, I love that name! I can't wait to meet her! Are you guys excited?"

Michael and Vicki looked at each other.

"She's excited but really nervous now that we're so close," he said.

"Oh, don't worry, everything is going to be great." Samantha smiled. "Just make sure you have the anesthesiologist in the room at all times!"

Vicki smiled, giggling. "I guess so. Sam, you'll be there for me, right?"

"You betcha!"

Watching his nephews reach into their stockings, Michael began laughing.

"What's so funny?" Vicki asked.

"I remember this one time when we had our stockings in the basement. I couldn't have been more than four or five years old. I woke on Christmas morning before everyone else and snuck downstairs to the stockings. I looked at all the stockings and decided that Santa wouldn't know if I moved all the presents into my stocking."

Vicki started to laugh.

"So I reached up as high as I could. I was pretty small so I had to get a chair. I stood on top of the chair and started pulling out the presents from everyone's stockings. Then I moved the chair over to my stocking and jammed in as many presents as I could. It was overflowing. Then I snuck back upstairs and pretended to be asleep. My mom almost caught me in the hall."

Vicki turned in her seat. "What did your parents do?"

"Well, they told me years later that they heard me get up. After I got back into bed, they went downstairs to survey the scene. They told me they laughed a lot and took a picture. Then they returned the presents to the rightful owners. Here I thought I could trick Santa, but I couldn't trick my parents."

"My goodness!" Vicki giggled. "I'll have to keep Elizabeth's and my stockings away from you from now on."

She paused. "You know, you laughed just now when you were talking about your parents. It's important to remember the good times. It's what life is all about.

"Hey, do you want to open your present?" Vicki handed Michael a small box, neatly wrapped with red paper and a bright green bow. She always put green bows on his presents because it reminded her of the color of his eyes. Inside the box was a silver bowl with the engraving FOR MIKE ONLY.

"Gee, thanks?"

She laughed. "Don't you get it, you ice cream fiend? Your pregnant wife can't steal your ice cream any longer."

Michael squeezed her hand and kissed her gently on the cheek. Reaching into his pocket, he pulled out a small box, also tied with a green ribbon.

"For *me*?" she inquired through raised eyebrows and a huge grin.

"For *you*. . . . Don't expect me to get down on my knees for this one."

"Ooh, this one might be better than I thought." Vicki slowly untied the ribbon, smiling up at him one last time before she opened the box. Hanging from a delicate gold chain was a panda mother holding her baby.

"Let me put it on you, Vick." He lifted the necklace from the velvet insert, unclasped it, and fastened it around her neck.

Vicki reached up, covering it with her soft, delicate hands. "It's beautiful. I love the way it feels. Thank you."

Michael placed his hands on top of hers, feeling the warmth of her skin. She leaned down, gently brushing his knuckles with a kiss.

Looking then at the bowl on the table in front of them, Vicki smiled. "Oh, my gift was so silly."

"No, I love it."

"Well, I hoped it would make you laugh."

"It does," he reassured her. "So, does this mean that you'll run out and get me ice cream whenever *I* want?"

"Of course. Once, maybe?"

"Wow, did I get the better end of that deal or what?" he teased, laughing.

"Hey, everybody, dinner's ready," Ken called from the dining room.

"C'mon, lady, let's get you to the table," Michael said as he helped Vicki to her feet.

Throughout dinner, Michael kept rubbing Vicki's hand gently, unaware of the numerous conversations around him. He loved her so completely and was delighted that they were soon going to be parents together. She was his world. Toward the end of the meal, he noticed she was speaking less, preoccupied and anxious again.

"Are you okay?" he whispered. "Maybe we should have gone straight home after visiting my dad."

Vicki shook her head. "No, don't worry about that. I just need some air."

Samantha noticed them talking quietly. She got up from the far end of the table and walked over to Vicki. She whispered a few words and Vicki nodded.

"We're going for a drive," Vicki said.

Michael looked up at her, concerned.

"Don't worry," she said, standing up. "Hey, I'll get you some ice cream if we find a store that's open."

She leaned over and kissed him on his cheek. Her hair fell in front of her face and she brushed it back behind her ear.

"Don't worry. I know everything will be fine. You make me believe that."

Putting on her heavy wool coat and Black Watch plaid scarf, Vicki said to Samantha, "Let's use your car. You drive. I'll talk."

The rain started to fall harder, pounding the ground. Michael wandered aimlessly, lost in thought.

What have I done? What have I done?

He looked up, letting the rain pelt his face. It felt good. Immediately, Michael put his head down again.

He staggered into a vacant marketplace, seeking shelter from the storm. He flopped down against a wall, letting the rough surface scrape his back. He noticed that his right sandal had torn nearly in two, but he no longer cared.

"My Lord, I'm so sorry," he repeated over and over.

His shoulders heaved deeply as he shook his head from side to side. "No, no. I can't believe it. What have I done? Lord, what have I done to you?"

Michael stood up. He slammed his fist into the unrelenting wall. He took off his torn sandal and hurled it across the street.

"Why does it always have to be me? Why did I have to carry that cross?"

He swung his bare foot against the wall but he barely felt the pain. "What have you ever done for me?" he shouted, looking up. "I've got no wife. Do you know that? Do you?"

Michael raced across the street and picked up his sandal. He threw it hard against the roof that covered the marketplace. "Your son died, my wife died. I guess we're even now, huh? Is that what you wanted? Is *that* what you wanted? *Did you? Answer me!*"

His screams echoed through the deserted streets.

"Why can't you answer me, Lord?" he wailed, dropping to his knees in the mud. "Look at me. Look at me! I'm pathetic. You've humbled me. Is that what you wanted?"

Bracing himself on his elbows in the middle of the street, his legs sprawled out to the side, Michael sobbed uncontrollably. He didn't care about the soldiers, his bruises, or his pain. All he knew was that he was alone, and Vicki was never coming back.

Michael stumbled to his feet and staggered over to his torn sandal. As he picked it up, he uttered the only words he had left.

"How can my daughter lift my burden, Lord? Please tell me. Why can't *you* lift it?"

The doorbell rang. Peering through the peephole, Michael saw the police officer looking down at his feet. When Michael opened the door, he heard him say, "Evening, sir. I'm Officer Stanton. Is it all right if I come in for a moment?"

Michael's stomach tightened. "Sure," he replied, turning and yelling down the hallway, "Ken! Come in here!"

"I'm looking for Kenneth Fontana."

"That's me!" called Ken, who raced in from the kitchen.

"I'm afraid there's been an accident." Turning to Michael, the policeman asked, "Are you Michael Stewart?"

Michael felt his stomach drop. "Yes."

"Your sister said you would be here."

"Is Samantha all right?" Ken asked, moving closer to the officer.

"Yes. She'll be fine."

"Thank God!"

"What about Vicki?" Michael asked. "What happened?"

Placing his hand on Michael's shoulder, the officer said, "You need to come with me to the hospital."

Michael pushed the officer's hand away. "What happened? Is she okay? Is she hurt? Tell me. Please, *tell me!*"

"We need to go now, Mr. Stewart."

Ken felt Michael look at him and nodded. "I'll be right behind you, Mike. Let me run the boys over to the Henrys'."

Michael stayed silent on the ride to the hospital, holding the door handle tightly. The officer had nothing more to say, leaving Michael to his terrible thoughts.

I don't want to be alone. Oh, Vicki. Oh, Vicki . . . please be okay.

"Mr. Stewart, we're here," the officer said, opening his door.

The car had barely pulled up to the emergency-room entrance

when Michael jumped out and bolted through the automatic doors. Sammie was standing in the corner. When she saw him, she raced over and fell into his arms crying.

"I'm so sorry. I'm so sorry," she kept repeating through tears.

"Are you okay?"

"Yes, I'm fine." She pulled away to look at him.

"You've got blood on your face." Michael hugged her again.

"I'm fine. Please, Mike. Please. I'm so sorry."

Michael whispered, "Please tell me she's okay."

Samantha cried harder, pulling away from him.

"I can't live without her, Sammie," he begged. "You know that."

Samantha was silent. After a moment, she whispered to him in a voice far deeper than normal, "She wasn't conscious when I saw her being taken in."

"Oh, God, no." The words seemed to escape him as he stood there, holding his little sister, trying to make her not say what he already knew in his heart. His head fell on her shoulder, and he became aware only of how her heaving sobs kept bobbing his head slowly up, then down. He took a deep breath, then let her go.

He walked over to the nurses' desk and announced to no one in particular, "My wife, my wife was brought in here a few moments ago. Please . . ."

All other words left him as he waited for someone to answer.

"What's her name?" one of the nurses asked.

"Vick. Vicki. Victoria Stewart."

The nurse typed a few words into the computer in front of her before asking, finally, "Mr. Stewart?"

"Yes."

"Please sit and wait for the doctor to come out."

Michael turned and found Samantha and Ken directly behind him, holding each other.

Nice, Michael thought.

It felt like only a few seconds later when Michael felt a hand on his sleeve.

"Mr. Stewart? I'm Dr. Brennan. Please come with me out into the hall."

Without thinking, Michael stood up and followed him blindly to a spot near a water fountain.

The physician turned to him. He looked as if he would rather be anywhere else than in this hallway talking to Michael. "I'm sorry to tell you that we were unable to save your wife. Her injuries were far too grave. But we were able to deliver the baby. You have a girl. She's doing fine upstairs."

The doctor said many other things, but Michael heard nothing else. He stood motionless, gazing at the bright ceiling lights. Again, it seemed only seconds before Samantha and Ken were next to him, asking what the doctor had said.

"Vicki . . ." He stopped, unable to continue.

Samantha fell into Michael, hugging him tightly.

After a few moments, he finally looked down at her. "I can't cry right now. There's just no time. The baby's okay. I have to go see my daughter."

"They saved the baby?" Samantha asked through her tears.

He nodded. "Elizabeth's here now."

Michael limped around on one sandal while holding the other torn one in his hand. He attempted several times to place the broken sandal back on his foot but it kept slipping off when he tried to take a step.

"Great," he muttered under his breath.

He took the other sandal off as the rain continued to pound down. His feet felt relief as he waded through the puddles. The raindrops massaged his bruised shoulders while cooling off his head and neck. He looked skyward and opened his mouth, letting the water collect there. He swallowed gratefully.

"Thank you."

He stopped near a large puddle, then stepped into it as if he were getting into a bathtub. He rinsed the mud off his feet and legs, thinking how he needed to get out of this rain and see Elizabeth.

Michael started back toward Leah's house, looking for familiar landmarks. The sky was still dark gray, making it difficult for him to determine the time.

When the rain let up, he began to shiver. He looked to his left— the aqueduct! His heart raced. Michael started to run hard, not caring that his feet were bare.

Soon Leah's house appeared in the distance. He could make out two figures standing near the front gate.

"Dad!" Elizabeth sprinted to meet him. She threw her arms around him and held on tightly. "Oh, Dad, did they . . . ? "

"They did . . . they did . . . and I helped . . . I carried the cross they nailed him to."

Michael tried to push Elizabeth away but she clung to him. "Daddy, no," she murmured. "You helped *him* . . . you helped him."

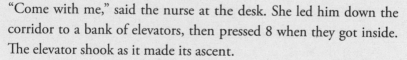

"Come with me," said the nurse at the desk. She led him down the corridor to a bank of elevators, then pressed 8 when they got inside. The elevator shook as it made its ascent.

"This way," she said when the doors opened. They made a left turn and went down another series of hallways that led to a security door that read NO ADMITTANCE WITHOUT PROPER IDENTIFICATION. The nurse entered a code on the accompanying keypad, and the doors opened automatically.

Balloon paintings covered the walls as she led him toward the nursing station. A man and woman stood with their arms around each other, cooing and tapping on the glass. Michael stopped near them.

"Not here," the nurse said, motioning him to continue walking.

She led him down a dimly lit hallway past a door that bore the simple inscription CHAPEL. As he approached this other nursing station, Michael noticed the bare walls and the hushed tone of the staff.

"Wait here, please," the nurse said kindly. She picked up a phone on the wall. "Mr. Stewart is ready to see his daughter. . . . Okay, okay. We'll go over there."

She led him past the nursing station and around a corner to a small window. Michael peered through it into a large room with only four incubators. He noticed all the equipment inside: machines, tubes, monitors. A nurse came up to him on the other side of the glass and pointed at a baby lying in an incubator.

Oh, Vicki. Oh, Vicki.

She looked so small to him. She was only wearing a diaper and had an IV connected to her left heel. Where her belly button would be was now clamped off by a yellow tag. On her right ankle was a plastic band that read STEWART, BABY GIRL—STEWART, VICTORIA (D).

Michael stared at the band. Vicki's middle name didn't start with a *D*.

He paused and looked at Elizabeth moving her arms and stretching her legs.

"Vicki's middle name doesn't start with *D*," he said, turning to the nurse next to him. "It's Evelyn."

When the nurse only looked at Michael, he knew immediately what it meant.

"Oh my God. *D* for 'deceased'?"

The nurse stood silent.

"Answer me, please."

Michael began fervently tapping on the window, trying to get the attention of the nurse inside the room. "Take that off," he said, pointing to the ankle band.

"Take it off *now!*"

The nurse inside couldn't hear him. He slammed his hands against the glass again.

"Mr. Stewart, please," the nurse next to him said. "Stop. Please."

"No!" Michael looked down the hall for the door to the nursery. He didn't see any entrance.

Turning back to the window he tried again to get the nurse inside to understand him. "Take it off!" he said, pointing angrily at the ankle band.

"Mr. Stewart, please stop," the nurse said, touching his shoulder. "Please. I'll have to call security. Please, sir, I don't want to have to do that to you."

Michael looked at his hands pounding against the glass. Suddenly exhausted and embarrassed, he covered his face and slid to the ground.

The nurse looked at him for a few moments before reaching down to lift his arm. "Mr. Stewart," she said gently, "it's time to get up."

Michael found his feet again but couldn't feel his legs. He stood up and smiled at the nurse oddly. Then, turning back to the window, he looked again at Elizabeth.

She's so small.

"Oh, Elizabeth, I'm so sorry," he said under his breath, pressing his face dejectedly against the window. "I'm so sorry. I'm not sure I can take care of you now. I don't know how I'm going to do this. I don't know how."

Michael began banging his head gently against the glass but saw Elizabeth start to cry. He turned to the nurse.

"Is she okay?"

"She was born a few days too soon but she'll be fine." The nurse touched Michael gently on his right arm. "I'll be back in a couple of minutes to take you inside. If you need me, I'm at the nurses' station. Would you like to see a priest?"

"No."

Michael watched the nurse walk away. He turned back to look into the NICU window. Michael could see a sticker on the baby's tiny chest, monitoring her heartbeat. Her eyes were bright blue and her cheeks were puffy and red. She continued to cry.

"Oh, Elizabeth, please stop," he said, starting to cry, too. "Please, I'll be strong for you. I promise you I won't ever leave you. You'll be the only person in my life now. The only person. No one will ever get between us. I promise . . . I promise."

"If you don't want me to go, I won't."

He lay there, surprised at his own words and thinking about the consequences of his statement. He remembered falling into a deep sleep, but now, in the early-morning hours, he was surprised to find her next to him.

"Well, maybe you can come back with us, Leah," he whispered, not wanting to wake her. He held her hand more tightly, pulling it up slightly so he could kiss it. It was intoxicating lying there, so close that he could feel her every breath. His heart beat rapidly.

"I don't want to be alone anymore, Leah. It's been too long. Elizabeth has grown up so quickly. She's become such a beautiful person. Each day that comes is one less day she needs me, or, in some cases—wants to be around me."

He laughed quietly, unaware that Elizabeth had woken and was standing at the foot of the ladder to the roof.

"For the longest time I didn't know how to love again, Leah. You taught me that love is worth having. I just didn't think I would find it here—in Jerusalem—in this time."

He shook his head in disbelief. He couldn't believe he'd just uttered those words.

Michael kissed the back of her neck. "What do you think about going back to Northport with us? It's a beautiful town, Leah. The people are friendly. The neighbors do care about one another. We're by the Sound, the beach. You can smell the ocean during the winter some nights where we live. We could take walks at night there, watch the sunset. I promise to be as romantic in our old age as we can be now. I promise I will never forget to say I love you."

Elizabeth's mouth dropped open. She'd never heard her father talk like this. She knew that he spent most of his time dismissing any romantic possibilities, using her as an excuse—which she found both humiliating and annoying. When she was younger, she used to wonder if he would ever marry again, and the thought upset her. But here, on this warm evening in a small town outside Jerusalem, she felt nothing but happiness.

He shook his head again, thinking about all the times he'd thought about going down to the beach to look at the sunset, but never did. "If you don't know how to swim, I could teach you," he promised into the darkness. "I'll teach you to ride a bike. I'll even go to the mall with you."

The last promise made him pause. He actually hated the mall. "Well, I'll have to think about that one." He tightened his hold. "I can teach you to play baseball. I tried it with Elizabeth but she was more interested in playing the piano."

Elizabeth winced at the memory. She had kept holding up the mitt, turning her head, and shutting her eyes whenever the ball came near her. Michael had finally given up, afraid that she would get smacked in the face, and she'd skipped happily back into the house to practice "When Johnny Comes Marching Home Again" on the old upright in the den.

"I promise always to let you into my heart. I promise. I really do."

Suddenly Leah stirred. His body quivered with excitement. "Hey, Leah. Good morning."

She turned over and lay flat on the bedroll. Her eyes fluttered and she moved her lips as if seeking some water. "Yochanan? Yochanan?" she mumbled drowsily.

Elizabeth turned away quickly and ducked back toward the dining area. Michael lay there for a moment, stunned. Then he jumped to his feet, tripping on some of the tangled blanket. He fumbled his way down the two ladders and into the kitchen. He braced himself against the wall as if it were a life raft. He looked down stoically at the worn floor, letting his tears fall freely.

After a few minutes, he took a deep breath and straightened. He knew now the important thing was to get his daughter back home safely. He repeated that to himself for several minutes until he felt composed enough to check one more time on Elizabeth.

When he reached the second floor, he saw her lying peacefully on the mat in the far corner. In the moonlight, he noticed that her eyes were closed, and he stood there listening to her rhythmic breathing. Then he quietly left the room. A moment later Elizabeth's eyes opened and she dabbed them with the blanket.

Michael wandered back down to the kitchen and stood for a moment. Perhaps she was just dreaming, he thought hopefully. After all, hadn't he had dreams about Vicki, too? Yes, that must be it. It was just a dream. He turned resolutely and headed for the ladder.

14

FOUND
YOU

Michael awoke to find Leah's head resting on his chest and his arms draped around her body. The sun had yet to make an appearance, but in the gray early-morning light, he could see everything so clearly.

Last night as they sat together on the roof, he thought something had changed. She was so near, her shoulder touching his and her hip against him. When he put his arm around her, she didn't resist. Instead, she leaned her head against his shoulder and her hair brushed his cheek when he breathed in deeply. What he remembered most clearly was how when he kissed her on the forehead, she had turned to him, placing her hands on his face.

But then she had called for Yochanan during the night. *Was it just a dream or her deepest wish?* He shook himself free of the blanket and struggled to stand up. Awaked by the sudden movement, Leah opened her eyes.

"Sorry, Leah, I fell asleep. I should have brought you back downstairs."

Leah stood up silently, placing her hand on his cheek. "Michael, I chose to stay."

"Really?" Michael whispered to her.

"Yes," she said, cradling his face now with both hands.

He looked around shyly. "Would you . . ."

Leah looked puzzled. "Would I what?"

Michael paused. He gently removed her hands from his face and turned away. He walked to the other side of the roof. He took a deep breath, watching the sun break over the mountains.

What are you doing, Mike? Especially after last night . . .

He could hear Leah's footsteps approaching behind him. Turning to face her before she got too close, he whispered, "This is all so confusing. You know I've got to get Elizabeth back home, right?"

"I know," Leah said, leaning forward and touching his arm.

Michael pulled her close to him. "Leah, if I could . . ."

"I know."

She wrapped her arms around him, and he held her tightly. His head was now down on her shoulder as he breathed in the scent of her hair and neck.

She started to rock back and forth, a simple dance between them.

"Have you ever done this?" she asked, reaching down to hold his hands.

He smiled. "Many, many years ago."

Michael held her hands up to his chest and leaned lower so that their foreheads touched. "How long have you lived here?"

"For as long as I can remember."

"Do you want to live here the rest of your life?"

Leah stopped slowly and pulled back from him. "Why, Michael, why do you want to know?"

He paused, releasing her hands from his. "Oh, Leah, it's a crazy thought . . . I'm sorry. I really should go get Elizabeth up."

"Of course," she whispered back, heading toward the ladder. "Let me get you some clean garments."

Michael followed her down the ladder. He could see to the right that Elizabeth was still peacefully sleeping.

Leah handed him a fresh robe. "I will get Elizabeth up for you."

He smiled warmly at Leah before descending the ladder with the fresh garment in hand. Before he headed to the back alley, he could

see a flickering of sunlight coming through the fig leaves in the courtyard.

Another morning, another day.

When he closed the door behind him, he paused to look around at
the washing tub and the toilet beyond. He shook his head in amazement.

This seems so normal now. He stopped abruptly, uncertain if he
could laugh on a day like today.

He took a chip of soap from the bowl and lathered it up on his
chest with the water from the tub. *Am I really here? Nobody would ever
believe this.*

After he finished, he put on the clean robe and walked quickly
back inside. As he climbed the ladder to the second floor, Michael
could see Leah sitting beside Elizabeth, rubbing her back.

"Come on, Elizabeth. Wake up. Daddy wants you to wake up."

Michael smiled. "Come on, sleepyhead," he called up to her. "It's
time to go."

"Huh?" Elizabeth said as she stretched out of her blankets. "Go
where?"

"Go home."

"Oh . . . really?"

Michael walked closer to her. "Yes. C'mon. Get ready now. We
need to leave soon."

"Okay, okay."

"I'll be back in a few moments," Leah said, patting Elizabeth one
last time on the back.

Elizabeth watched Leah climb down the ladder before turning to
Michael. "Daddy, why are we leaving now? What about the soldiers?
What about Jesus?"

"What about him?"

"Well, we can see if he really rises from the dead, right? If we stay
another day, we would—"

"I don't need another day to know what I saw. What I need is to
get you home."

Leah made her way back up the ladder and stood behind them now with a white shirt in her hand.

"Michael, perhaps you're right to leave now. With Passover finished, Pilate has gone back to his palace by the sea. There won't be any of his soldiers around."

"Well, then, that's it. We'll leave this morning." Michael retreated down the ladder to grab a cup of water.

Leah handed Elizabeth the Springsteen shirt. "I cleaned this for you."

"Thank you." Elizabeth gave Leah a hug. "Thank you for everything."

Leah smiled and handed her another garment and veil. "Be sure to wear these."

Elizabeth thanked her again.

Michael was sipping from a cup of water out in the courtyard and marveling at the well-constructed house when he felt a hand on his shoulder.

"Michael?" Leah asked. "Would you like something to eat before you go?"

"No, thanks. I'm really sorry we have to go. I need to get Elizabeth back."

Before he could finish, Elizabeth came downstairs wearing her new garment but with the veil in hand. "Could you help me with this?" she called out to Leah. "I'm having trouble with it."

Leah took the veil and lovingly wrapped it around Elizabeth. "I will miss you, Elizabeth."

"I'm really going to miss you, too." She handed Leah her Springsteen T-shirt. "Please take this. It's something to remember me by."

Leah hugged her closely. "*That's* something to remember me by."

"Okay, are you ready, Elizabeth?" Michael called out from the kitchen. He had seen them holding each other, but now needed to turn away.

"Yes, Dad, I just want to say good-bye to Cassie."

Michael watched Elizabeth sit down next to the lamb. She was whispering softly while petting the animal. He couldn't help but chuckle.

"Please, whatever you do, Leah, please take good care of Cassie," he said, trying to lighten the moment.

Leah turned away. "Of course."

"Bye, Cassie." Michael patted the lamb on the head. "Okay, Elizabeth, let's get going. It's getting really light now."

Elizabeth gave Cassie a big hug.

"Baa," the lamb cried as she walked away.

"Baa back at you," Michael said with a smile.

Leah walked with Michael and Elizabeth out the front gate. "Are you coming with us to town?" Michael asked.

Leah shook her head. "I can't. I just can't."

"Bye, Leah," Elizabeth said, turning to her.

Leah leaned over and kissed her on the cheek. "Be well. Take care of your father."

"I will. Thank you. Thank you so much." Elizabeth smiled at her, then walked away.

"I'll catch up to you," Michael said to his daughter.

A moment passed before he turned back toward Leah, looking down at her bare fingers.

"Thank you for everything." Michael reached over to hold her hand, which she took in her own, placing it over her heart. He bent over slightly and kissed her softly on the lips.

"Good-bye," he whispered.

Leah nodded and stepped back. Quietly, before she closed the gate between them, she said under her breath, "I found you, Michael."

Michael watched Leah walk across the courtyard until she was out of sight. He turned back to the road and saw Elizabeth waiting for him. He walked slowly to her, his head down.

"Dad, I know you always said it would be just us two forever, but, you know, I can deal with three—"

He stopped her in midsentence. "We come from different places, Elizabeth." He looked back at Leah's humble home and shook his head. "It would never work."

"Oh, Dad. How do you know it wouldn't work if you never try?"

"Sometimes trying can really hurt," he said, looking back at the house and seeing Leah now up on her roof. *She's watching us.*

Michael waved, but instead of waving back, Leah pointed at them and placed her hands over her heart.

He wrapped his arm around Elizabeth's shoulder, turning her back to the road.

"C'mon. Let's go."

They walked in silence for the next twenty minutes or so. Finally Michael noticed a familiar building with flowers growing over the ornate front gate. "We're getting close!" He squeezed Elizabeth's arm in excitement.

She picked her head up and looked into his face. "Dad, how did you know Mom was the one for you?"

Michael stopped, surprised at her timing. "Why are you asking me that *now*?"

"Because you never told me how you met."

Michael started walking again, looking skyward. "Not a cloud in the sky today, Elizabeth."

"Yes, Dad, not a cloud in the sky." She rolled her eyes. "But back to Mom. How did you meet?"

"If I tell you, can I call you Liz in front of your friends?" he asked, teasing.

She frowned and took a deep breath. "Okay."

"Wow. You must really want to know if you're willing to suffer that public humiliation."

He took a deep breath. "Okay, I met your mother on the dance floor at Aunt Sammie's wedding. Your mom was an old college friend of Uncle Ken's. I was walking back from the bar with a Diet Coke when I bumped into her and spilled the soda all over her. Boy, was I embarrassed."

Elizabeth giggled. "Nice first impression!"

Michael laughed again. "So I spent the next few minutes getting napkins and seltzer to try and wash the stain out of her dress. Safe to say your mother wasn't impressed with my cleaning skills."

Elizabeth stared at him. "Was she mad at you?"

"She tried to make me think she was. She told me it was her favorite dress. But she started to smile so I knew she was just razzing me. After we got most of the soda out, she said I owed her a dance. I could never turn down a lady asking for a dance, Elizabeth."

She gazed up toward the sky, smiling. "What song did you dance to?"

"'Summer Wind.' Sinatra. I'll never forget how she felt the first time I put my arms around her. When the song ended, I didn't know what to do, but she took the lead."

"Well, what did Mommy do?"

"Well, the soda had left quite a stain on her dress so she wanted to get a sweater from the car to cover it up. I offered to come along. Seriously, it was my fault." Michael gave Elizabeth a sly smile.

"When we got outside, the parking lot was covered in snow. She had these big high heels on and started to slip. I tried to catch her so I grabbed her arm. But instead I slipped, falling flat on my back, pulling her down with me!"

"No way!"

"Oh, yes way!" Michael said with a big smile.

"Were you hurt?"

"Only my pride. Your mom had landed hard on top of me." He winked at Elizabeth. "Then we shared our first kiss."

"Really?"

"Well, no, not really," he said, laughing. "I was so embarrassed I started apologizing over and over and over."

"What did Mom say?"

"Well, she didn't say much. She struggled to get up, pushing down on me. But as she stood up, her feet slipped out from underneath her and she fell back down on top of me again."

"Did you kiss her then?"

"Well, no, not quite. When she fell, she was sitting on my chest."

"What do you mean?"

"I was pinned underneath her. And she just sat there, totally stunned, looking at her high heels. One of the heels had broken off. She turned around and looked down at me. 'Isn't this great?' she asked. 'You broke my heel and stained my dress. How am I going to go back inside?'"

"She sounded like she was mad."

"I was definitely afraid. But then she told me that there was only one thing left to do. So I asked her what that would be. She didn't say anything but just leaned over, picked up the other high heel, and broke it right in front of my face."

"Oh, she was mad!"

"No, she wasn't. After we struggled to get up to our feet, we both stood there for a second and then she just kissed me."

"Really?"

"Really."

"Did you go back to the wedding?"

"Nope."

Elizabeth looked at her father slyly. "What did you do?"

"I don't know if you realize this, but broken heels make for great ice skates. We skated around the parking lot until people started coming out."

Elizabeth hugged her father. "Wow, that's cool."

Michael leaned over so he could get closer to Elizabeth's right ear. "Your mother always knew how to make a great moment out of an embarrassing one. And, you know what, so do you."

He looked skyward again, surprised by how good it felt to share his memories of Vicki with Elizabeth.

"Is Uncle Brian like that, too?" she asked curiously.

"Oh. Elizabeth. Let's save my brother-in-law for another day."

They walked a few more blocks before Elizabeth turned to him again.

"What did you really think of Leah?"

"I thought she was nice."

"Well, I really liked her. I spent a lot of time with her. She taught me how to weave. She always asked me how I was doing and whether I needed something to eat or drink. I liked it when we sat down and had dinner together, the three of us. She made me laugh a lot, not because she was different or funny or anything. But, I don't know, she always seemed to know how to make me smile."

"Yeah, I know what you mean."

"Yes, Dad, you know *exactly* what I mean," Elizabeth said with a coy smile.

"What are you getting at?"

"I went up to check on you last night, and Leah was up there with you."

Michael stopped walking. "You did what?"

"Relax, Dad. You were both sleeping when I went up there. I didn't see anything."

"Elizabeth, nothing happened."

"Well . . . do you love her?"

Michael rubbed his forehead, looking down at the ground. "There's no easy answer here, Baboo. I don't know if it even matters. . . ."

Suddenly he started walking at a faster pace. "Let's get home. We're almost there, right through this alley. Man, it's kind of eerie no one's around."

"Leah said it was the Sabbath, Dad. And she was right: I haven't seen any soldiers."

"Good, because the tunnel is right around this corner."

They took a few steps out into the street.

"Hold on!" Michael gasped, pulling his daughter back into the alley. "Look!"

Elizabeth leaned in close next to him so that she could peer around the corner, too. "Oh, no!"

A soldier was stationed about twenty feet away on their side of the street with his back to them. His weapon glistened in the morning sun, the shiny blade glaring back at them. The metal helmet disguised his face, but they could clearly see the white cloth attached to it.

At this close distance, Michael could also see the scar on the back of the soldier's leg. Finally, he could make out the design: a Roman coin branded into his skin.

How sick, Michael thought, totally repulsed by him.

"He's waiting for us," Michael said, looking at the bank of six half-mooned sewer grates embedded in the side of a building across the street. "The tunnel's right there, I think. But I don't see the shirt!"

"What shirt?"

"I tied a piece of your T-shirt to the grate we came from." Michael kept his eyes on the soldier. "This isn't good, Elizabeth. We're the prey. We're the prey!"

They watched the soldier leaning there comfortably against the wall, not making a move.

"Dad, how are we going to get back now?"

Michael shook his head. "I don't know. I really don't. Let me think."

He watched Elizabeth peer around the corner again, obviously terrified that the soldier would find them. Pointing in the opposite direction, Michael said, "I'm going to make a run for it over there. You stay hidden in this doorway. When he passes you, I want you to sprint to the tunnel."

"No!"

"Shh," said Michael, placing his hand gingerly over her mouth. "Quiet!"

Elizabeth shook her head several times.

"I'm not leaving you," she said, wrapping her arm around his.

"Please, Elizabeth." He hugged her close. "Please!"

She began to cry. "What if I can't make it? What if he hurts you?

How will you get to me? I don't want to be alone. Please, Daddy, please."

"Okay, okay. Please, don't cry. I need you to be strong. Let's think of something else."

Michael felt a hand on his shoulder. He jumped.

"I can help."

"Leah?" Michael said, turning around. "What are you doing here?"

"You and Elizabeth need to get home. Let me help you."

"How?"

"Listen to me. I'm going to get the soldier to follow me. I know what he's capable of and I'm not afraid," Leah said defiantly as she pulled the ripped Springsteen T-shirt out from under her robe and put it on. "You must not let him stop you."

"Elizabeth, give me your veil," she demanded, taking the white veil and handing Elizabeth the black one. "Put this one on."

"We can't let you do that. You'll be in too much danger. That soldier would kill you when he finds out you're not Elizabeth."

Leah fastened the white veil around her, then helped Elizabeth with the black one.

"Please don't do this," Elizabeth begged. "There has to be a better way. Right, Dad?"

"Yes, we'll think of something," he said, turning to Elizabeth. He felt a quick kiss on the cheek before realizing that Leah had walked into the street.

"No!" he gasped, watching as Leah strutted straight toward the soldier.

As she passed him, the soldier's head snapped up, though the rest of him didn't move. He was staring at her like a tiger ready to pounce. After a moment, he pulled off his helmet and tossed it to the ground. He let her get about ten yards in front of him before he started in pursuit.

"Daddy, do something!"

Turning to her, as if just realizing she was still there, he yelled, "Elizabeth, go to the tunnel *now.*"

"No, Dad, no!"

"I'll help her, but you go, now! Do you know which grate it is?"

"I think it's the third one."

"Halt!" the soldier shouted to Leah. "I've been expecting you."

The soldier held up a piece of the T-shirt, the one that Michael had tied to the grate.

"Oh, no," Michael muttered.

Terrified, he implored his daughter to run. "Go now!" Michael motioned to Elizabeth, who immediately sprinted across the street.

Michael followed her for a few steps, then stopped. He could see her ahead, struggling to open one of the grates.

The soldier was nearly upon Leah. "Where have you been hiding?" he hissed. "I've been waiting for you. I knew you'd come back to me."

He tore at Leah's veil, then stepped back in surprise.

"Leave her alone!" Michael screamed, taking several steps toward him.

Leah spun around, shrieking, "Michael, go!"

"Shut up!" With the shaft of his spear, the soldier knocked Leah to the ground. He fell down on top of her, holding the spear across her neck.

"Dad! Daddy, I can't open it!" Elizabeth shouted from the grate, struggling to break it.

The soldier spun around, lifting his spear from Leah and staring back at Elizabeth. "There she is."

"No!" Michael yelled.

"Go!" screamed Leah, hitting the soldier on the back of the head. He staggered a moment, then rushed toward Elizabeth.

"Oh, Lord, oh, Lord, please help us," Michael repeated over and over, fumbling at the grate. He slammed it once with his shoulder, jarring it open slightly.

Elizabeth stood up and kicked it with her foot. The grate fell through.

"Get in!"

"Stop!" the soldier yelled. He threw his spear at them. It skidded off the ground past Elizabeth's head, striking the wall behind them.

Michael pushed Elizabeth into the tunnel. Turning one last time, he got a quick glimpse of Leah as she darted into a side alley and was gone.

Michael jumped down through the opening, landing on the grate. "Go, go ahead, *now,* Elizabeth!"

"I'm going, Dad! I'm going!"

"Keep your hand on the wall, but run!" He watched her disappear into the darkness ahead.

Michael sprinted after her, his fingertips outstretched against the walls to try to guide him through the dark tunnel. He heard footsteps all around him.

Is he following us?

Michael didn't stop to listen. He heard only the pounding of his own feet. After a while, he slowed down, out of breath.

Michael was no longer running, and it surprised him when he realized that he was barely walking. *Where am I?*

He stopped for a moment, trying to examine the sore fingertips on his left hand, though in complete darkness, it was impossible to see anything. He kept his right hand pressed against the wall, afraid he would lose his way if he let go. He couldn't hear any footsteps behind him or in front of him.

"Elizabeth? You there?"

After what seemed like an eternity, a faint voice called back through the darkness, "Daddy, I can hear you but I can't see you."

"Stay where you are."

"What about the soldier? Can you see him?"

"Elizabeth, I can't see anything. I can't hear anything. Are you okay?"

"Yes, Dad. I'm just really scared."

"Okay, don't worry. I'll be right there. Just stay put."

He stumbled forward a few feet, his steps echoing around him. "Are you moving at all, Elizabeth?"

"No, Dad. I want to. It's so dark . . . please hurry!"

"Okay, I'm coming."

He started to run but quickly got winded again.

"Elizabeth?"

"Yeah, Dad, you're getting closer. Please don't stop. Please!"

"I'm coming, don't worry. Keep your hands out. . . . Are you doing it?"

"Yes!"

Michael propelled himself forward, stumbling and breathing heavily until he collided with her.

"That's my arm!" Elizabeth yelped.

He put his hand out and felt her face, putting his hand softly over her mouth. "Quiet, let me listen for a few moments."

"I can't hear anything, Dad," she said, her voice muffled by his hand.

"Okay, okay, turn around and keep walking."

"Shouldn't we run?"

"I can't."

They took several more strides forward.

"There, look." Elizabeth pointed to a dim light ahead.

"Elizabeth, how can you be so certain? We could be walking to a whole different world. Does any of this seem familiar to you?"

She stopped. "I'm not sure."

"Did it take us this long before to walk through the tunnel?"

"I'm not sure. I didn't keep track."

"Let's be careful. Just in case, okay?"

The light became brighter with each step forward. Michael put his hand on Elizabeth's shoulder, protecting her. As they got closer to the light, he grabbed her more tightly.

"Stop."

"Why?"

"Let me go first. If you don't hear me calling for you, go back."

"What?" she yelped. Elizabeth shook free from her father's grip and raced toward the light. "Stairs!"

"Elizabeth, please. Wait!" He watched Elizabeth's dark figure disappear through the opening. "Great, here we go again."

When he reached the lit area, he saw steps before him. Climbing them, he found himself back in the basement of Our Lady by the Bay.

He stood there and looked in wonder at the boxes of food that were stilled piled up everywhere.

"Elizabeth, where did you go?"

"Up here, Dad!" She was making her way up the stairs to the church.

"Elizabeth?"

Michael watched the basement door close behind her, then looked around at the empty room. It was quiet. Even eerie.

He fell to the floor and immediately slammed the trapdoor shut, worried that the soldier might still get them. He got up and ran to the corner, pushing a pile of boxes onto the door. Next, he ran to the other side of the room and grabbed more boxes, frantically dragging them to the center of the room.

"Let's see him get through this!"

Satisfied with the mound of boxes he had made, he started up the stairs to get Elizabeth. When Michael reached the altar area, he saw Father Dennis by the vestibule.

"What happened, Michael?" he said, pointing to his robes. "When did you get these clothes? Your shoulder, it's bleeding. Did any of the boxes fall on you? My Lord, where are your shoes! Look at your feet! What happened?"

Michael walked swiftly over to him. "Father, Father. I really need to speak to you. You're not going to believe this."

"Calm down, son. Where were you?"

"Elizabeth? Where did she go, Father?"

"She went outside, Michael."

"Oh, okay. Follow me." Michael started to run back toward the basement.

"Is everything okay?" Father Dennis asked, running after Michael. "Slow down. You're scaring me. What happened?"

Michael stopped abruptly, grabbing the priest by the shoulders and staring intently into his eyes.

"Father, I saw Christ!"

"Okay," he said calmly, "Christ is everywhere. How did he reveal himself to you?"

"No, no, you don't understand. I saw him. I actually saw him. Down there!" Michael pointed over to the basement door.

"Down where?"

"In your basement."

Father Dennis looked at Michael. "Have you been hurt?"

"No, Father. Listen to me." Michael opened the basement door. "Come here, I'll show you."

"Okay, Michael." Father Dennis trailed Michael down the stairs and watched him as he ran to the huge pile of boxes in the center of the room.

"What are you doing?"

Michael didn't respond. He started shoving boxes two and three at a time away from the disorderly pile he had made just moments before.

"What exactly are we looking for, Michael?"

"The trapdoor to your subbasement, Father."

Father Dennis slowly walked over to him and reached down to place a hand firmly on his shoulder. "Michael, there is no trapdoor, there is no subbasement. Please, please get up."

"But, Father," Michael said, moving his hand frantically across the floor, "we just came from it a few minutes ago."

"I'm sorry, but I don't know what to say." Turning away from Michael, he added, "Let me go get Elizabeth for you. Will you be okay while I'm gone?"

Michael stood there looking at the floor, then sat down heavily. "Yes, yes, Father. Get Elizabeth."

Michael sat stunned, leaning his head against a pile of boxes while watching Father Dennis walk back up the stairs.

I must sound crazy. Father probably thinks I've finally lost it.

He decided that he couldn't be making this up: there was no way that he and Elizabeth could have imagined the same thing. He started to tear up but quickly wiped his eyes when he heard footsteps.

"Dad! Dad, are you okay?" Elizabeth said, running down the stairs. "Father Dennis said you might have hurt yourself." She ran over to him and knelt beside him.

"I'm fine." His voice was weaker than he intended.

"Why are you crying then?"

"Look." He pointed at the floor. "The trapdoor isn't here. It's gone! He doesn't believe me."

Elizabeth looked around the room before she stood up and started pushing aside piles of boxes. She stamped her foot from one area of the room to the other, searching. Finally, she shook her head and came back to sit down next to him.

"No one will ever believe us," he said. Then, under his breath, he whispered, "I lost her forever."

Elizabeth didn't hear his last statement. She said weakly, "No one believed me, Dad. They thought I was making a joke wearing these clothes and telling them about Jerusalem." They stared at each other. "But we both know what we saw, right?"

Michael looked over at her. She might be strong and brave, but she still needed him. Pulling Elizabeth to her feet, he said gently, "Yes, we know. C'mon, Baboo, let's get home."

They walked through the now deserted church. Father Dennis was nowhere to be seen. Michael picked up his keys and cell phone from the box near the altar, and they made their way down the front steps.

"Car is still here," Elizabeth said, seeing their Camry parked exactly where they had left it.

Crossing the street, Michael stopped abruptly and looked down Main Street. "You know what, Elizabeth? Today is a good day for a walk. I owe you something."

Elizabeth looked horrified, pulling him back to the sidewalk. "In these clothes? And you with no shoes?"

Michael smiled. "Yeah, in these clothes. What's worse, walking with your father or being dressed like this?"

"Wow, that's a tough one. Hmm. Well, my friends think I'm crazy anyway. Maybe crazy is cool?"

"Darn right it is." Michael put his arm around her and started walking down the sidewalk toward the water.

"When did that place open?" he asked when they passed a toy store on their right.

"Dad, that's been there my whole life! Aunt Sammie used to take me there all the time."

"Hmm," he said loudly.

Elizabeth started to giggle.

"What, what's up?" Michael asked as he tightened his grip around his daughter's shoulder.

"They're looking at us, Dad," she said, pointing.

Michael looked ahead, seeing a group of boys laughing, obviously watching them. "So they are, Elizabeth."

"Hey," he shouted out to the group of them, "what do you think of these fine robes?"

The boys looked around at each other before one shrugged his shoulders and gave them a thumbs-up. "Hey, mister, where are your shoes?"

Michael laughed. "Today I don't need them."

"Dad, cut it out! You're embarrassing me!"

"Oops, sorry, *Liz.*"

Suddenly they were startled by the sound of a car horn honking on the other side of the street. Michael stopped.

"What's wrong, Dad?"

He shook his head and slowly walked to the other side of Main Street. An old man was struggling with his cane and a bag while attempting to press the crosswalk button. His hand shook visibly.

"Hold on. I've got that, sir," Michael called out as he jogged over and pushed the button. He turned to the man. "You look familiar . . . Mr. . . . ?"

The man smiled. Michael could see his pink gums. "Szymanski." He looked at Michael inquiringly. "I'm not sure I know you."

Michael shook his hand. "I'm Michael Stewart. Can I give you a hand with that bag? Do you need some help?"

"You know, son, today I could use it. I hope you don't mind."

Michael grinned. "No, I don't mind at all."

He put his shoulder under the man's outstretched arm. As a car approached, Michael grabbed the bag and put his hand out to stop the vehicle. "Quite an adventure, don't you think, Mr. Szymanski?"

"Oh, every day is an adventure for me now."

From across the street, Elizabeth grinned broadly and waved. When Michael and Mr. Szymanski had safely crossed, the old man cheered, "Woo-hoo!"

Michael and Elizabeth laughed. "Elizabeth, this is Mr. Szymanski. Can you please take this," he said, handing her the bag.

"Sure."

"Which way are you going, sir?"

"Not sure. Just taking my time and enjoying the day."

Michael thought a moment. "Would you like to join us?"

"That all depends. Where are you going?"

"Yeah, Dad," Elizabeth chimed in, "where are we going?"

"Baboo, I'm taking you and Mr. Szymanski for the biggest, baddest ice cream sundae you can get!"

"Ooh!" she squealed in delight. "I can see the shop!" She ran ahead down the street and in through the parlor doors.

Michael rolled his eyes. "There she goes again."

Mr. Szymanski chuckled. "They all do that. Always in a hurry."

"Well, we'll take our time." Slowly they walked down Main Street. The track for the cable car was still visible in the middle of the road, a vestige of bygone days. Michael took in the beautiful architecture of the quaint, old town. "This is nothing like Jerusalem," he muttered. "But it's just as beautiful."

"What's that, Michael?"

"Ah, nothing. Maybe someday I'll explain it."

Michael could see Elizabeth seated on one of the stools at the front counter when they walked in. The shop was painted in shades of white and pink, with candy displayed at the entrance. Booths lined the walls and an old jukebox played in the back.

This is perfect, he thought.

"Hey, Dad," Elizabeth whispered, smiling surreptitiously, pointing to the woman behind the counter. *"No ring."*

Michael looked down at his left hand. He felt a momentary sense of panic and loss as he remembered, then pushed the feelings aside. They were home. His daughter was safe. It was all that mattered.

"I've already ordered, Dad." Elizabeth twirled around twice on her stool, underscoring her statement.

"Okay." He sat down next to her and took an experimental spin himself. Michael looked at his beaming daughter. *I can't believe I didn't do this sooner.*

"Are you going to share with your father?" he asked, needling her.

"Aw, do I have to?"

Michael laughed. "You can do whatever makes you happy. What would you like, Mr. Szymanski?"

The old man thought a moment. "You got enough money in your wallet for a banana split?"

Instinctively Michael put his hand in his pocket, then drew it out again quickly. "Elizabeth, look at this!" he exclaimed, holding out his palm. There were the silver coins he had taken from Judas. He was still gazing at them in wonder when the woman behind the counter turned around to greet them.

"Your daughter said you had never been here before. I'm so happy you found us."

Michael smiled as he looked up into the most beautiful green eyes he had ever seen.

ACKNOWLEDGMENTS

On a warm May night in 2007, a couple of decades of indecision ended. I arose with purpose, filled with ideas on how to finally complete my novel, which had gathered dusty bytes on my computer for far too long. I had never been so excited about the concept of writing. I shook my normally hard-to-wake wife, Debbie, out of her sleep and shared my thoughts. When she got excited about the plot, I knew then I had something special.

Based upon some emotional childhood experiences, I had been pondering two questions: If we had an opportunity to cleanse our sins, how would we go about achieving that, and whom would we seek to help us?

As I began to work on the first draft, the creative process became therapeutic. It gave me an opportunity to understand why my body and mind were experiencing certain emotions as an adult and how the joys and pains of childhood transformed me into the person I am today.

When you write, it's rarely an absolutely joyful experience. But from the first word I wrote in my notebook to the last correction made on the proofs, *Necessary Heartbreak* enabled me to believe in the goodness of the human character.

I do believe there are people walking the earth who step into your lives for reasons. Many have done so along the way to help push me along in this project.

After the first draft was written, I sought out an editor to sit down and work with me paragraph by paragraph. While the concept and general ideas were already down on paper, I needed to shape this book with more details, dialogue, and tension. I searched for someone locally who could work with me, but I hit a dead end. I was fortunate to have a friend like Dee Karl, who badgered me to get off my backside and use Monster.com.

Although I received over thirty responses from my Monster.com experience, I interviewed only one person. I didn't need to see anyone else after meeting Jenn Kujawski.

Jenn was a significant influence during the self-publishing process. She helped move this book in a direction I could feel proud of, spending many hours sharpening my creative skills and offering several suggestions that are part of this book today.

I was fortunate enough to sign with my book/movie agent, Irene Webb. With her enthusiastic support, I was able to revise the original manuscript into a more developed story.

While on a vacation trip to Orlando, I was contacted by Simon & Schuster VP Anthony Ziccardi, who expressed an interest in publishing a revised edition. He was the perfect fit for me and this trilogy, and I'm grateful for his support.

Anthony placed me in the very capable editing hands of Mitchell Ivers, who steered me in new directions, and I welcomed his suggestions on how to give the story more depth. I consider myself quite lucky to have him as my editor.

During the year it took to write, re-write, revise, and re-write the book, my wife has had to endure my many moods. Sometimes she had to take the kids out of the house for weekends so I could focus. Often we would sit side by side for hours, going over each line and paragraph. She was a big part of helping move this project forward, and I'm grateful for her ideas and support.

Last, I must acknowledge the many book clubs, reviewers, librarians, readers, friends, clergy, ministers, pastors, and nuns whom I've corresponded with via email or phone, or met in person. Each and every one of you is a part of helping me forge this first book of the trilogy into what it is today—a story printed by one of the world's top publishing houses. Your support and kindness will never be forgotten.

READING GROUP GUIDE

NECESSARY HEARTBREAK

INTRODUCTION

Necessary Heartbreak tells the story of Michael, a single dad from New York who has lost his faith after his wife's death and is struggling to raise his feisty fourteen-year-old daughter, Elizabeth. When Michael and Elizabeth stumble upon a trapdoor in their church basement, they discover a portal leading back to first-century Jerusalem during the tumultuous last week of Christ's life. There they encounter Leah, a grieving widow; a menacing soldier who is determined to take Elizabeth as his own; Judas on the last night of his life; and a close-up of the man Jesus. Unable to return to the present, Michael comes face-to-face with some of his most limiting beliefs and realizes he must open himself up to the possibility of a deeper faith in people, in himself, and in love if he is to find his way home.

DISCUSSION QUESTIONS

1. Compare Michael and Elizabeth's relationship with Michael's relationship with his own father. How are their power struggles and communication difficulties similar and different?

2. Discuss Michael's relationship with religion. What changed his once-strong faith? How is his belief in God different at the end of the novel? How do Elizabeth's and Leah's faith change throughout the novel?

3. Is Michael too overprotective, or just a concerned parent? Does Michael use his fear for Elizabeth to hold himself back from life? Why does he push people away?

4. Why does Michael consistently avoid women and feel almost uncomfortable with them? What is he afraid of? Why does he have so much trouble letting go of Vicki and moving on, going so far as to search for her in Jerusalem?

5. Talk about the different ways Michael and Elizabeth deal with losing Vicki. Throughout the story, they hide their emotions from each other. Why can't they talk about her with each other? Why do they each blame themselves for her death, when clearly it's neither one's fault?

6. How did the narrative format of the novel, incorporating flashbacks throughout, impact your read?

7. Why does Leah take Michael and Elizabeth in so easily? How are they able to accept life together so quickly? What do they learn from each other? What do Michael and Leah see in each other of their missing spouses?

8. Leah and Michael discuss having a "reverence for life," in both Leah's time and Michael's. Michael admits that not much has changed. Reread the passage on pages 157–158 and talk about how the two cultures respect life.

9. Discuss the difference between "kill" and "sacrifice." Why does Leah ultimately decide not to sacrifice Cassie? What does Elizabeth learn from Cassie? Discuss Cassie's significance to the story and what she symbolizes.

10. What does Michael make Leah believe?

11. How is the second time Michael denies Christ different from the first?

12. Why do Michael and Elizabeth keep finding excuses to stay in Jerusalem one more day? Is it because they're drawn to Jesus or do you see another reason?

13. Why are Michael and Elizabeth so intent on helping Jesus even though they know how the scene will play out? Why must Michael shoulder his burden? How can Elizabeth lift Michael's burden?

14. How does Leah break through Michael's façade? Why doesn't he ask her to come home with them? Did you like the ending of the book? Why or why not?

15. How does heartbreak shape each character? Do you agree with the title, that heartbreak is sometimes necessary?

ENHANCE YOUR BOOK CLUB

1. When Michael is a teen, he repeatedly listens to Bruce Springsteen's album *The River* and relates especially to the song "Independence Day." Listen to that song or just look up the lyrics. Is there a song in your own life that has particularly resonated with you or helped you through a difficult situation? Share with your book club.

2. Leah shares a Passover feast with Michael and Liz. Research the history of Passover and try making some dishes for your own feast, such as charoset and matzos.

3. Read the story of Jesus' crucifixion in the New Testament of the Bible. How do the descriptions in *Necessary Heartbreak* change your impressions of those events?

AUTHOR Q&A

1. **What inspired you to write this story, mixing time travel with ancient times and customs?** I grew up with a romantic, idealistic view of the church. Over the course of many years, this view eroded, especially during the winter of 1983–84. I was without money and a roof over my head, riding the E train in New York City at night. I sought help from

many, including a family friend who helped run a church. He turned me back into the cold New Year's Eve night in 1983. As I sat on the train pondering, I started to write this novel, drawing on some of the key childhood experiences that still touch my soul today. And I wondered whether this was the church I wanted to be part of in the future. I found myself questioning the wrong person—Jesus Christ. So I wanted to send my characters back in time to restore the meaning of life to myself. I wanted my characters to be part of history's most important moment. I wanted them to experience what the true meanings of love, faith, and sacrifice really are.

2. **Tell us about your research on Roman and Biblical times. How much is real and how much is enhanced by your imagination?** I tried to stay faithful to the actual events, but I wanted to look at those events from the perspectives of the characters. My first editor, Jenn Kujawski, was instrumental in the research. We dedicated many weeks, even months, to this particular part of the process. The great benefit of this experience was that I learned so much about Jesus Christ, the person.

3. **Can you tell us about your personal faith?** It continues to evolve. I'm human. I question certain aspects of it. As I go along in these books, I learn more through the research process. I continue to gather a greater understanding of what an incredible role model Jesus is for me and for anyone else. **Has your faith ever faltered, like Michael's?** Yes, many times. It was at an all-time low after I watched my mother die from cancer at the age of forty-seven. She suffered so greatly, and I wondered why she had to endure so much pain at such a young age.

4. **Michael and Elizabeth both have rather volatile relationships with their fathers. How were you able to capture teen angst so well?** I have two daughters myself. As they get older, they become more independent emotionally. I utilized some real-life experiences and allowed them to unfold on the page.

5. **How did you create the character of Leah?** I first wanted the character to be of a background different from Michael's so I could show that people have much more in common than they realize. In addition, I incorporated several personality characteristics of women I've met and admired. **Is the story of Leah's husband based on real events?** No. I wanted to take the emotional temperature of the times, when confrontation between Jews and Roman soldiers erupted daily. I wanted to show the reader some of the normal tragedies a woman would have had to endure.

6. **The novel captures the viewpoints of a middle-aged father, a teenage girl, and a woman from Biblical times. Which character was the hardest to write?** The most difficult character was Leah, because extensive research was involved. Being of Christian background, I needed to

pay particular attention to this character. We spent many, many weeks researching every little detail of Leah's home, how she would make a living, and the relationships she would have. **Which character was easiest?** Michael. Most of the material associated with him comes purely from my heart: my experiences, my emotions, and my feelings regarding past and present relationships. **Which is your favorite?** Leah is no doubt my favorite. She is intriguing, strong, possessed with the ability to understand the reality of any situation. I built this character from many different women I've come across in my life. It was fun to revisit those particular experiences.

7. **You have a successful career as a sportswriter. What made you decide to start writing fiction?** I've sat on this story idea for a very long time, over two decades. I've tried to revisit it on several occasions, but could never find the proper angle. I spent many nights wondering why my mother was dealt such a severe fate, suffering the ravages of cancer. There were days when a feeling of hopelessness engulfed me, and I wouldn't know where to turn for answers. One hot May night I awoke with my answer. I dreamed I was on that street when Jesus was riding the donkey, Palm Sunday. I was chasing Him, trying to ask Him why we have to suffer.

8. **Do you lay out your plots beforehand or are there surprises in the writing process?** I would say both. The Biblical scenes were prepared in an outline. And then the characters took over: their personalities evolved, their strengths and weaknesses were unveiled. Some of the flashbacks were written a couple of decades ago, refined and polished over the past couple of years. **Was there ever an ending when Michael and Leah ended up together?** Good question. I'm in the process of answering that in the next book.

9. **Which authors and/or books have most impacted your own writing?** *The Power of Positive Thinking,* by Norman Vincent Peale, is one book I could read or listen to over and over again. His ability to simplify what life can be to us all motivates me to try and make every day a great one.

10. **What advice do you have for aspiring writers?** When you're writing, give yourself ample opportunity to absorb yourself in the story. And it's fine to incorporate the experiences that move you. There'll be some rejection—all writers have to listen to many different opinions about their work. But remain faithful to yourself and the work.

11. **Can you tell us about what you're working on next?** I'm currently writing the sequel, called *The Greatest Christmas Gift.* It picks up with Michael and Elizabeth in Northport seven months later.